Skyler

A Walker Brothers Novel

Seven Sons Ranch in Three Rivers Romance™
Book 6

Liz Isaacson

ISBN-13: 978-1-63876-367-3

1

M allery Viera woke the morning after Christmas, the fact that she had a live, breathing man in bed with her still foreign and strange.

Number one, she and Skyler didn't sleep in the same room in his huge, posh, luxury apartment in Amarillo.

Number two, her feelings for Skyler had her wanting to slide closer to him under the sheets and go back to sleep within the warm safety of his arms.

And that absolutely couldn't happen.

He was doing her a favor, that scorching kiss in her kitchen from weeks ago notwithstanding.

She wasn't going to make a bigger fool of herself.

She and Skyler weren't supposed to be in Three Rivers, but after his announcement about their marriage at lunch yesterday, they hadn't been able to leave.

His momma was a Southern giant through and

through, and Skyler hadn't been able to deny his mother the opportunity to take them to breakfast and "get to know Mal."

Mal had held Penny's gaze, but she'd probably have wilted had Skyler not warned her about the intensity his momma possessed.

And Mal was certain all of their secrets would be exposed at breakfast. Penny was like an FBI agent, and there were as many words spoken in the times of silence as there were when she was speaking.

On the other side of the bed, Skyler shifted, a groan coming out of his mouth. He lifted his head, and their eyes met.

Pure anxiety flashed inside her, but she managed to smile.

"This bed is terrible," he complained.

"It's not great," she agreed. Everything Skyler owned was the finest and most expensive. He hadn't told her how he'd come to be so wealthy without a college degree and within the first thirty-five years of his life.

She hadn't asked.

But the evidence of his money was everywhere, from the huge, brand-new pickup truck he drove to the four-bedroom apartment on the top floor of a downtown high-rise in Amarillo.

Mal hadn't stepped over such luxurious carpet in all her life. And her bed was like sleeping on clouds and cotton candy and the exhalations of unicorns.

The first couple of nights had been hard for her, but she had a door that locked. She wasn't truly afraid of Skyler. She just couldn't believe the situation she'd gotten herself into.

"So," he said. "What did you think of my parents?"

Mal found the conversation while they lay in bed intimate and sweet. Living with Skyler had been quite different than running with him or being friends with him or laughing while he tried to fold his body into yoga positions while she taught the class from the front of the room.

He was more reserved. Serious in a way she'd never seen from him before. He seemed to have two sides—the public Skyler he wanted others to see.

And the real Skyler, who didn't really know who he was. The real Skyler didn't show himself to very many people, but Mal had seen him, especially around his family.

"I actually liked them," she said. "And you weren't kidding when you said your brothers are loud."

He smiled at her and propped his head on his hand. Did he find it odd they were lying in the same bed? Just because they had a piece of paper that said they were married didn't mean they really were.

They'd kissed the one time in her kitchen, and then a quick peck four days later when they'd met at the courthouse for their wedding.

"Yeah, we're all loud," he said with a smile. The same smile she'd seen him flash to others during parties, lunches, or other social occasions. "You have to be when you're growing up with six brothers. If you weren't loud, you didn't eat."

Mal giggled and looked up at the ceiling. "Do you think we'll go back to Amarillo today?"

She was very careful not to say home. She wasn't even sure where her home was right now. She needed to get her courage up though, and she needed to start thinking and acting like Skyler's wife.

Her hearing with an immigration judge was only sixteen days away now, and she'd need to be convincing enough to get an extension on her green card.

Skyler had dived into the issue, and he told her some new fact he'd read that day almost every day. He'd said that the judge would likely set another hearing in the future until the immigration agents could determine whether or not their marriage was real.

"It's usually a year," he'd said.

"But I can't work," she'd said.

"You don't need to work," he said. "I have plenty of money." And that was the closest he'd come to saying anything about the finances.

Mal didn't know what to do with herself if she didn't have school and work. She'd petitioned the judge to be able to continue her classes īand her jobs, but she wouldn't know until the hearing happened.

She was slowly going insane, she knew that.

"We have no clothes," Skyler said. "So yes, I'll tell Momma we're going home today."

Mal didn't mind sleeping in her clothes—in fact, she slept in her clothes almost every night, but that could've been from her pure exhaustion more than anything else. Skyler had borrowed a pair of basketball shorts from his brother, Micah, and a T-shirt with a horseshoe printed on it.

He was as sexy as ever, and Mal rolled away from him and sat up, hoping he hadn't been able to see her attraction to him.

She wasn't sure why she was trying to hide it. He'd been the one to kiss her, as she reflected on every day. Every single day.

He'd said he wanted to kiss her again, the one and only time they'd talked about the episode, only minutes after it had happened. But he hadn't.

She hadn't known how to bring it up. How to put her hand in his. How to cuddle into him on the couch while they watched movies and studied and went running.

Their lives had simply gone on, but she was now on his lease, and she'd filed all kinds of papers to get her new name on all her legal documents.

"Mal," Skyler said, his voice that quiet, contemplative one she'd only heard a few times now. This was the real Skyler Walker talking, and she wanted to hear what he had to say.

"Yeah?"

"Would you go out with me tonight?"

For some reason, his vulnerable question struck her as funny. She tried to hold back her laughter, but that only made it burst from her mouth in more of an explosion.

He got up and came around the bed, sitting next to her and taking her hand in his. That got Mal's laughter to dry up, because now her heart raced like a champion horse.

He wore a playful smile on his face, and when their eyes met, showers of sparks cascaded down her back. "What's so funny about that?"

"We're married," she said. "What am I going to say? No?"

"You could," he said. "Do you want to say no?"

Mal swallowed, the dark depths of his eyes searching hers. She shook her head. "No."

"Great." His eyes dropped to her mouth, rebounding back to hers quickly. "That Japanese place? Sushi?"

Mal didn't get sushi and vegetable tempura as often as she'd like, because it was expensive. But Skyler didn't worry about that.

"Sure," she said. "I haven't been there in forever."

Skyler nodded. "Awesome. And uh...never mind."

"No, say it," Mal said.

"It's just...we've been married for five weeks now."

"Yeah."

"And I'm fine. I am. I just...." He hung his head. "I'd like to try that kiss again."

Mal's pulse rippled, and an icy excitement spread through her. "You would?"

"Yeah." Skyler looked up and met her eyes. Mal didn't know what to say. She didn't know what to do.

So she commanded her mind to stop trying to figure everything out, and she just acted.

She leaned toward him, and he leaned toward her. In the next moment, Skyler Walker kissed her, and Mal pulled a breath in through her nose.

This kiss wasn't as wild, or as uninhibited, as the one they'd shared in her kitchen weeks ago.

It was just as passionate, and Skyler once again threaded the fingers on one hand through her hair as he kissed her. Mal sure did like that. She liked kissing him.

She simply liked *him*.

———

"Morning, Momma," Skyler said an hour later, releasing Mal's hand as he stepped over to his mother and embraced her. He dwarfed her, just like all of his brothers did.

Mal honestly wasn't sure how Penny Walker had carried any of the Walker men to term, especially twins. She was probably five-foot-four at the most, and Skyler could likely lift her up and throw her as far as he wanted.

Of course, he did spend a lot of time in the gym on the bottom floor of his apartment building, as he didn't have a job like most students. He only had four classes, and two of them were throwaways—like floral arrangement and bowling.

His mother laughed as she hugged her son, and Mal wasn't surprised when the woman embraced her next. She'd hugged Mal yesterday too, though her shock had kept her at bay for a few minutes.

"I've got pancakes in the oven," she said, stepping back. She wore a wide smile that didn't seem fake at all, and she put off a warmth Mal basked in.

A keen sense of missing her own mother hit her, and she hurried to put a smile on her face too. She was a lot like Skyler in that she put on a mask to hide how she really felt.

"Smells like bacon," Skyler said. "Oh, and sausage."

"Daddy likes the bacon," his mother said. "It's not my favorite."

"I'm with you, Momma." Skyler smiled easily at her and turned as his father came down the hall. "Mornin', Daddy."

They also embraced, and Mal got a hug from the freshly showered Gideon Walker too.

"What are you two up to for the rest of the holidays?" Momma asked as she gripped a pair of tongs and started pulling the strips of bacon from the pan.

Mal's mouth watered, because out of sausage and bacon, she definitely preferred bacon.

"Just going back to Amarillo," Skyler said, his voice a touch too casual.

"You don't have family, Mal?" Penny asked, glancing over her shoulder.

Mal suddenly realized how hard it was to lie to the woman, and she didn't want to fib anyway. So she said, "My family is all down in Mexico, ma'am."

"We'll go see them in a couple of months," Skyler said.

Penny didn't ask any more questions about that, thankfully, but she did say, "How many siblings do you have, Mal?"

Mal could easily talk about her two sisters and two brothers, and that got them through the setting up of breakfast, the prayer, and getting their food.

The four of them sat down at the kitchen table, and Mal felt a sense of peace she hadn't in a long time. She'd always been comfortable with Skyler, and they'd had a good time together in the two years since she'd known him.

She laughed and smiled, contributed to the conversation by talking about the beaches in Mexico. Penny's face lit up then, as she loved the beach.

By the time she and Skyler left the house, Mal almost wished they could stay longer.

Not really, but almost.

She threaded her fingers through Skyler's, let him open the door and help her into the truck, and then while he walked around the front of the vehicle, she slid over on the bench seat so she'd be sitting right next to him.

He looked at her when he got in beside her, and Mal decided if she was going to be married to this man for at least the next year, she should get to kiss the devilishly handsome cowboy whenever she wanted.

So she did.

And while she knew she was his wanna-be wife, he sure did kiss her like maybe, just maybe, they could have a real relationship...someday.

2

Skyler Walker used to have thirty-five-hundred square feet to himself. Somewhere he could escape the façade he carefully crafted for everyone and everything in Amarillo. But within the walls of his own home, he was able to be himself.

Except Mal lived in the apartment now too. And he wanted her there. It just meant he needed a few minutes to himself in his own bedroom as he tried to figure out how to be the Skyler Walker she'd known and the Real Skyler Walker.

Honestly, playing both parts was utterly exhausting. Only a few people knew who he really was, and two of them—Micah and Wyatt—had been texting him all morning.

During breakfast, during the drive home. He'd muted

their conversations after telling them he'd be driving for an hour as he and Mal made their way back to Amarillo.

That hadn't stopped his brothers from continuing their conversation without him. Normally, he'd be annoyed at the slew of messages he had to wade through. But he needed their support in this moment, and he sat down on the edge of his bed to read through the string.

Breakfast on Saturday? Wyatt had asked.

Yes, Micah had said. *I'm in. I'm going to lose my mind over Simone.*

And Skyler can tell us about Mal, Wyatt had said. *Sorry about Simone, Mike. What's going on with that?*

They continued to go back and forth, and Micah had finally admitted that he'd been the one to break up with Simone Foster, because she didn't want anyone to know about their relationship.

And I'm just not sure why she's embarrassed of me, Micah had ended with.

Wyatt, who had literally been well-liked by everyone for his entire life, went on to tell Micah there was nothing about him she could possibly not like.

Skyler smiled at that. When he wanted to feel good about himself, he could go to Wyatt. His older brother definitely didn't have a confidence problem.

"And why should he?" Skyler asked himself. Wyatt had been a cowboy billionaire even before he'd inherited part of Daddy's money. Everyone in the rodeo scene adored him, and even more-so now that he had his own line of western wear.

He hadn't had a failed business. He hadn't had a girlfriend steal from him and cause the federal authorities to come asking questions about fraud and embezzlement.

He sighed as his thoughts always seemed to come back to that situation in Dallas. He wondered if there'd ever be a time when he didn't think about all that had happened there and end up angry.

Or if he could possibly ever truly feel happy. He'd experienced some of it at the homestead at Seven Sons, he knew that. The ranch there seemed to have a dome around it that kept negative things out. And Skyler really liked going there.

He thought he was the brother wearing the black sheepskin, but at Seven Sons Ranch, everyone just accepted him. After his announcement yesterday before lunch, every single person had come over to hug him and Mal.

Yes, they'd been shocked. There were definite questions in Jeremiah's eyes, and Momma's, and out of all of them, Micah had seemed the most leery.

But he'd still said congratulations, hugged him and Mal, and not demanded to know the truth.

He'd have to tell him and Wyatt on Saturday, and the thought didn't terrify Skyler. Someone should know. Someone who could help him know what to do.

At school here in Amarillo, Skyler felt like he knew

what to do to be liked, to get someone to laugh at something he'd said, to get a woman's number.

But with a marriage to Mal...he had no idea what he was doing.

Saturday breakfast is fine, he said. *Here? Or are you going to make me drive to Three Rivers?*

Three Rivers, Wyatt said. *You're not doing anything anyway.*

Ditto Wyatt, Micah responded. *Amarillo doesn't have anything good for breakfast.*

Skyler scoffed, because that was so false. But he smiled, didn't argue, and said, *Fine. Breakfast at ten on Saturday. No women.*

No women, Micah said.

Wyatt took slightly longer to confirm the female-free breakfast date, but he did a few minutes later.

Skyler showered and changed his clothes, as he'd been wearing the same set for over twenty-four hours now. When he finally opened his bedroom door and went down the hall to the kitchen, he felt like he could face Mal again.

He sure did like kissing her and seeing her sitting on the couch in the living room, lifting a mug to her lips, actually made his heart lighten and start tap-dancing.

"Hey, pretty girl," he said, bending over the back of the couch and placing a kiss on Mal's cheek.

"Hey." She sounded surprised, and Skyler wanted to kick himself in the teeth. She looked at him, but he turned and went into the kitchen to get his own drink. He wasn't terribly fond of coffee though, as he wasn't sure what was so alluring about the stuff. He drank it though, because it was normal. Common. And in some circles here in Amarillo, the trendy thing to do.

"Why do you do that?" she asked.

"Do what?"

"Pretend."

"I'm not pretending." But he kept his face turned away from her as heat rushed into it. Embarrassed heat. He poured himself a cup of coffee, stirred in sugar and cream, aware that Mal had gotten up from the couch and approached him.

"You've literally never said, 'Hey, pretty girl,' to me," she said, frowning.

"You didn't like it." He nodded and stirred his coffee. "Got it."

"It's not that I didn't like it," Mal said, sighing. "Okay, look, we've got to talk."

Talking. One of Skyler's least favorite things to do.

"Okay," he said anyway.

"I think we rushed into this marriage thing, because of my court hearing." She groaned as she sat on the barstool at the kitchen peninsula. "I've got a charley horse."

"Want me to rub it out?"

"Would you?" She looked at him with a hopeful look on her face, and Skyler smiled. A real smile. One that brought true happiness to his soul.

"Sure, get that lotion you like." He held up one hand. "Wait. I'll get it. Can you get back to the couch?"

"Yeah."

Skyler went into the bathroom she used and found the lotion labeled *Energy*. Skyler could admit he enjoyed the citrus smell of it, with a hint of lavender.

Fine, maybe that was what the bottle said. But it smelled good.

He sat on the ottoman in front of Mal, and she lifted her foot into his lap. He'd rubbed out her charley horses in the past, but there was something sensual about the action this time. He kept his eyes down as he put lotion in his hand and started massaging it into her calf.

"Can I keep talking?" she asked.

"Sure," he said.

"So I know we had a hurry-up marriage. But we've been living together for five weeks, and I feel like I know you less than I did when we were just friends."

Skyler didn't know what to say. She was probably right, because he'd retreated inside his tortoise shell the moment they'd said, "I do."

There had been no honeymoon. They'd been married on a Thursday, and he'd helped her pack and move everything she owned on Saturday.

He'd put her name on the lease. He'd printed all the forms she needed to fill out to get a new driver's license and the forms she should've filed but didn't. He'd done anything he could to make it look like he and Mal had started to merge their lives. That their marriage was real.

He'd read a lot online, and it seemed like everything would be examined, from all angles, and he wanted to leave no stone untouched.

Why?

He'd asked himself that question a million times. And the truth was, he didn't know, other than helping Mal felt like the right thing to do.

"So I think we should establish a few rules," Mal said.

"Okay," Skyler said.

"Inside these walls, we are who we are. We're honest with each other in all things. Anything we're worried about, we get to say. Anything we don't like about the other, we can talk about."

She flicked her foot, and Skyler looked up. "Skyler, you don't have to pretend with me."

Being real was something he longed for, and all he could do was nod.

"We're messy, and sometimes we stink." She smiled at him. "I mean, I can only imagine what your running shoes smell like, and it's not good. And that's okay."

"Okay," he said.

"You don't have to go hide in your bedroom."

Skyler's heart jumped over itself. "Sometimes I need some time to myself after something stressful."

"Fair enough." She gave him another soft smile, and she really was beautiful with her big, brown eyes, all that dark hair, and her olive skin. "But you don't have to then come out and be fake with me."

"What if I think you're pretty?" Skyler kept his hands moving along her calf, up and down and around. Mal *was* pretty—more than pretty. Beautiful.

"Do you?"

"Yes." He looked at her. "I might be out of my mind here, Mal. But I really like you. I fought against a relationship with you for a long time, because well, just because." That wasn't entirely true. He knew the reason for the "because," but he wasn't ready to detail it for Mal. At least not right now.

"You're thirty-five," she said. "You've had girlfriends before."

"Yeah." He cleared his throat. "And I'm not really interested in love and marriage." In fact, he pretty much thought they were both fake. Unattainable.

"Oh."

"I mean, I wasn't," he said. "So I never asked you out. I never let myself do more than think you were beautiful and run with you and text you."

"Do you think you could change how you feel about love and marriage?"

Skyler wanted to. His whole soul ached to be able to feel normally about women again. Maybe with Mal....

He could only nod.

"Okay," she said. "For full disclosure, I've had a crush on you for months now, even before you offered to solve my problems and support me through this." She ducked her head and tucked her hair, and a powerful satisfaction moved through Skyler.

"Thanks for telling me," he said. "I like you too, in case you haven't figured that out."

"I figured." She grinned at him. "When you asked me out while we were lying in bed this morning."

He chuckled. "There's so much about this that's awkward, isn't there?"

"Not if we don't want it to be." She leaned forward. "And Sky, I don't want it to be."

"Me either," he said, still massaging her calf. "I'm going to breakfast with my brothers on Saturday."

"Oh? What are you going to tell them?"

"The truth," he said. "I think they could help me."

A panicked look marched across her face. "Skyler, I don't think that's wise. You said the immigration agents would interview family and friends."

His morals began to battle. He didn't want his brothers to have to lie for him. He didn't want to lie to them.

"I think we need all the love and support we can get," he said, trying to search for the right thing to do. Maybe his gut would tell him. But Skyler knew it wasn't his gut that talked to him. His momma would be down-right mortified if she knew he'd given God's glory to his gut.

Skyler was mortified at that too.

He dropped his eyes back to her slender leg, trying to

work through how he felt. It was impossible. Not something he could do in a few minutes.

"I don't think that's wise," she said, gently pulling her foot back. "My leg feels much better. Thank you, Sky."

He lifted his eyes to hers. "I like it when you call me Sky."

Mal slid forward and touched her lips to his in a sweet kiss. "Just think about Saturday, okay? You're smart, and I trust you."

Skyler nodded. "Thank you, Mal." He hadn't felt very trustworthy since Shayla had stolen from him, skipped town, and left him to deal with the authorities on his own.

Bumbling, and shocked, and unsure of what to say, Skyler had narrowly escaped getting arrested. He'd been questioned multiple times, and the FBI agent he'd spoken to the most had given him a card and said, "Answer if I call, Mister Walker."

Theron Oaks hadn't called, thank the Lord above. In that moment, Skyler realized he needed to do a lot more thanking of the Lord above. And talking to Him. Pleading with Him. Finding out what God wanted him to do. Because if God wanted him to do something, Skyler knew the Lord would provide a way.

And he should enlist Mal in his endeavors.

"So," he said. "Let's talk about religion."

"Religion?" she asked.

"Yeah," he said. "Because I have a feeling we're going to need all the help we can get."

3

M al hadn't been to church since she was thirteen years old. She cocked her head at Skyler, trying to see something in him she hadn't seen before.

"Do you believe in God?" he asked. Just like that. Point blank.

"Yes," she said, just as easily.

"I've never seen you go to church."

"You either." She wasn't sure why her defenses were so high. It wasn't like he was accusing her of something.

"I go when I go to Three Rivers," he said, dropping his chin to his chest. "It's kind of a family expectation."

"If you believe, why don't you go?"

Skyler looked at her, those eyes so open and so dark. He'd spent so much time deceiving others with those eyes, but Mal felt like she was once again seeing the man behind the mask.

"Honestly?"

"I think we're to the point of being completely honest with each other, yes." She crossed her arms and leaned back into the couch, suddenly too close to him. All she could think about was kissing him, and that didn't seem super appropriate for their talk about religion.

"I had some...trying things happen in Dallas. I kind of lost my faith." He drew in a big breath and took several long seconds to push it all back out of his lungs. "Not past tense. I have lost my faith."

Mal nodded, because she knew what that felt like. An urgent curiosity wanted to ask him what had happened in Dallas. Until that moment, she hadn't even known he'd lived in Dallas. The reminder that she barely knew him felt like a bucket of ice water to the face, and she blinked, blinked, blinked until her voice wasn't quite so tight.

"But I'm thinking I'd like to go back to church," he said, reaching for her hand. If he knew how tender and vulnerable such simple gestures made him, he probably wouldn't do them. Or maybe he would. Skyler seemed to know exactly the power he held over women. Mal thought she'd done a good job of hiding all of her feelings for him, but now she wasn't so sure.

"What do you think?" he asked. "Will you go to church with me on Sunday?"

Mal found herself nodding, though she'd had some trying things in her life too. They weren't the reason she'd stopped going to church though. She supposed she'd just become too busy. Too focused on other goals in her life.

Which sounded ridiculous inside her own head. If there was anything she should focus on, it was her relationship with the Lord.

Maybe that's why everything in your life is in ruins, she thought, and her throat tensed right back up.

Skyler stood up and stretched backward. "Great. I might go take a nap. That mattress really jacked up my back." He groaned as he moved, finally leaning forward and placing a sweet kiss on her cheek that was too close to her mouth to be casual. "We're still on for dinner?"

"Yes," Mal said. He nodded, that sexy smile on his face, and headed back toward his bedroom. The moment the door closed, Mal relaxed. She wasn't sure what that said about her—or Skyler—but she didn't think it was good.

"Yeah, because you're *married* to that man." The impossibility of the situation hit her in that moment, as it had in others, and tears gathered in her eyes.

Her phone rang, and Julia's name sat on the screen. Mal sniffed and pulled back on her emotions. Her younger sister would be able to hear them, even across the many miles between them. Mal had learned about her sister's hound-like qualities from a young age. There was nothing Julia couldn't sniff out, nothing she missed, nothing she didn't know. And not just about everyone in their small village, but seemingly everywhere.

Mal swiped on the call, hoping her sister had some good news. "Hey, Julia," she said as cheerfully as she could. She couldn't believe it, but she was actually ready to do something with her life. She'd longed for a Saturday off, for an afternoon to herself. But now that she didn't work and didn't have anything to do, she still wasn't happy.

"Oh, holy frijoles," Julia said, already into the gushing. She could speak faster than any human alive, and Mal actually smiled at the level of drama in her voice. "You'll never believe what just happened to Jorge."

"I'm sure I won't," Mal said. She always found herself slipping back into a slightly more Hispanic accent when she spoke with her family. Almost like she was ashamed she hadn't stuck more true to her roots, the way they all had.

"First, Mami wants me to say *gracias* for all the money you've been sending. It's helped with Papi's medicines so much."

"Of course," Mal said, leaning further into the couch and closing her eyes. She hadn't told Skyler a single thing about how much money she sent back to Black Canyon, and how sometimes she resented it.

No wonder she'd stopped going to church. She had bad feelings about her own family. She wished she didn't, but she didn't know how to get rid of the toxic emotions.

"Second, Jorge just got proposed to!" Julia shrieked

and started laughing, as if getting engaged was the funniest thing on the planet.

Surprise streamed through Mal, if only because Jorge was as traditional as traditional got. He wouldn't want his long-time girlfriend to propose to him. "Wow," she said.

"And he said no!" Julia laughed again. "It was *so* funny. You should've seen his face. You'd have thought Valeria had just cursed him and all of our ancestors. Then he stomped out of the room, yelling something about how he had a plan and she couldn't just ruin it."

"Oh, wow," Mal said, because she didn't know what else there was. She missed her siblings in moments like this, because she'd love to be able to tell everyone to hang tight in the tiny kitchen where most of their conversations took place while she went to talk to Jorge.

Her family's house in Mexico would fit inside Skyler's apartment, but they were lucky to have it. The town of Black Canyon was actually one of the wealthier seaside towns in Mexico, due to the black coral reef that brought a lot of tourists. Her father's family had started a restaurant in the area generations ago, and almost all Viera's stayed and worked it. They needed people to serve, people to cook, people to fish, people to take care of the boats.

Mal had left to get an education, and the years had kind of just melted away.

Julia continued the story, and how Valeria had actually started crying, and Mama had made huevos rancheros to calm everyone down. That was her mother. Always trying to make everyone feel better with food.

No wonder Mal ran every day and considered everything she put in her mouth. She didn't want to feed her feelings—she wanted to deal with them.

"Anyway." Julia sighed, and Mal was tired after the conversation, and she'd only said a few things. "What's new with you?"

Her eyes flew to the door where Skyler had disappeared. "Uh, not much," she said.

"Well, you should see this new dog Paulo got. It's so cute." Julia went off again, this time talking about how hot her husband was, and how much they both loved this dog.

By the time Mal hung up, pure exhaustion pulled through her. Talking to Julia should be an Olympic event, and Mal would win the gold medal every time.

Without anything else to do, she switched on the TV and got up from the couch. If she didn't have homework to do, a nap to catch before she ran off to another job, she might as well fill the fridge with something good to eat.

Her mama wasn't the only Viera who knew how to cook, and Mal had learned at Mami's knee since the time she was old enough to hold a wooden spoon. Not only that, but cooking a traditional Mexican dish soothed her, and by the time she slid the chile rellenos into the oven, she felt more settled than she had in a long, long time.

She glanced at Skyler's door again, not nearly as much anxiety skipping through her system at the thought of him behind it. She wondered if he'd tell his brothers about the legitimacy—or lack thereof—of their marriage on Saturday.

She hadn't told Julia, but that wasn't because she couldn't. The US ICE agents weren't going to interview her family. She hadn't told her sister, because she was....

"Embarrassed," she muttered to herself. She couldn't believe she'd forgotten to file the right paperwork at the right time.

Only fifteen more days until everything would be sorted out. She could only hope she wouldn't lose her heart—or cause too many problems for Skyler—before she could get out of this mess.

———

"Are you going to tell me about Dallas?" she asked later that evening. They'd just been seated at the Japanese restaurant, and the scent of tempura and soy sauce filled the air. Mal loved it, and her stomach grumbled at her for depriving it of food all afternoon. She and Skyler had enjoyed an easy, casual lunch together of her chile rellenos, but he'd gone into his bedroom to change his clothes for dinner, and Mal had had to text him to find out how fancy they were going for their date that night.

Business casual, he'd said, but Mal didn't know what that meant. She worked at a gym, for crying out loud. If she wasn't teaching yoga or selling gym memberships, she was making specialty sodas for people in such a hurry they couldn't even get out of their cars to get a drink.

She'd sorted through her closet for fifteen minutes before just texting him again, asking him to send her a picture of what he was wearing.

His laughter had filled the apartment then, as he'd already left his bedroom. She'd ducked out of her bedroom to find him cackling at his phone.

"What?" she'd asked.

"Did you seriously just ask me what I was wearing?" He grinned at her mischievously. "Is that a pick-up line, Mal?"

"No," she'd said, feeling foolish. "Nothing sexual. And I can see now anyway."

Business casual meant pressed slacks. A button-up shirt in the most delicious shade of blue. Just the right color to make his dark hair seem darker. His tan skin even more desirable. He'd covered most of his hair with a cowboy hat before they'd left the apartment, and Mal had hardly known how to breathe as they rode the elevator down to the parking garage, his hand firmly in hers.

She'd managed to find the only dress she owned, and it was only a little bit odd-fitting. It was all black, and she thought she'd need to get another one before Sunday so Skyler wouldn't know she only owned one dress.

"I suppose I'll tell you about Dallas eventually," Skyler said, bringing her back to the moment.

"Where else have you lived?" she asked. "We could start there."

"Let's see," he said, sighing. "I grew up on a little ranch down by San Antonio for a couple of years. Daddy was trying to get his tech stuff off the ground. We lived with his parents for a while, but I was too little to remember much." He smiled, and Mal thought his childhood probably held a lot of happy memories.

"Then we moved to Austin. Daddy's firm took off from there. I took some classes there about airplane mechanics and stuff, and the woman I was seeing lived in Dallas. So I moved there."

"She lived in Dallas, while you were in Austin?"

Skyler swallowed, the movement in his throat on the nervous side. "Yeah, I met her on a dating app."

"Ah, got it."

"And I was in Dallas until I moved to Three Rivers, after Rhett bought Seven Sons. And then I decided to come to school here." He nodded like that summed up all thirty-five years of his life.

"And Rhett is the oldest," she said.

"That's right." He looked up as the waiter arrived, and he ordered everything for them flawlessly. Mal would never admit it out loud, but she sure did like being taken care of by Skyler Walker. He had a way of making her feel like a queen, and that hadn't happened very often. Not for her.

Don't lose him, she told herself, and she smiled and

asked him to tell her a story about his childhood. She wanted to know everything about him, and somewhere in the middle of the story, as he detailed how it was not his fault the grape sodas had exploded in the back of his mother's minivan, she started pleading with the Lord to allow her to keep him in her life.

Somehow, she prayed. *Somehow make this work.*

Skyler drove to Three Rivers on Saturday morning, the highway between the two places almost entirely his own. A sense of calmness accompanied him, at least until the outskirts of town started to come into view.

He wasn't sure why. He was only meeting Wyatt and Micah. They hadn't even told any of the other brothers, and he didn't have to drive through town and south fifteen minutes to Seven Sons. He wouldn't have to face the twins, or the oldest brothers who could sometimes gang up on him like twins, even though Jeremiah and Rhett weren't the exact same age.

He pulled into the hipster breakfast joint Wyatt had chosen, his stomach already angry with him. He shouldn't have let Wyatt pick. The man had a personality larger than life, and he didn't mind waiting in line just for a table.

He was never covert, as he stood out everywhere he went. Skyler wanted to blend in, especially when with Wyatt.

His brother didn't get what it was like to stand in his own shadow. But Skyler knew exactly how that felt, and he honestly wasn't sure he was up to it today.

"You're already here," he said to himself as he swung his huge truck into a parking space way out on the edge of the lot. It wasn't full, so maybe this experience wouldn't be as painful as Skyler thought.

He crossed the parking lot while the Texas Panhandle wind tried to steal his cowboy hat. Keeping one hand pressed to the top of his head, he bent into the breeze until he was safely inside.

The noise hit him like a punch in the nose. He blinked against the chatter, the laughter, the clinking of silverware against plates. The shop only had about fifteen tables, and they were all full.

Skyler had arrived first, and he stepped over to the counter, which had a pastry case beside it, and said, "How long is the wait for a group of three?"

"Five minutes," the guy there said. He didn't wear a cowboy hat—not surprisingly—over his hair. It was long and he'd pulled it back into a man-bun. Skyler might have stared a little longer than was socially acceptable, as part of him wanted to grow his hair out like this guy's. Just to see what Momma would say. And maybe Rhett.

Definitely Jeremiah, who didn't hold his opinion back, that was for sure.

A smile touched his lips, and he put his name on the waiting list.

Only sixty seconds later, Wyatt and Micah entered the shop, and Skyler sucked in a breath. There was no waiting area in a place like this, and Wyatt and Micah were as broad and tall as Skyler. Fine, Wyatt was a little taller than them all.

"Skyler," he boomed, and if everyone hadn't already noticed the bull riding celebrity, they did then. Wyatt pulled Skyler into a hug, and Skyler couldn't help smiling. It was simply impossible to be upset with Wyatt.

"Hey, guys," he said, knocking knuckles with Micah once Wyatt let him go. All of his anxiety was gone now. These were his brothers. He loved them. He trusted them. The three of them had banded together over the years, especially after the twins had come along and created a natural divide between the older brothers and the younger ones.

"Did Daddy text you?" Wyatt asked.

"I don't know," Skyler said. "I keep my phone on silent almost all the time, and I was driving." He pulled his phone out of his back pocket, not shocked when he saw he had twenty-four texts.

Twenty-four.

The massive family text string was definitely a con for Skyler, and he had a moment where he wondered what it would be like to be an only-child. Or maybe a brother to one person. He couldn't even imagine it, and he simply swiped to read the texts.

At least Daddy hadn't put his message on the family text, so it was easy for Skyler to find. He read the message quickly, saying, "He thinks he can raise miniature horses?" He looked up at Wyatt and Micah, who both shook their heads.

"Perfect response," Micah said with a grin. "That was exactly what we said when Wyatt read me the message on the way here."

"Skyler," the man-bun guy said, and they paused their conversation until they were seated at a table in the corner. Skyler sat next to Micah, pressed against the wall, and he was sure he wouldn't be able to use both hands to eat. So he better not order something that required more than a fork.

"Rhett will go help Daddy," Wyatt said.

"I can too," Micah said. "Lord knows I barely have anything to do at Seven Sons."

Skyler didn't miss the bitterness or unhappiness in Micah's voice, and he exchanged a glance with Wyatt.

"What does that mean?" Wyatt asked, quite delicately too. Skyler wished he could be that gentle when asking questions.

"It means that I'm there," Micah said. "But I honestly do odd jobs. I don't have a real purpose."

"Sure you do," Wyatt said.

"I have to ask Jeremiah for my chore list every morning." Micah glared at Wyatt, who held up one hand in surrender.

"So what are you going to do?" Skyler asked. "Get your own place, like Wyatt? Or Rhett? Or a little farm like Momma and Daddy? A whole ranch?"

"I don't want my own place," Micah said. "At least not that kind of place."

"So open a shop here," Wyatt said. "You're good at what you do, Mike. There are tons of homes being built; you could be the premier cabinet-maker in Three Rivers."

"I don't want to build cabinets."

"What do you want to do?" Wyatt asked.

Skyler was tired of the game already. Micah just needed to say what was on his mind, instead of making them guess.

"I want to build custom furniture."

"Then do it," Skyler said at the same time Wyatt did. They grinned at each other, and Skyler's annoyance settled down again.

He should've known that the moment Micah's problem was out, Wyatt would turn to him. After all, Wyatt didn't have problems.

Not fair, Skyler told himself. He hated these poisonous thoughts about seriously the nicest man on the planet. He quickly cleared his throat and said, "When's your surgery, Wyatt?"

"End of January," he said, lifting his water glass to his lips. "We have to get moved into the new house, and I need to find a nurse who's willing to come live up in Church Ranches." He said it so nonchalantly, but Skyler wondered who would possibly be able to do that.

"You're going to have someone live-in?" Micah asked.

"Yeah," Wyatt said. "Marcy has to fly every day, and she'll have to leave super early to get in the air at her usual time." He shrugged one shoulder like he hadn't thought through this until he was blue in the face. "And I don't want to be up that early."

"Yeah, no joke," Skyler said. "I hate getting up early."

Both of his brothers looked at him, and he realized how fake he'd sounded. "I mean—"

"I thought you said you run," Wyatt said, a knowing look in his eyes. "Don't you do that early in the morning?"

"Well, sometimes," Skyler said, though he'd put in four miles with Mal before making the hour-long drive to Three Rivers that very morning.

"Why do you do that?" Micah asked.

"Do what?" Skyler hid behind his water glass too, wishing the waiter would come ask them for their orders.

"Pretend you're something you're not," Micah said.

"You aren't the black sheep," Wyatt said, leaning forward and flipping the brim of Skyler's cowboy hat.

Instant heat flared to life inside Skyler. Angry heat. "Don't, Wyatt."

Wyatt grinned at him, but he didn't go into full joy mode. "I'm not sure why you think you have to be so different. Seriously."

"I *am* different," Skyler said.

"No," Wyatt and Micah said together, their eyes locking onto each other. They seemed to have everything synchronized, and Skyler tried not to feel ganged up on. But Wyatt and Micah had grown closer over the past year and a half while they'd lived together in the homestead at Seven Sons.

And Skyler—ever the black sheep, no matter what they said—had been off at school in Amarillo.

"You're wearing the hat," Wyatt said.

"And the boots," Micah added.

"That doesn't make me a cowboy." Skyler leaned back in his chair and folded his arms, his shoulder brushing the wall beside him. He felt too broad and too big, and surely everyone would see it.

"All right," Wyatt said in a highly false voice. "We can talk about that later. Let's talk about—"

"Are you boys ready to order?" a woman asked, and Skyler's relief was unlike anything he'd ever felt before.

"I haven't even looked," Micah said, reaching for a menu in the middle of the table.

Skyler hadn't either, but it didn't matter. This place served breakfast, and he knew what he wanted. "I'll have the western omelet," he said. "Lots of veggies."

Wyatt's mouth played around with a grin as he

watched Skyler for a moment to make sure he was done with his order. He nodded, because he was.

"I'll have the special," Wyatt said, and they all looked at Micah.

"I have no idea," he said, closing the menu. "I want a lot of bacon, a Belgian waffle, and over-easy eggs."

"You got it," the waitress said without making a big deal out of Micah creating his own order. And Skyler supposed he'd gotten lucky that this hipster place even had a western omelet.

She walked away, and Micah adjusted his chair a couple of inches away from Skyler. Then he looked at him. Skyler looked right back, switching his gaze to Wyatt. Back to Micah.

"What?" he asked.

"Mal?" they said together. "You're married?" Wyatt added, reaching for his glass and draining the rest of the water. "Start talking, cowboy. I sense a good, long story."

———

"CALL MAL," he told the truck as he drove away from the fancy breakfast joint.

"Calling Mal," the truck said, and a few moments later, the line connected. His heart boomed in his chest as the phone rang, and finally Mal answered.

"I didn't tell them," he said in lieu of hello.

"You didn't? What did you say?"

"They asked about you," Skyler said, realizing he was yelling. He often did when he allowed the phone to connect through the radio. He wasn't sure why, and he always felt like a fool afterward. "And I just said we'd decided to get married quickly."

He turned onto the highway and accelerated, ready to be back in Amarillo. He wasn't sure why the air in Three Rivers was so full of expectations. But it was. And that was exactly the same reason Micah felt so stilted here. He'd come to Seven Sons to contribute to the family ranch, but there wasn't anything for him to do.

None of the brothers had to work, as their bank accounts were all huge since Daddy had sold his company. But a man still needed to have something to fill his time with. Something good.

"They didn't question why?" Mal asked.

"Wyatt tried," Skyler said. "But I played my black sheep card and said I didn't want to make a big deal out of it." His throat hurt, because his brothers' words wouldn't leave his mind.

You aren't the black sheep.

Skyler had always marched to the beat of his own drum, and he might not be a total black sheep, but it was something he'd embraced to make himself stand out in a family of loud, personable boys that had grown into insane, elbow-throwing men—especially if there was food in sight.

"Out of what?"

"Out of the wedding. Have everyone come. That kind of thing." Skyler swallowed again, wishing he'd stopped for a drink before starting down the highway. There was literally nothing between Three Rivers and Amarillo, and his throat was so dry already.

Wyatt had said Momma felt bad she couldn't be there for all the weddings, and that had only added to Skyler's guilt about not telling the complete truth. And for depriving Momma of being there to watch him get married.

It isn't real, he told himself. And he'd rather not deceive her—and everyone else—right to her face by throwing a big wedding...that wasn't real.

"Okay," Mal said, and she sounded relieved. "And you think they bought it?"

"I didn't try to sell them anything," Skyler said, looking out his window. He really needed a way to not let simple comments annoy him so much. His feelings went up and down like a roller coaster, often leaving him feeling bad that he'd had negative feelings for whoever he was talking to.

He needed help, and he resolved to call...someone as soon as he could. Who, he didn't know.

"Okay, I'll see you when you get here," Mal said, and Skyler noted she didn't say "home." She never did.

And that added to his frustration too.

"Yep." He let her end the call while his fingers

clenched the steering wheel. A few miles passed, and then he said, "Call Jeremiah."

"Calling Jeremiah," the truck echoed back to him.

"What's up?" Jeremiah asked.

"I think I need...." Skyler blew out his breath, unsure of how to admit this out loud.

"You need what?"

"Nothing, I—"

"Oh, it's something," Jeremiah said, and though there was activity on the other end of the line, Skyler felt like he had Jeremiah's full attention.

Skyler stared out the windshield, trying to find the strength he needed.

"Sky?"

"Help," he said. "I need help."

"What kind of help?"

"Like, someone to talk to. Or...I don't know."

"Ah, got it." Jeremiah fell silent for several seconds, and then he said, "I've got a great counselor. I'll forward you her number."

Ultimate relief and gratitude moved through Skyler. Jeremiah hadn't asked any questions. He didn't think Skyler was weak.

"Sent," he said. "Listen, can I call you back in ten minutes? I've got a goat problem that is really annoying me right now."

"Yeah, sure," Skyler said, and this time he ended the call and continued on his way home.

Home.

He wondered if Mal would ever feel like her place with him felt like home. He sure hoped so. He didn't know how to make that happen, but he sure hoped so.

He also hoped he never had to use the words "goat problem," and he chuckled the rest of the way to Amarillo.

5

Mal stood in front of the mirror mounted to the wall in her bedroom. This was easily the nicest apartment she'd ever lived in, with a bedroom that actually took several steps to cross. The shower never ran out of hot water, even when she got in right after Skyler got out. A proper heater worked all the time, and she couldn't even imagine what the summer months would bring—AC that always kept things cool?

What a dream.

She thought of the man moving around in the kitchen just down the hall, and she'd definitely fallen into a great dream.

But the dress she wore wasn't part of that dream. She'd gone to the mall yesterday morning while Skyler was off in Three Rivers, breakfasting with his brothers. He'd given her a credit card with a metal name she hadn't even known existed, but she didn't want to use it unless she absolutely had to.

That day was coming, she knew. She wasn't working anymore, and she wouldn't be able to keep buying her own groceries for much longer. He'd fixed her car. He paid the rent. They hadn't talked about any of it.

"Unhealthy," she murmured to herself, and she looked into her own eyes. "This isn't what you want."

She did want to stay in the country. She didn't want to have a marriage that was a complete sham, with the only guy she felt like she could ask to do this huge favor for her.

She needed to talk to Skyler, about real things. She'd always dreamt of her wedding day, and it wasn't while she wore jeans and a tank top, standing in front of a stranger who had the power to make her union legal.

Tears filled her eyes. A knock sounded on the door, and she jumped as if she'd been shocked.

"Mal?" Skyler said through the door. "We're going to be late."

"Coming," she said, swiping quickly at her eyes. She'd spent all morning in the bathroom, showering, shaving, primping, fluffing, straightening, and brushing on the exact right amount of makeup.

She drew in a deep breath and went to the door. Skyler had already started to retreat back down the short hall that led into the main living area. He turned back, nearly stumbling before he came to a stop.

"Wow," he said.

But Mal didn't believe him. There was nothing *wow* about the dress she wore. Number one, the color was all wrong for her complexion. Number two, it also didn't fit quite right. She was a little more petite than the standard size, and the waist of most dresses never actually fell at her waist.

Should've gone with a skirt and blouse, she thought as she walked toward him.

He wore something in his eyes she hadn't seen in him before. When she realized it was desire, Mal's throat turned dry.

"When did you get that?" he asked, reaching for the sleeve and pinching the fabric between two fingers.

"Who says it's new?" she asked.

"It has a tag on it, Mal." He grinned at her and plucked the tag from the sleeve.

Horror filled Mal, because then he'd see just how inexpensive the dress was. His smile didn't slip though. He simply fisted the tag and brushed the other end of the small plastic piece to the floor.

"Yesterday," she said, her voice creaking. "While you were in Three Rivers. I don't, uh, actually own a lot of dresses."

"Well, this one looks great. The green is nice." He turned and continued into the kitchen, and such warmth filled Mal that she had the fleeting thought that she'd been wrong for the past thirty-six years of her life, that she did look good in green.

She gave herself a little shake before following him. No, she did not look good in green. It made her olive skin actually look greener, like she was about to throw up. Which was about how she felt in this moment.

"Hey," she said. "So I wanted to have a little family meeting with you after church."

His eyebrows lifted as he reached for his keys. "Family meeting?"

"Isn't that what you and your brothers call them?"

"Yes, but—" His voice muted as surprise filled his expression. Color instantly appeared in his cheeks, and Mal found a blushing Skyler to be even more handsome than usual.

"What?" she asked.

"Are we a family?"

"We're *married*," she said, some of her Latina fire shooting to the top of her head. She folded her arms and settled her weight on her back foot. "So yes. Family meeting after church." She turned and walked toward the front door, glad when Skyler followed.

Awkwardness also accompanied them into the elevator down the hall, and it wasn't until she dared to glance at him that the tension broke.

"Sorry," he said.

"For what?"

He shrugged. "I don't know. Whatever you're mad about."

"I'm adding that to our agenda," she said.

"Adding what?"

She turned fully toward him, wishing they didn't have to go to church before their meeting. "You just apologized for something, and you don't even know what. What's with that?"

His eyes took on a fiery quality, but Mal simply glared right back.

"I had this girlfriend once," he said. The elevator dinged and another couple got on, both of them dressed for church too. Skyler put a smile on his face, and just like that, Mal watched the real Skyler Walker disappear.

He edged closer to her in the elevator and took her hand in his. She squeezed it, but it wasn't a casual or romantic squeeze. More like a *you'll finish this conversation as soon as we're alone* squeeze.

Skyler got the message. In the two years they'd been friends, they'd always had a special way of communicating with each other. That was one of the reasons Mal liked him so much. He was easy to talk to. Fun to laugh with.

She relaxed as they flowed out of the elevator and into his truck. He'd picked a church that was just a short drive away, and difficult conversations about ex-girlfriends couldn't happen in only five minutes.

Mal tugged at her dress once she got out of the truck, and she didn't feel like she could walk into the church. Then Skyler came to her side, and together, they faced the thick, wooden double doors that stood open, welcoming everyone to come and worship there.

"All right," Skyler said, exhaling heavily through his nose. "I don't know if this pastor is good or not. I just asked around to find this place."

"Who did you ask?"

"Jerome," he said.

"Jerome?" The incredulity in Mal's voice shot into the atmosphere. Skyler looked at her, and in the next moment they both burst out laughing.

"Okay," he said among the chuckles. "Maybe that wasn't the wisest choice."

"Yeah, because Jerome has never opened a Bible in his life," Mal said as they started up the steps.

Skyler secured his hand in hers, and Mal settled a little bit. It still took effort for her to take that final step to enter the church, but she let the music playing from the organ wash over her. She closed her eyes and took a deep breath, trying to find the deep part of herself that had used to enjoy going to church.

She did like singing, and she decided that even if that was all she enjoyed that day, this would be worth it. Her legs got her out of the small foyer and into the huge chapel. The ceiling stretched at least two stories tall, with huge stained glass windows along both sides.

The benches ran perpendicular to the windows, and up at the front, the dais rose to a pulpit and the choir seats, where the organist sat.

She let out her breath, not having realized that she'd been holding it.

"You okay?" Skyler asked, his voice barely loud enough to be heard.

"Yeah." She glanced at him. "You?"

"I'm good," he said, not going very far toward the front of the congregation. He stepped out of the aisle only a couple of rows from the back and sat down, leaving room for Mal on the end of the pew. She looked around, as if she'd see someone she knew there. She didn't, and she gave a little jolt when Skyler lifted his arm and put it around her.

She looked at him, their gazes locking. How she'd ever fought the magnetic force drawing her to him, she wasn't sure. He smiled, but it wasn't the same false one she'd seen from him in the elevator.

"Thanks for coming with me," Skyler said, pressing a kiss to her temple.

Mal leaned into the touch, a sense of comfort threading through her. This was good. This was the right place to be. With him.

And if they could have a real talk during their family meeting, Mal thought that maybe, just maybe, they'd be able to make a real relationship work.

If Skyler can be real, she thought. Before her thought patterns could zig and zag, the pastor stood up and walked over to the pulpit. The organist didn't stop playing, though, and Mal startled mightily when the choir suddenly burst into song.

"Oh, wow," she said right out loud. She hadn't bothered anyone though, because the choir was so loud. They stood from the first several rows at the front of the chapel, clapping and swaying as they turned around and faced the church-goers.

Joy filled the air from the smiles on their faces and the sounds coming from their mouths. Skyler pulled his arm away and started clapping along with them, albeit a half-hearted effort.

Mal just sat and stared. This wasn't like any church she'd ever been to before. And she couldn't say she hated it.

By the end of the joyful song, she wore a smile. And when the pastor said, "You are in the right place this morning, my brothers and sisters in the Lord. If you were worried about that, I implore you to stop. This is where you should be. The Lord wants you here. The Lord loves you."

And Mal believed him. She sat enthralled through the whole sermon, her soul warming and warming until she realized how starved her spirit had been. Before she knew it, the pastor invited everyone to stand to sing the closing song. Mal and Skyler did, though neither of them knew the words.

As she left the church, Mal felt lighter than she had in a long, long time. "That was great," she said as she stepped outside into the sunshine.

"Yeah?"

"Yeah," she said, looking at Skyler. "Did you like it?"

"Yeah," he said slowly. "It was all right."

"You didn't like it?"

"I—do you really think the Lord even cares where we are right now? What we're doing?"

Mal blinked and focused on the steps leading back to the sidewalk. When she reached the bottom, she said, "Yes, Skyler. I believe that."

He nodded but stayed quiet all the way back to the apartment. He loosened his tie in the elevator, and Mal wanted to watch him perform such a sexy move many more times in her life. With her heart racing, she walked down the hall to their apartment and waited for Skyler to unlock the door.

Acting cool and calm, she asked, "How about I make chimichangas for lunch?"

"Ah, trying to soften me up." Skyler chuckled and took Mal into his arms. The moment sobered between them, and Mal's pulse pounced through her body. Skyler ducked his head and pressed his cheek to hers. "Tell me what you're thinking."

"I want to talk about money," Mal said before she could tell herself to stop. "I want us to be united on things. I want an open, honest marriage, where we can talk about how we feel, and what we want out of life."

Skyler pulled away from her, keeping his head turned to the side. "All right."

Mal stood helplessly by the door as he started through the living room toward his bedroom. "That's it?"

"I'm going to get my computer," he said. "And change my clothes." He paused before entering the hall that led to his bedroom. Mal had only ever peeked down it, the first day she'd come to live with him when he'd given her a tour of the massive apartment. That whole wing of the apartment held his bedroom and bathroom, along with fancy artwork and a thick rug on the floor.

"You wanna start on those chimichangas?" His teasing smile made all of Mal's insecurities dry up.

"Oh, jeez," Mal said, giggling. She went into her room and changed into a comfortable pair of yoga pants and an oversized T-shirt. In the kitchen, she pulled some containers out of the fridge that held the pulled pork she'd made for dinner on Friday night.

She could make her own refried beans, but she was just as happy with canned ones when she was really hungry. If she wanted authentic Mexican food, it required more than a few minutes for a menu she'd thought of ten minutes ago.

She poured oil in a pan and set it on the stove and started filling flour tortillas before Skyler returned, his laptop under one arm. He sat at the counter and opened the laptop. "All right. Do you want to come look at this?"

Mal wiped her hands on a kitchen towel, suddenly nervous again. "Yes." She left the oil to heat and rounded the counter to sit beside him.

He typed and clicked, and a few seconds later, his bank account came up. He turned the laptop toward her.

"I have a lot of money." He cleared his throat and shifted on the stool. "My daddy was a huge tech mogul in Austin. He sold his company and all seven of us sons became billionaires overnight."

Mal swallowed as she finally realized how many numbers she was looking at on the screen. Skyler had half a dozen accounts, and they all had nine figures in them. She blinked, thinking the information on the screen had started to blur and that was why there were so many numbers.

Not so.

"I know you're not working right now," Skyler said. "I have no problem helping you out."

"Sky, this is more than helping me out," she said, her voice made mostly of air.

"I know that," he said. "And Mal, I know I haven't graduated from college or anything, but I'm not stupid. I've thought a lot about this, and us, and I know this is the right thing to do." He gazed at her with such intensity that Mal had no choice but to believe him.

She had no idea what to say, and tears filled her eyes. The scent of hot oil started to tickle her nose, and she should get up and roll up the meat and cheese she'd spooned over the tortillas and get them frying.

She couldn't look away from Skyler.

"You're on the account," Skyler said. "There's plenty to share. I don't want you to think of it as my money or your money. We're married, like you said. It's *our* money."

Mal shook her head, a tear splashing her cheek. She reached to wipe it, but Skyler beat her to it. He leaned toward her, his fingers so warm against her skin. His breath drifted across her cheek, and then his lips touched hers.

Mal kissed him, a completely new experience as he moved slowly, kissed sweetly, and didn't hold a single thing back.

6

Skyler wanted what he'd said to be true. He wanted to share what he had with Mal, but it was more than that. He wanted to build a life with her. He knew he had more to tell her, and she had plenty to tell him too. They didn't know each other as well as most people who were married probably did.

Once they went to the hearing, they'd have time.

He had time now.

He finally pulled away from her and pressed his lips together. He sure did like kissing her, and they'd shared a different kind of kiss every time. He sure did like that, as it told him Mal had many sides and a lot of layers. And he'd never wanted a simple woman.

"So if you need a new dress, Mal, that costs more than fifteen dollars, go get it."

Her cheeks colored, and she nearly toppled the stool

she stood up so fast. She kept her head down as she got back to work on the chimichangas, and Skyler wished he'd thought before he'd spoken.

"Sorry," he said.

"For what?" she asked again.

"For being a jerk," he said. "I shouldn't have said that. You can buy whatever kind of dress you want."

She eased the first chimichanga into the hot oil, and the sizzling and spitting was quite satisfying to Skyler. He was also starving, and had he known Mal would start feeding him delicious Mexican food most days of the week, he might have asked her out for real, months ago.

The image of Shayla's face floated through his mind, and he knew he wouldn't have.

"Is money the only thing?" he asked.

Mal didn't answer immediately. She babysat the chimichangas for another moment, and then she turned back to him. "How many brothers and sisters do I have?"

"Four," he said.

"One older brother. One younger. Two younger sisters."

"What are their names?"

Skyler wondered if he was taking a test. "Jorge is the oldest. Then you. Then Julia, Marcus and Raquel." He folded his arms on the counter in front of him. "Can you name my brothers in order?"

A challenge sat behind her smile. "Rhett, Jeremiah, the twins, Wyatt, you, Micah."

"Which twin is older?"

"Liam."

Skyler grinned at her. "So we know a little bit about each other." He stood up, wanting to kiss her again. In fact, they had all afternoon with nothing to do. His hormones raced, but he pressed on the brakes. "For example, I know you're a good cook. I know you have a good singing voice, and you love to sing. I know you hate shopping. I know you're good at your job, and good with people because you genuinely care about them."

He joined her in the kitchen, hoping she'd say a few things about him, so he'd know he wasn't crazy.

She just gazed up at him. "I know we know each other."

"You can tell me anything."

"I'm sure you'll regret that," she said with a smile. She turned back to the stove and carefully flipped over the chimichangas. She kept her eyes down as she said, "I'd love to know why you apologize without a reason."

"Ah, that goes back to the ex-girlfriend," he said, hating Shayla's presence in his life. But she'd been there, and Skyler couldn't just erase those years, even if he wanted to.

Mal didn't say anything, and Skyler took that as his cue to keep talking. "Her name was Shayla, and she always seemed to be mad about something. So I learned to apologize, even if I didn't know what I'd done." He shrugged, the familiar foolishness and embarrassment filtering through him. He wondered if he'd ever be rid of it.

Just like he wondered if the Lord really cared if he'd gone to church that day. Mal did, and his brothers did, and Momma and Daddy had always taken them to church on Sundays. Momma volunteered at the church on Tuesdays and Wednesdays too, sorting donations and teaching a class on how to make jam, among other things.

He simply felt so small among such a huge world, among so many people.

"Well," Mal said. "You don't have to do that to me. If you don't know why I'm upset, ask me. I'll tell you. Probably in two languages." She flashed him a smile. "I'm not sure you've seen upset from me yet."

"Oh, boy," Skyler said with a smile. Easily, as if he'd been born to do it, he slipped his hand along her waist. "Thanks for calling this family meeting. I'm, uh, not great at the whole talking thing."

"You don't have to be good at it with anyone else," Mal said. "Just me."

"Deal." Skyler slipped away from her, because though they were married, he wasn't in love with her. And if they weren't married, he wouldn't even be considering leading her to his bedroom.

He sat back at the counter and logged out of his banking website. "That card I gave you is connected to one of these accounts," he said. "I know you haven't used it, but you really can. For groceries, and all that. You probably shouldn't even have your own account. They'll want to know why."

"I'll go close it tomorrow," she said.

Skyler nodded, suddenly tired for no reason at all. "Do you want to go for a hike this afternoon?"

"Let's see how I feel after I eat this chimichanga." She pulled the two of them out of the oil and put them on a plate with a paper towel on it. "Let me get some toppings out, and we'll be ready."

Skyler watched her work, and she was so welcome in his life, in his apartment. He thought about telling her about the therapist he was going to call tomorrow, but when she turned from the fridge, laden with sour cream, salsa, and guacamole, he decided it could wait for another day.

After all, they didn't have to talk about everything in their first family meeting. At least that was what he told himself.

THE NEXT MORNING, Skyler woke at six, even though he hadn't set his alarm. He lay in bed, trying to go back to sleep. But the endeavor was fruitless, he knew that. He rarely napped during the day, and once he woke up in the morning, that was it for the day.

He got up, put on his running shorts, his basketball shorts after that, and was pulling a T-shirt over his head when he went into the kitchen. He started making coffee, though he wouldn't drink it, and wondered if he could go knock on Mal's door and ask her to go running with him. With all the food she'd been making since she'd stopped working, Skyler definitely needed to hit the gym even if he didn't run.

"Morning," Mal said, and Skyler's heart rate jumped. "Oh."

"Scared you, didn't I?" She wore her Spandex and a sweatshirt with a white feather on it—and a smile.

"Yeah," he said. "You want to go running?" He pushed the power button on the coffee maker, and it started to click.

"I'm already dressed," she said.

"I'll get my shoes." He had nothing to do the rest of the day, and he could easily go lift weights after lunch. Or that evening. Or whenever, really.

Mal's phone chimed, and she picked it up off the counter where she'd set it. "I think it's...your mother."

Skyler almost dropped the coffee can he was putting back in the cupboard. "What?"

"Yeah, it says, *You two will come for the New Year's Eve light parade, right?*" Mal looked up, complete surprise on her face.

Skyler crossed the kitchen and took the phone from her. He didn't have his momma's phone number memorized, but the messages certainly seemed to be from her. He met Mal's eyes. "What do you think?"

"We don't have anything else going on," she said.

"And it's over by ten," he said. "We can still get back here for the ball drop."

"They don't have an afterparty at the ranch?" She accepted her phone back from him. "And I can't remember the last time I stayed up until midnight by choice."

"We could go back to the ranch, if you want," he said. "Or stay at Momma's. She'd die and go to heaven, then come back and make us New Year's breakfast." Skyler smiled, and he suddenly wanted to do exactly what he'd outlined. Going to breakfast with his brothers had been really fun. And going to church had opened a door Skyler had closed a long time ago.

He knew it wasn't as simple as just re-opening the door, and everything between him and the Lord would be magically okay. He thought of his own phone, and the call he needed to make later that day, wondering if he should tell Mal about it now or after he'd made an appointment.

His throat dried up, because he wasn't even sure what to say when he made that phone call.

Maybe you should ask Mal for help.

The thought existed in his mind, and Skyler didn't want to dismiss it. "Mal?"

She looked up from her phone, her expression open. She wouldn't judge him. At least he hoped she wouldn't.

"I...I got the name and number of someone from my brother."

Mal's head cocked to the side. "Okay."

Skyler realized that what he'd said was beyond vague. "A therapist," he said next.

"A therapist?" Mal pointed to herself and then him. "For us?"

"No." He sighed. He really wasn't great at this. "For me. I get irritated really easily, and I don't know. Jeremiah swears by his therapist, and I thought maybe it would help me work through some things."

Mal put her phone back on the counter, her attention on him solely now. "Skyler."

"I'm fine," he said. "I just want to not be so grumpy all the time. And you didn't know Jeremiah before, but he was worse than me."

Mal didn't smile. Skyler didn't either.

"Okay."

"I'm going to call today," he said. "And I wondered... what do you say when you call to get an appointment like that?"

Mal wrapped her arms around Skyler's waist and leaned into him. "You just say, I need to make an appointment to see Dr. Mal." She smiled then, though it was small and mostly playful. "They won't ask you why. If they do, you say you just need to talk to a therapist as soon as possible."

"Okay." Skyler held her—his wife—in the kitchen, glad he'd decided to say something. "Let's go running. All these chimichangas are making me slow."

"You don't have to eat until you feel like you're going to pop." Mal swatted at his chest and backed up. Skyler laughed, glad he'd decided to confide in his wife. No, he hadn't told her everything about himself or his past yet. But no one could drink from a fire hose.

They ran; he showered; he skipped breakfast as he usually did. When Mal went to get in the shower, Skyler pulled out his phone and tapped to Jeremiah's text that held the information he needed.

He took a deep breath and tapped to make the call.

"Windsor Counseling," a woman chirped, and Skyler wanted to hang up. He took another breath. He *wanted* to do this. He wanted to feel whole again. He pushed against the sheepskin he'd been wearing since the fiasco in Dallas, and cleared his throat.

"Yeah, hi," he said. "My name is Skyler Walker, and I'm looking to get an appointment with Dr. Haskell."

"Okay, is this for a medication appointment?"

"I don't know," Skyler said.

"Is this your first time in?"

"Yes, ma'am," he said, and at least Momma would be proud of his Texas manners.

"We're booking out a couple of weeks right now," the woman said. "Holidays and all that. Let's see...I can get you in on January eighth?"

Skyler didn't need to look at his calendar. There wouldn't be anything on it. He'd already decided not to go back to school for the winter semester. He only had three semesters left to finish his degree, but he honestly didn't need one. He could do the finances and keep the books for Seven Sons with what he knew now.

"Sure," he said. "That works."

"Do you know where we're located?"

"No idea." Skyler's stomach growled, and he made his way toward the kitchen to get a protein bar.

"We're in the new office building on the north side of town," she said. "Third floor. Suite two thousand; it's only one of two offices on the third floor."

"North side of town?"

"Yeah, up by the highway that goes out to the ranches."

"What town?" Skyler asked, realizations clicking around in his brain.

"Three Rivers."

"Of course." Instant irritation exploded inside him, but he managed to thank the woman, say he'd be there on January eighth at ten-fifteen, and hang up without shattering his phone.

"Three Rivers," he said in disgust. But Jeremiah lived in Three Rivers, so it made sense that his therapist did too.

Mal came out of the bedroom, freshly showered, her hair still damp. Skyler said, "I got an appointment on the eighth. It's in Three Rivers."

"The eighth? When's the hearing?"

Skyler's heart shriveled and re-expanded in less than a breath. "Shoot." He swiped on his phone, quickly getting his calendar open. "The tenth. Thank the Lord." He didn't want to make that call again, and he absolutely could not miss Mal's hearing.

Mal's whooshing breath met his ears, and he looked up at her. "Did you want to come with me? We can go to breakfast beforehand. Go see if there's something to do in Three Rivers after. Make it a whole day if we're going to drive there."

"Sure," she said. "I need something to do."

"You and me both," he muttered. He'd never had a problem filling his time before. He didn't have to account to anyone, but he didn't want Mal to know he sometimes literally sat on his laptop, fiddling around with whatever.

Mal pulled a banana from the bunch and opened the fridge to get a piece of string cheese. "Okay, I'm going to go call my brother. Word on the street is that he got engaged over the weekend."

"All right," Skyler said. She went back down the hall to her bedroom, and Skyler went toward his, already texting Jeremiah.

Thanks for warning me the therapist was in Three Rivers, bro.

I live here, Jeremiah said. *Can you talk now? I want to know who you're seeing.*

Skyler sighed, because he barely wanted to talk to a therapist, and he certainly didn't want to answer his brother's questions.

"It's Jeremiah," he told himself as he crossed into his bedroom. "He's your brother. He's not going to judge you."

He closed the door and tapped the phone icon, his chest laced tight. Only when Jeremiah said, "Sky," did he relax. It was so nice to have someone he could say anything to and feel like he could show his face to them again.

And he had more than one someone like that. He had Wyatt and Micah. Jeremiah. And honestly, any of his brothers. His parents. They all loved him he knew.

You aren't the black sheep.

"Hey, Jeremiah," he said, and he tried to focus on the conversation. But his mind kept moving through the apartment to Mal, and if she could be one of the someone's in his life that he could say anything to and still look her in the eye.

7

Wyatt held the box while Marcy stretched the tape across it to secure it. She sniffed, and Wyatt said nothing. He wasn't sure what to say anyway. He and Marcy had talked about moving many times over the course of the past month.

She *did* want to move into the house at Church Ranches. She did. She'd insisted on it. She just had a lot of feelings about leaving the house where they currently lived. She'd bought it herself, and she'd lived on this street for thirteen years. It was the only home she'd known other than her childhood home, which she and her brother had sold a few months ago.

So, since Christmas, Wyatt had helped her go through cupboards and closets. He hauled things to Goodwill or the dump, and he listened whenever Marcy had a story to tell about something in her house.

Cleaning out his bedroom at the homestead had been easy, a thirty-minute job that was mostly him packing up his clothes and making sure he hadn't left something crucial in the bathroom.

He'd been living with Marcy since their reconciliation right after Thanksgiving, and he fell more in love with her every single day.

Tomorrow was New Year's Day, and they were moving into their new home. New year. New start.

Wyatt was terribly excited about all of it.

"I'll get these in the truck," he said. Even with his bad back, he could carry more than Marcy, usually in one arm. She was strong in other ways, but hefting packed boxes and getting them over the tailgate of his big truck wasn't one of them.

"Okay." Marcy sniffled again, and she bent to pick up the hamster cage, following him outside. They'd already gotten the keys to their place, and they were moving everything they could today.

Tonight, they'd spend New Year's Eve with the family at the light parade, something they were supposed to have done last year. Wyatt didn't want to dwell on what had happened exactly one year ago tonight, so he pushed the memories out of his mind.

"Buy me lunch?" Marcy asked as she put her hamster in the back seat.

Wyatt looked at her from across the truck bed. "Yeah, of course." Wyatt liked going to lunch more than almost anything, and Marcy didn't even have to ask. "This should be the last load, besides the furniture we're taking."

Marcy nodded and climbed into the truck.

"What do you want for lunch?" Wyatt asked, trying to get her talking. He didn't like it when Marcy shut down, but he didn't know how to avoid it.

She's fine, he told himself. And it wasn't his job to fix her anyway. This was just how she dealt with stress.

"They delivered the patio furniture yesterday," he said. "And the new bed and everything for upstairs."

"I know," Marcy said. "I can't wait to see it."

Wyatt couldn't either, and he reached over and took Marcy's hand in his. "You okay, sweetheart?"

"Yeah." She gave him a small smile, her eyes still a bit teary. "Wyatt, I have to tell you something."

His heartbeat flailed for a moment, and the world around him swooped. "Okay."

"Wait. No, not yet."

"Not yet?" Wyatt's curiosity exploded. "What does that mean?"

"It means I forgot I had a plan."

"A plan?" Why was he repeating everything she said? "Marce, just tell me if you don't want the house. Or if you want to split up once we get to our anniversary."

"Wyatt Walker," she said, her voice full of shock. "Of course not."

"Well, you just said in this super serious voice, 'Wyatt, I have to tell you something.' It sounds bad."

"It's not bad," she said, giggling. Ah, there was his Marcy, the woman he loved. He loved the woman who needed to work through her emotions too, the woman who wasn't embarrassed to cry in front of him.

"Okay, well, what's the plan?"

"If I told you, it wouldn't be a surprise."

"Oh, come on," he said, grinning at her. He lifted her hand to kiss her wrist. "Just give me a hint."

"You'll see at the house."

He normally didn't drive over the speed limit, but he suddenly wanted to get to the house. Quickly. He pressed down the accelerator, and Marcy squealed as the truck lurched forward.

He laughed with her, but he really did want to get there. Church Ranches was an exclusive, gated community in the swells above Three Rivers, and it normally took about twenty-five minutes from Marcy's house to get there.

Today, it only took Wyatt twenty.

"All right," he said, practically leaping out of the truck. "Let's go see what we've got."

"You're going to ruin it," Marcy said, following him much slower.

Wyatt chuckled and stepped to the back of the truck to collect a couple of boxes. "These go in the kitchen."

Marcy took the hamster and opened the front door ahead of him so he could carry the boxes and not have to wrestle with the door. He walked through the huge foyer and then the living room to the kitchen, which sat in the front corner of the house, behind the garage.

Wyatt put the boxes on the island countertop and exhaled. "I love this house," he said.

"The hot tub is here," Marcy said from the French doors that led into the backyard, and Wyatt practically sprinted over to her.

Sure enough, the hot tub he'd ordered sat there. "It's beautiful," he said, putting his arm around his wife. "Is that the surprise?"

"You ordered it, cowboy." Marcy rolled her eyes and stepped out from under his arm. "Let's get the truck unloaded and go see the furniture."

"Fine," Wyatt called after her. But he took one more look at the hot tub, already anticipating the first soak he could take and how glorious it would be.

Eventually, he and Marcy got all the boxes and bags into the house, and Wyatt stepped into their bedroom with her. The master suite was massive—even bigger than the one at Seven Sons—and he'd ordered a couch, an armchair, and an armoire to hold a television in addition to the bed.

Everything was there, just not necessarily where he wanted it. "Should we move it where we want it?"

"Yeah," Marcy said, tossing a bag on the bed. "I brought the new sheets too. We can get the bed set up so we won't have to do it tomorrow."

"Yes, ma'am. Tell me where you want all this stuff." He put the couch in front of the window, where he hoped

Marcy would perhaps sit and relax with a book. A lamp went next to it, then the armchair.

The bed got positioned on the longest wall, with a pair of matching nightstands made with a beautiful, dark wood. Wyatt thought of Micah as he adjusted their position and Marcy plugged in a lamp and put it on her side of the bed.

"We should have Micah build us something," he said.

"Is he going to open the shop?"

"I think he's meeting with a building owner in a couple of days," Wyatt said. "To find out about leasing the space. So yeah."

"What about a dining room set?" Marcy suggested. "We didn't buy one of those."

"Nope." Wyatt hadn't seen the need. He and Marcy weren't the ones who were going to entertain the family at their house. Though it was easily the biggest out of any of the Walkers, neither of them cooked, and he hadn't seen the point of buying a big dining room set.

Together, they made the bed, and Marcy wadded up the packaging and said, "All right. Let's go check out the stuff upstairs."

"Do we have to set all of those beds up too?" he asked.

She smiled at him. "Not today, cowboy."

He pressed a kiss to her forehead, and together, they went up a wide set of steps to the second floor. This really was way too much house for just two of them. They had an office on the main level, just off the entry way. A huge living room, kitchen, dining room. Three bathrooms, plus laundry facilities on the main level. Their master suite, which could easily house three beds. The master closet itself could be a bedroom. The upstairs boasted a theater room, four more bedrooms, and three more bathrooms.

At the top of the steps, Wyatt's phone rang, and he pulled it out of his back pocket. "It's Grace," he said.

"Answer it," Marcy said, crowding in close to him.

But she didn't need to stand so close, because he put the call on speaker, tapped the button, and said, "Hello?"

"Wyatt?" Grace asked in her Texas voice.

"That's right," he drawled back to her. He took a breath and held it, because he really needed her to agree to come to Three Rivers and be his nurse following his surgery.

It had been much harder than he'd thought to find someone who was willing to move in with him and Marcy, and basically dedicate twenty-four hours a day to helping Wyatt with whatever he needed.

He hadn't been prepared for the first couple of interviews, and when the home-care nurses asked what days they'd have off, Wyatt had just blinked, his mind blank. He'd turned to the Internet after that, and he'd learned what they would expect from him. And he wanted someone good, not just whoever would take the job.

Grace Hardy was his last chance.

"I'm so sorry, Mister Walker," she started, and a hiss came out of Marcy's mouth. She walked away, going into the first bedroom that sat just off the landing, which over-looked the foyer below.

"But I just can't leave Oklahoma City by the end of January. If the surgery wasn't until April, I could do it."

"All right," Wyatt said, disappointment cutting through him too. "I understand." And he did. "I'll talk to my doctors."

"All right," she said. "Thank you for the opportunity to interview."

The call ended, and Wyatt let his hand fall back to his side, his phone still clutched in his fingers. Out of all the nurses he'd interviewed, he'd liked Grace the best.

Wyatt walked across the loft and into the bedroom. "It's okay, Marcy," he said. "We'll find—"

He stopped talking when his brain short-circuited.

This room wasn't just holding a mattress and a night-stand thrown haphazardly in here by the furniture store delivery guys.

This room had been set up. Lovingly set up.

And the only mattress was only big enough for a small child.

Marcy stood next to the crib, which was fully assem-bled and made up in pale green sheets, with a quilt inside that had a giraffe on it. "Hey," he said. "I've seen that quilt."

"Your mother made it," she said.

"She said it was for someone special."

Marcy put her hand on her still-flat stomach. "It is, Wyatt. It's for your baby."

He wanted to take in the rest of the furniture. The fact that Marcy—or someone—had been here to hang curtains in this room. But he could only look at Marcy, her words sinking deep into his ears.

"My baby," he said, but it wasn't a question.

"I'm pregnant, Wyatt." Her grin stretched as wide as the Mississippi. "I'm due in July."

A roar started in Wyatt's head, and he swept into the room, taking Marcy right into his arms and off the ground. He laughed, the joy pulling through him so much better than anything he'd ever felt before.

Marcy squealed and laughed too, and Wyatt just held her tight. When they quieted, he set her on her feet and leaned his forehead against hers.

"Are you happy?" she asked.

"Beyond happy," he said, letting his emotions swirl around inside him however they wanted. "This is so great." He kissed her, maybe a bit more gently than he normally did. He suddenly understood why Jeremiah took breakfast to Whitney in bed, and why Tripp had been crying at the hospital the day his son was born.

"When can we find out if it's a boy or a girl?" he asked.

"Months, baby," Marcy said. "I think I'm only five or so weeks along. I just barely missed my period."

"Okay," he said, keeping her within the circle of his arms. He breathed in the scent of her hair, and she suddenly smelled different. She was going to be the mother of his child, and Wyatt couldn't stop smiling.

"When did you put all this together?" He looked around at the curtains and the fully made-up crib.

"Saturday," she said. "While you were at breakfast with your brothers."

Wyatt swayed with her, happier than he'd ever been.

"I was thinking," Marcy said, stepping back. "Why don't you call Skyler and ask him to come live here and take care of you?"

"Skyler?"

"Yeah." Marcy gestured for him to follow her, and he did as they went to the next room. This one had the mattress and box springs leaning up against the wall, as he'd expected. "I mean, you don't really need a trained nurse. You just need someone to steady you as you climb in and out of the hot tub." She flashed a smile in his direction and helped him get the bed put together.

"I mean...yeah." Wyatt wondered if Skyler would come. "You know, he's married now."

"And we have four bedrooms up here no one will be using," Marcy said. "You'd have someone here to help. I could still fly." She lifted one shoulder in a shrug and added, "I want that nightstand over there."

Wyatt put it where she wanted, between the bed and the window seat, and sat down on the window seat, a sigh leaking from his mouth. "How long are you going to fly?" he asked.

"Until I can't fit in the cockpit," she said. "And I'm going to hire someone as soon as possible and start training them."

"That needs to be done anyway," he said.

"Maybe two people," Marcy said. She joined him on the window seat and took his hand in hers. Wyatt loved touching her, even something as simple as holding her hand. "I still want Payne's Pest-free," she said.

"Of course," he said. "It's a family heirloom."

"But someone else can fly for a while," she said, tucking herself into his chest.

"Skyler," Wyatt mused again, and Marcy nodded. "All right. I'll call him and see what he says."

8

Mal's anxiety grew with every mile that brought her closer to the entire Walker family. She'd met them all before, of course, but there was something different about having dinner for a holiday and just hanging out for hours while they waited for the sun to go down.

They weren't stupid people, that was for sure. And while she sure did like Skyler, she wasn't in love with him. And she'd need to pretend like she was. For her, she wasn't even sure what that looked like or sounded like, as she'd never been in love before.

Skyler had fallen silent about ten miles ago, and as they passed a sign that said they still had ten miles until they reached Three Rivers, he finally cleared his throat. Mal looked at him, wondering if he could simply feel her anxiety.

"Wyatt called this morning," he said.

"Oh?" It wasn't completely usual for Skyler to have so much contact with his brothers. He'd told her they went long periods without talking, and then there'd be a flurry, and until he'd announced to everyone that they were married, it seemed like they were in the middle of the flurry.

"Yeah, he's having a hard time finding someone to come help him after his surgery."

"Oh." Mal didn't know what that had to do with Skyler. Maybe Wyatt just wanted to blow off his frustration.

"Mal, I don't think I'm going to go back to school next week." He shifted in his seat, and Mal's whole world shifted.

"You're not? I thought you had three semesters left." She stared at the side of his face, but he kept his attention out the windshield, despite the fact that there was hardly any traffic in the middle of the afternoon.

Momma had invited them for dinner before they were going to head over to Main Street for the light parade. No, Mal had never been. Skyler said he hadn't either, and she had not looked at the website link one of his brothers had sent him, which he'd forwarded to her.

Mal swallowed, still waiting for Skyler to explain. If neither of them had a job or went to school, what was their life going to be like? She'd actually been counting down the days until he went back to school, because then she'd have some time to herself to figure out how to...she didn't even know what. Be herself again?

No matter what, she felt lost.

"I don't need a degree to manage the ranch money," he said. "I can work there any time I want, and I don't like school." He finally glanced at her, though it only lasted a moment. "I never have."

"Yeah, I know," Mal murmured, trying to work out what next Monday would look like when Skyler didn't leave for class. A mile passed. Then two. "So, wait," she said, trying to piece together how this conversation had started with Wyatt calling him, and then Skyler saying he could work for the ranch without a degree.

"Skyler," she said. "Are you saying you want to...what are you saying?"

"I don't know," he said.

"Why did Wyatt call?" she asked.

"He's having trouble getting someone to come stay with him to help him after the surgery."

"And?" Mal prompted.

"And he wondered if maybe we wanted to come live with him and Marcy." By the time Skyler finished speaking, Mal could barely understand the words.

"Live with him and Marcy?" Mal almost started laughing, but she was so shocked, she didn't.

"They're moving into a big house up in a gated community tomorrow," he said. "The surgery isn't until the end of January. We could take the next thirty days to pack up, move things here on the weekends...." He trailed off, and Mal was glad.

She had too many words to chew on right now. He wanted to move to Three Rivers.

She couldn't even imagine doing that, though she had no real ties in Amarillo, other than the fact that she'd lived there for the past fifteen years. She had other friends in Amarillo—Skyler did too. He'd expressed frustration with his brothers in the past, and Mal couldn't imagine *living* with one of them.

"What are you thinking?" Skyler asked.

"So much," she said. "I—I don't even know where to start."

"You don't want to move to Three Rivers."

"Not particularly." She turned toward Skyler again. "And certainly not if we don't have our own place."

"My goal was always to come back to Seven Sons and do the finances," he said. "You knew that."

"Yeah, but...that was years down the road."

"We'll have to be married for at least two years," he said. "I'd be done with school by then."

"I know." She blew out her breath. "I guess I just hadn't thought about it."

"Let's go by Wyatt's place this afternoon," he said. "Before we go to my parents' house. You want to?"

"Okay," Mal said, because she wasn't sure what other choice she had. She ran her hands through her hair, already feeling it start to frizz though she'd spent time with a flat iron and lots of hair products this morning so she'd look as good as possible for his family.

"He said it's huge," Skyler said, reaching for his phone in the middle console. "Will you text him for the address?" He handed her his phone.

She swiped, feeling a bit off to be handling his device. She supposed married couples could look at each other's phones without finding it odd, but Mal was still trying to figure out how to be married.

She found his texting app, and Wyatt's name sat at the top. She asked him for his address, and he started responding instantly. It popped up, and she said, "It's here."

"Ask him if we can come by in about twenty minutes," Skyler said.

Mal did, and Wyatt gave a thumbs up. She told Skyler, and then she got his map program navigating them to Wyatt's new house. "It's outside of town," she said, wondering how she felt about that.

She'd come from a small village, and she liked the city of Amarillo. It wasn't a huge city, but it was about ten times bigger than Three Rivers.

"Yeah, it's up in an exclusive new development," Skyler said, glancing at her again. "You know Wyatt was a celebrity bull rider before my daddy even sold the tech firm, right?"

"No," Mal said. "I did not know that."

"He's got his own clothing line and everything."

"Wow." Mal zoomed in on the map, and sure enough, it looked like they were driving out into the middle of nowhere.

Skyler drove through the middle of town, and Mal noticed a bakery on Main Street. All the old buildings possessed a charm she hadn't seen in a while. She liked the snowflakes protruding out from the tops of them, even though it hardly ever snowed in Texas, though the Panhandle did get some white stuff from time to time.

A red, white, and blue barbershop pole was stuck to the side of one building, and Mal saw boutiques, a movie theater, diners, shops, and more.

"Here's where the parade will be," Skyler said, pointing to the grand stands already set up on the side of the road. "We have a reserved spot near the announcers. I guess Jeremiah is a sponsor, and so is his wife's family."

"Sounds fancy," Mal said, swallowing as she realized that every single person in the Walker family was very wealthy. She thought about how much she could send to her family, and she had to swallow again.

Skyler chuckled, and they drove by a fountain and a dog park.

"Do you still want a dog?" she asked, watching a couple of people who had their dogs out that afternoon.

"Always," he said. "I think the only person who loves dogs more than me is Daddy."

Mal smiled, but her nerves wouldn't allow her to truly relax.

They wound out of town, leaving the vibrancy of Three Rivers behind, and started up a slight incline into some hills. Skyler's phone directed them where to turn, and sure enough, a set of blue flags with the word FLAGSHIP printed on them welcomed everyone to the new development.

Skyler pulled up to the gate, which was shut though most of the homes Mal could see were still in various stages of construction. "Look," she said, spying a sign. "They still have lots for sale. We could buy a place here." Her voice was full of false suggestion, though, and Skyler scoffed and shook his head. Thankfully.

She couldn't even *imagine* living here. Pure awe filled her as Skyler leaned out the window and keyed in a code to get the gate to open. He didn't seem to think anything was out of the ordinary at all, but Mal couldn't get her heartbeat to settle down.

They went past all the construction to a house in the back corner of the development that was clearly done. A big, black truck sat in the driveway, and Mal realized she'd have to put on her loving wife skin right now to be able to interact with Wyatt and Marcy.

Skyler pulled his fancy truck next to Wyatt's, and Mal saw money everywhere now that she knew more about Skyler's family and situation. "Ready?" he asked. "This place looks plenty big, Mal."

"It sure does," she said.

"I don't want to live here though," he said. "It's at least

a half an hour to the ranch, and I'll be working there every day."

Their eyes met, and Mal nodded. "I didn't know we'd be moving to Three Rivers so soon."

"I didn't either. It's just...Wyatt might need my help, and he said something the other day at breakfast, and I don't know."

"What did he say?"

Before Skyler could answer, Wyatt and Marcy came out the front door, and Skyler nodded to them. "Later," he said, opening his door and sliding out of the truck. Mal did the same as Skyler started to laugh. He and Wyatt embraced, clapping each other on the back.

They almost looked like twins, though Wyatt was slightly broader and slightly taller. He carried himself with supreme confidence, and Mal felt nothing but genuine happiness from him. He grinned at Mal over Skyler's shoulder, and then he stepped around him to hug her too.

"Ooh," she said as he picked her up in a hug. She couldn't help laughing and patting his shoulder too.

He set her down quickly, and said, "Okay, so I guess you maybe want to see where you two will be staying if you decide to come live here?"

"Something like that," Skyler said, reaching for Mal's hand. She gladly slipped her fingers in between his, needing and finding the anchor he provided. They exchanged a glance at the same time Marcy and Wyatt did.

"Well, we have a secret in the house," Wyatt said. "And if you don't want to know it, that's fine. But if you do, you have to solemnly swear to keep it a secret until we announce it."

"Solemnly swear?" Skyler laughed, and Mal smiled too. He looked at her, and he beamed with joy. She liked seeing him like this, and she felt every muscle in her body soften. "Do we want to solemnly swear not to tell anyone?"

"I don't know who I'd even tell," Mal said. "It's not like anyone knows—"

"Remember, this is Wyatt we're talking about," Skyler said. "Even a casual mention of the secret could end up somewhere he doesn't want it." He looked at Wyatt and Marcy, who waited expectantly. "We're out on the secret," he said. "I don't want that kind of pressure."

"All right."

Marcy said, "Give me a minute," and went back in the house.

"They're still working on a few things out here, too," Wyatt said. "The yard won't go in until spring. I'm having them do the back fence though, because I want to get a dog."

"Oh, Skyler wants a dog too," Mal said.

"Of course he does." Wyatt chuckled and slowly started moving toward the front door. "Has he told you the story about the turtle?"

"Wyatt," Skyler said with plenty of warning in his voice.

"Or the snakes. And there's at least three about dogs."

Mal looked at Skyler, who wore that adorable blush in his face. "Do tell."

"This guy has a heart of cotton," Wyatt said. "He'll bring home anything wounded, helpless, or crying." He grinned like he'd just revealed an amazing thing about his brother.

But Mal felt like Wyatt's words had formed spikes and were stabbing, stabbing, stabbing right through her lungs.

9

Skyler chuckled with Wyatt, though he noticed an immediate change in Mal. All at once, he realized what Wyatt had said.

He'll bring home anything wounded, helpless, or crying.

And wasn't that exactly what he'd done with Mal? She *had* been crying the night he'd gone to her hovel of an apartment. He *had* brought her home. But she wasn't wounded or helpless.

She pulled in an audible breath, but Wyatt didn't notice or didn't care as he turned to open the front door and walk inside.

Skyler didn't need another thing to put on the conversational back burner, so he didn't follow Wyatt inside. "You're not one of the animals I used to rescue growing up," he said.

Mal simply looked at him. "Feels like it."

"It's not true." He gathered her into his arms. "Honestly, it's not."

She clung to him, and Skyler wondered if she could feel how much he needed her too. He was the one who was wounded and helpless, and she'd always been the one to pick him up, pound on his door at six-thirty and get him out the door for a run, and make him laugh.

In that moment, Skyler fell a little further along the path toward loving her, and they breathed in together. "Okay, so let's go see where we *might* stay *if* we decide to come here and help Wyatt."

"If?" Mal asked, stepping back and straightening her shirt. She looked into the house like it might swallow her whole.

"Yeah," Skyler said. "We make decisions together now, Mal. That's what married people do." He took her hand again and led her into the house. A huge foyer had doors leading off both sides of it, and directly in front of him opened up to an enormous living room. This was definitely high-end living, and he wondered how much Wyatt had paid for this house. It honestly didn't matter. His brother had so much money, he'd never be able to spend it all, even if he bought a hundred houses like this.

"Marcy's office is here," Wyatt said, coming back into the foyer and indicating the room on the right. "The steps are right around the corner here, and you guys will be upstairs. But main living here. We have a hot tub back there already." He grinned, and Skyler did too.

"For your back, of course," he said.

"Of course." Wyatt laughed, and it felt good to be surrounded by so much joy. Skyler sure could use more of that. With Wyatt, he didn't feel like he couldn't be himself. With Wyatt, he wasn't the black sheep.

"Formal living here," Wyatt said, indicating the other side. "If either of you need an office, you can have it. I don't even know what to do with a formal living room."

"That's where you meet with people you don't want to bring all the way into your house," Skyler said. "You know, like the pastor, or someone who just drops by."

"I don't think many people will drop by," Wyatt said.

Thank goodness, Skyler thought. In his opinion, there was nothing worse than a pop-in visit. He'd opened the door for anyone over the past two years in Amarillo, and he'd hosted parties where he couldn't get people to leave when he wanted them to. Anything to be in the spotlight, be the guy everyone loved.

Since marrying Mal, he'd dropped that persona completely, and he didn't miss the Skyler Walker who'd been so concerned about hiding who he really was.

You still haven't told Mal a whole lot about Dallas, his mind whispered, and he pushed the thoughts away. They had plenty of time for her to learn his deepest, darkest secrets.

Not that long, filtered through his mind. His almost-arrest and the accusations against him could be brought up in her hearing. He honestly didn't know what happened at a hearing like this, and he thought about hiring a lawyer while Wyatt showed them the living room, the fireplace, the bathrooms, the master suite, and the kitchen.

"This is beautiful," Mal said, dropping his hand and moving into the kitchen more fully. Her eyes glowed with wonder as she took in the granite, the six-burner luxury stove, the double ovens. "I could make so much Mexican food in here." She laughed—truly laughed—and Skyler's heart took flight.

"Neither Wyatt or Marcy cook," he said. "And I'm sure they wouldn't mind you taking over the kitchen."

She looked at Wyatt with pure hope in her eyes, and Wyatt swept his hand toward the enormity of the kitchen. "It's all yours, Mal. I haven't had good, authentic Mexican food in a while."

Skyler shook his head and rolled his eyes.

"What?" Wyatt asked. "I haven't."

"Sure," Skyler said. "Show us the upstairs."

Marcy met them on the bottom stair, turned, and went right back up. They all followed, bypassing the first room on the right and continuing through the loft.

"Three bedrooms up here," he said. "All yours, even if you only need one. Three bathrooms, all connected to bedrooms. Big loft. Theater room. I'll probably move into the theater room and never leave, honestly." He chuckled, but Marcy protested.

"He won't be able to climb stairs for a while after the surgery," she said. "Don't let him fool you. He'll watch movies from bed or from the hot tub."

"Which has stairs I'd need to traverse to get in it," he said, grinning at her.

"Where do you come up with these words?" Skyler asked. "Traverse?"

"He also started doing this vocabulary game," Marcy said, swatting at him in a playful way. Skyler watched them, because they acted like a married couple, and he knew he and Mal were much more stiff. They acted like they were dating, still unsure about each other and where they stood.

Because that was a completely accurate description of where they were in their relationship.

"So now he uses all these fancy words no one understands."

"They understand them," Wyatt said. He looked back at Mal and Skyler. "And that's it. It's a big house. We're two people. I'll need a lot of help immediately following the surgery, and Marcy has to fly and run Payne's."

"All right," Skyler said. "We're gonna need to talk about it."

"Of course."

Skyler also wanted to talk to Jeremiah about a more permanent living solution...at Seven Sons. But he'd felt Mal's shocked energy when he'd mentioned moving to

Three Rivers, and he wasn't even sure he could get her to come right now.

They all went back downstairs, with Marcy chit-chatting with Mal about the holidays in Mexico. Skyler shouldn't have worried about her fitting right in with everyone else in the family. Mal was a pro at fitting in.

It was him who always seemed to be just on the outskirts, circling and trying to find a way into the bonds his brothers had created with each other while he hosted parties in the top floor apartment.

––––––––

"Hey, Momma." He held his mother tight, so glad when she did the same for him.

"My baby." She called all of her sons her baby, even Rhett, who was the oldest of them all. Skyler didn't mind, because he could feel his mother's love so keenly, and he needed it right now. "How was the drive?"

"Not bad," he said. "It's just long." He didn't dare bring up the idea that he and Mal might move here. They'd talked about it on the way from Wyatt's, and she seemed softer, more open to the idea now that she'd had some time to think about it.

And honestly, Wyatt's mansion in the hills had probably helped, especially the kitchen.

"Smells great in here, Mrs. Walker," Mal said, and

Momma stepped away from Skyler so she could hug Mal too.

"It's nothing to do with me," she said. "Jeremiah brought his barbecue meatballs. All I did was put rice in the machine."

"You make your rice in a rice cooker?" Mal asked.

Momma grinned at her as she stepped back. "It's so much easier. I used to make it on the stove, but everything they have nowadays is so slick." She moved further into the ranch house her and Daddy had bought several months ago. "Come in, come in. Rhett just texted to say they were just leaving."

A quick glance around told him everyone else was already here. Momma's house wasn't nearly as big as the homestead on the ranch, but she'd managed to bring in benches and chairs to supplement the couches so everyone had somewhere to sit.

"Sky." His dad came over and gave him a big hug too. "How's school?"

"Uh, good," Skyler said. "I'm thinking of taking next semester off to help Wyatt."

That got Momma to turn and look at him again. "You are?"

"Yeah, it's an idea," he said, glancing at Mal. He cursed himself for bringing it up. Because his parents weren't stupid, and they knew Mal was in school too.

"What will you do, Mal?" Momma asked. "Stay in Amarillo alone?"

"Oh, no, ma'am," Mal said with a shaky laugh. "If we decide to come here, I'll take a semester off too."

Concern rode in Momma's eyes and she looked at Daddy. "We could help Wyatt."

"Momma," Skyler said. "He wants someone to live-in with him. You can't do that."

"I have all the miniature horses," Daddy said. "We can't live with Wyatt."

Skyler almost started laughing about the horses. "I heard about these horses, Daddy. You want to show 'em to me?"

"Yeah, sure." Daddy's eyes lit up with an internal fire, and he moved faster than Skyler had seen him move—at least in the past few years. Skyler grinned at the others as he followed Daddy, pausing to give Micah a hug and bump knuckles with Tripp and Liam.

Jeremiah was buried in the kitchen wearing an apron while he pulled something out of the oven. The familiar, amazing Walker family energy filled the house, and Skyler could understand why Momma wanted them all there. When Skyler was with them, he enjoyed himself. It was the *thought* of getting together with almost twenty other people that he struggled with.

He didn't know how to describe it, and he couldn't wait to meet with Dr. Haskell to see if she could make sense of his tangled thoughts and feelings.

Outside, the wind tried to steal his cowboy hat, and

Skyler squashed it back on his head before Mother Nature could be successful.

"I got seventeen of them," Daddy said, reaching the fence and standing up on the bottom rung. "Look at 'em out there. They seem happy, don't they?"

Skyler had no idea how to tell if a miniature horse was happy or not, but he said, "Sure do, Daddy."

His dad wore a permanent smile, and Skyler realized that he probably missed being a cowboy. Or at least working.

"Daddy," he said. "Are you...happy?"

His father turned his head and looked at him. "Happy? Sure, I'm happy."

"What are you doing with your retirement?"

"Tryin' to keep up with your mother." He chuckled. "That's all I've ever done, son. Try to keep up with Momma. She has endless energy, and she dragged me to every beach in Grand Cayman. Twice."

Skyler wasn't sure why that was so funny, but laugher exploded from his mouth and flew up into the sky. Momma was a force to be reckoned with, that was true. "I'll bet she did." He put his foot on the bottom rung and pushed himself up too.

"Are you happy, Sky?"

"Happy enough," he said honestly. "Mal and I are thinkin' of moving here. You can't tell Momma."

Daddy chuckled and shook his head. "If you think you

can keep a secret from your mother, you need another year of college."

"Nothing's set in stone," Skyler said. "And it would be to help Wyatt, which I've already told Momma."

"She'll sniff out all the news," Daddy said. "She's been doin' it for years."

"That she has." Skyler sighed as he watched a brown and white miniature horse clip and clop closer to them. "Daddy, do you...I mean, do you think I *fit* in the family?"

Daddy didn't answer right away, and Skyler let his insecurities flow from him. The Good Lord took them and swirled them up into the sky, giving Skyler a few moments of respite from his terrible self-loathing.

"Why don't *you* think you fit in the family?" Daddy asked.

"Because," Skyler said, the words teeming beneath his tongue. He hadn't told anyone about what had truly happened in Dallas. No one. Not even Momma—so some secrets could be kept.

"They're all so *good*," Skyler said. "Rhett is practically perfect in every way. I swear the man has never had a bad thought or made a mistake in his life."

"Oh, that's not true," Daddy said. "You know it's not, Sky."

"Yeah, I know." Skyler sighed and looked up into the darkening sky. "Sometimes, I just feel like, if you guys all knew the truth, you wouldn't want me around anymore."

Daddy stepped off the bottom rung and edged closer

to Skyler. He put his arm around Skyler's shoulders and squeezed him tight. "I don't know what you're struggling with specifically, but I can guarantee you one thing: I will always love you. No matter what. Momma too. And all of your brothers." He cleared his throat and sniffed, but Skyler didn't dare look at him to see the emotions for fear his would break open like a compromised dam.

"That's what families do," he said. "That love is unconditional, Sky. Same as God's."

"Thanks, Dad." Skyler spoke very softly, and he welcomed the reassurance buzzing through him. "I was almost arrested in Dallas. Shayla stole a bunch of money from my business, which was why it failed, and the federal government thought I was embezzling funds, involved in tax fraud, and getting ready to skip over the border."

Daddy didn't say anything, and Skyler let him think through what he needed to say. Skyler was a lot like his father in that regard, and he never wanted to be rushed with a response. Because he wanted to give the *right* response and sometimes that took a few seconds to come up with.

"Were you embezzling funds?"

"No."

"Committing tax fraud?"

"Dad, no."

"Then I'm real sorry that happened to you." He lowered his arm and stepped only six inches away. "You don't have anything to be embarrassed about if it's not true."

"I lost everything," Skyler said. "And even if it wasn't my fault, it's still embarrassing."

"You were a little boy," Daddy said with a big breath. "But I lost everything once. And I had your mother, and all seven of you boys to take care of. We had to live with Grandma Lucy and Grandpa Jerry, remember?"

"Yeah," Skyler said. "I guess I never thought that it was because of a failure."

"Oh, I felt like *such* a failure," Daddy said. "I'd tried to get a new type of technology off the ground, and it just wasn't happening. No one trusted that their secure information would in fact, be secure. I lost the business, my partners, all our savings—and some money we didn't have."

"I didn't know all that."

"You were only seven years old," Daddy said. "I'm glad you didn't know." He bent down just as the little brown and white horse arrived, giving him a healthy pat through the rungs. "That means I did my job as a parent. But Momma knew. My parents. Everyone in San Antonio, it seemed." He sighed and reached into his pocket, where he withdrew a couple of baby carrots. "But I picked myself up, dusted myself off, and tried something else."

"I'm trying," Skyler said. "But I hate college, Daddy." He'd never said those words out loud, at least not after his second attempt at higher education.

"I know you do, son. Everyone knows you do."

"They do?"

"I actually have no idea." He grinned, and Skyler saw a younger version of his father shining through the weathered, wrinkled face. "But I'm pretty sure everyone knows you don't like going to school. You never have. You're more of a doer than a learner."

Skyler turned away from the horses getting treats from his dad. He leaned his back against the fence and looked up to the house. The cheery yellow lights coming from the windows framed in the smiling, happy people, and Skyler once again found himself on the outside looking in.

And he really wanted to be in. He wanted to be one of the seven sons that everyone was happy to see. He wanted to be *happy*, and he wasn't sure he even remembered what that felt like.

Momma opened the back door and waved to them. "Gideon. Everyone's here, and we're eating."

"Coming," Daddy called. He clapped his hand on Skyler's shoulder and met his eye. "You're a good man, Skyler. Don't live in the past. You've got a pretty wife in there, and the love of your family." He walked away then, and Skyler wondered if he should take his words at face value, or if he knew he and Mal's marriage was fake and that she didn't love him.

[illegible]

10

al sat in the most comfortable camp chair she'd ever been in. Skyler rubbed her hand with both of his, and the snacks and drinks flowed freely from the square next to theirs, where Whitney's family from Wilde & Organic sat.

Mal had enjoyed dinner greatly, as she missed her big and loud family and hadn't even known how much. But Skyler's family had filled a hole in her life that she'd filled with work and classes and trying to get through another week by stretching her salads into two or three meals or getting a discount shake at the gym.

Darkness had fallen, and Mal's excitement kept climbing and climbing as she anticipated the beginning of the event. She felt like a small child on Christmas morning, and she looked around at all the people in the park and lining the street.

Children ran and played. Some people had brought their dogs. Everyone seemed to have something to eat or drink, and a few people across the street had just lit sparklers for their kids. This place seemed to be touched with magic, and Mal sat back and drank it all in.

She could use some magic in her life, and she looked at Skyler, who still wore his cowboy hat, though there was definitely no sun to block from his face. She turned over her hand and slid her fingers easily between his. He glanced at her, and they smiled at one another. The moment lengthened, and it was so tender and so meaningful.

Mal had things she wanted to tell him, like how charming he was, and how good-looking, and how kind for picking up the pieces of her life and sheltering her in his luxury apartment. Yes, Wyatt's words had horrified her. But Skyler's instant reassurance had calmed her.

"And we're ready to begin!" someone practically shouted into the mic. A general cry of delight rose into the air, and Mal leaned forward with everyone else to see the first float coming down the street. It was a huge globe, done in blue, green, and white lights, and it was easily the most magnificent thing Mal had ever seen.

"Look at that," she said, pointing as if Skyler couldn't see it.

She sat, enthralled, as the floats went by. As a whole troop of dancers wearing black suits with lights on them did a hip hop dance right in front of their section. She'd never clapped so hard for a performance. She ate too much chocolate licorice, and drank too much diet cola, and enjoyed herself oh, so much.

"And now," the announcer said. "It may not be midnight yet, but it's time for our New Year's kiss cam."

Mal really wanted to kiss Skyler, and she leaned toward him, the biggest smile on her face. "You gonna kiss me, Sky?"

He grinned back at her as the announcer counted down, and at one, his lips touched hers. Happiness and excitement burst through her, and Mal cradled his face in her hands and kissed him.

"You're on the screen!" Liam said, hitting Skyler's arm and breaking their connection. "You guys were up on the big screen." He looked like they'd won the lottery by sharing their kiss with the rest of the crowd, and Mal giggled as she leaned back in her chair.

She had the very real feeling that this year was going to be one of her best. As long as she could make it through the hearing and stay in the country.

———

MAL HAD JUST SAT on the edge of the bed when Skyler came into the bedroom. He'd given her almost forty-five minutes to change and get ready for bed, and he now wore a pair of gym shorts and a navy blue T-shirt with two W's on it.

"It's Wyatt's," he said, turning in a slow circle, his arms spread out like there would be something special about the tee. "Wyatt Walker limited collection T-shirt." He wore a huge grin when he faced her again. "Just my size."

"Wow," Mal said with a giggle. "Does Wyatt have women's wear?"

Skyler walked over to the bed and climbed onto it, saying, "I don't even know. I doubt it." He settled against the pillows and sighed. "This bed is a thousand times better than the one at my mom's. We're never staying there again."

Mal's nerves buzzed with energy as she peeled back the comforter and got beneath the sheets. She stayed sitting up against the pillows and headboard too, folding her hands over her stomach. "That was an amazing light parade. I had a ton of fun."

"Me too." Skyler sighed again, and he seemed so happy. "I can sneak down the hall to the next bedroom in a little bit."

"It's fine," Mal said. They'd slept in the same bed before, and they *were* married. She'd rebelled against the idea of actually doing married things with him, because, well, she had a lot of reasons for that.

One was that she'd never been intimate with a man like that, and she wanted it to mean something when she did.

"So you were going to tell me something Wyatt said at breakfast."

"Yeah."

She waited for him to get his thoughts where they needed to be. He finally said, "He said I wasn't the black sheep of the family."

Mal turned to look at him while he spoke. He scooted down in bed, his eyes trained on the ceiling. He was the picture of perfection, his shoulders pulling against the T-shirt in all the right ways. "I don't think you're the black sheep. I mean, I think we kind of hang on the edge, because everyone else has lived here together for so long."

"We don't really fit," he said.

"Yet," she said. "We don't fit *yet*. But everyone is really nice."

"Oh, yeah, they're nice," he said. "They're actually pretty great. I'm...not so great."

"Skyler," she said, a bit of chastisement in her voice. She couldn't believe he thought that about himself. "You're great." She drew in a big breath. "Literally one of the greatest guys I know."

He met her eye, anxiety in the set of his jaw. "You barely know me, Mal. I mean, let's be honest. I had a mask for everything."

She nodded, trying to process that he'd admitted it. "So you knew you were sliding into a character."

"Oh, yeah. I'm really good at it, actually, and it's kind of fun to play someone else."

Mal looked down at her hands. "Have you been playing a character with me?"

"Sometimes," he said. "But not since you said we get to be ourselves."

That conversation was only a week old, but she had noticed him just being the Skyler Walker he was.

"Maybe your brothers don't need a mask either," she said.

"They don't."

Mal took a big breath. "If you're really not going to go to school, I think we should move here. Wyatt needs the help. His house is huge. And maybe if we're here, we'll be able to find where we fit in the family."

Skyler reached over and took her hand in his. "I think you're right." He pushed himself up on his elbow. "And beautiful." His eyes shone like stars, twinkling and dancing with desire. "And smart. And fun to talk to. And accepting." He kissed her, keeping it sweet and slow.

Mal kissed him back, a level of excitement in her blood that said she might be able to give this man her whole heart. And she wasn't sure if the satisfied buzz left in her system after Skyler said, "'Night, sweetheart," and rolled over was because he'd kissed her or because he had the power to carve out her heart and leave her grasping for a way to live without him.

———

They woke on New Year's Day in Three Rivers, and Mal

said, "I want to see what this town has to offer," the moment Skyler opened his eyes.

He smiled, and he was so beautiful in the weak morning light coming through the blinds. "I know just where to take you."

"Yeah?"

"Yeah, there's an amazing bakery on Main Street. And they have these amazing chocolate soufflés." He closed his eyes again. "But I need ten more minutes." He yawned, and Mal thought he was the sweetest man on the planet.

"I'll go shower," she said, sliding away from him before she kissed him with all the passion and desire streaming through her.

"I'll go after you," he said, his voice already halfway toward sleep.

Mal took her time in the shower, proud of herself for all the hard conversations she and Skyler had had over the past couple of days. While he got ready, she went downstairs to find Jeremiah and Whitney both sitting at the dining room table, mugs of coffee in front of them while Whitney tried to get their five-month-old to eat something creamed and green.

"Morning," Jeremiah said with a big smile. "Was that bed better than Momma's?"

"About fifty billion times better," Mal said, glancing into the kitchen. "Is there enough coffee for me?"

Jeremiah's chair scraped as he got up. "Of course. It's a bit old, though. I'll make some more."

"I'm sure it's fine," she said, thinking of Skyler's brew. "Skyler is terrible at making coffee."

"That's because he doesn't like it," Jeremiah said, taking the coffee pot and pouring it down the drain.

Mal almost opened her mouth to ask, "He doesn't?" but she sucked the words right back down her throat. She should know that about the man she was married to.

And now you do, she told herself. She couldn't be expected to know everything, right?

"It's fast," Jeremiah said. "We just got this new coffee maker for Christmas."

"I got it for him," Whitney said. "The man drinks coffee until ten p.m."

"If I were awake at ten o'clock at night," Jeremiah said as he filled some part of a coffee pot Mal had never seen before. "I would drink coffee. I work hard, and I need the caffeine."

"I know," Whitney said, smiling at him. "I'm just surprised you can sleep after all the stimulants you consume."

"I'm tired," he said. "I'm old."

"And JJ still doesn't sleep through the night." Whitney beamed down at the little boy, who flung out his hand and knocked the spoon way. "Do you, buddy? You need to sleep through the night so Daddy doesn't have to get up."

Mal thought they were the epitome of cute. Jeremiah asked Whitney if she wanted more coffee, but she waved him away. She eventually gave up on trying to get JJ to eat the mushy green stuff, and she started ripping up the left-over piece of toast in front of her and putting it on the baby's tray.

JJ was very interested in the toast, and watching him trying to get his chubby fingers around the pieces properly was entirely too enjoyable. When he got one and managed to get it in his mouth, Mal felt like cheering for him.

"He's adorable," she said to Whitney, who was watching him with the same level of adoration on her face.

"Do you and Skyler want kids?" Whitney asked, and Mal's throat dried up.

"Coffee's ready," Jeremiah said, rescuing Mal from saying something that would surely give away her false relationship with Skyler.

She flashed a smile in Whitney's direction and went over to the counter, where Jeremiah had no less than a dozen containers of flavored creams. She mixed up her coffee so it was full of caramel and cream, with barely any coffee flavor left.

She thought of herself sitting at a giant dining room table, trying to feed a chubby baby something they didn't want and then giving up and giving them toast. She'd thought about having children before, but she'd never had a boyfriend serious enough to think about turning him into a fiancé.

She could envision her and Skyler, married, children in the house. He'd do the ranch finances, and she'd teach all the kids how to make refried beans, and the best pulled pork, and how to season the guacamole just right. A small smile graced her face, and she sipped her coffee while standing at the counter.

"Morning," Skyler said, sliding his hand along her waist. Mal leaned right into him, pressing her head against his chest.

"Hey," she said, glad he was there. "Jeremiah made coffee."

"Yeah, I'll pass," he said. "They have a place here with the best hot chocolate ever—at least according to Wyatt. I'm going to get something there." He looked over to the table. "We're going to the bakery. You guys want anything?"

"Baklava," Jeremiah said. "And a few of those tiger tails. And a pecan pie."

"Jeremiah," Whitney said, chuckling.

"They're going," he said. "And Whit wants the chocolate iced doughnut with the Bavarian cream. Oh." He snapped his fingers. "And two maple long Johns."

"You're going to be in a sugar coma," Whitney said, getting up from the table. She swatted at Jeremiah's shoulder as she took the baby out of the highchair.

"It's a holiday," he said. "I'm barely going out to the ranch today."

Skyler nudged Mal, and she looked away from Jeremiah and Whitney. "We'll bring it all back," he said. "You might need to text me all that."

Jeremiah took out his phone, and Skyler shook his

head. His brother seriously liked his sweets. He started toward the front door, Mal at his side. "What else are we going to do today?" she asked.

"I don't know. Maybe you should Google to see what there is to do in Three Rivers on New Year's Day. Maybe there's a farmer's market or something."

"Pancake breakfast," Jeremiah called after him.

"And there's a Holy Cow boutique in the park," Whitney said.

Mal looked at Skyler, and Skyler looked at Mal. They barely made it out the front door before they burst out laughing.

11

Skyler got up every morning by six-thirty, but he could not beat Mal out to the main living area of the apartment. She was always lacing up her shoes or filling their running backpacks with water by the time he emerged.

They ran in the mornings, just like they had when they were just friends. He took care of errands and bills and other life stuff while she made him a new authentic Mexican dish every day for dinner.

She was dynamite in the kitchen, and Skyler grew more and more comfortable with her in his personal space.

They hadn't spoken of moving to Three Rivers again. Wyatt's surgery was still three weeks out, and he said he was still going to try to find a nurse to come live with them. He and Marcy hadn't revealed their secret, but Mal and Skyler didn't spend any time talking about that either.

He learned what her favorite color was—purple. He knew how she took her coffee now. They shared more about their hobbies, what they didn't like, and discussed movies they went to together.

Every day, he read something else about the immigration process to the US. Every day, he stood in the shower and prayed aloud that the Lord would provide a way for Mal to stay in the country. His feelings for her were inexplicable, but they were present nonetheless.

On Sunday, they didn't run, but instead, Skyler slept late, showered, shaved, and went to church with Mal. The second time was easier than the first, and Skyler liked the pastor and his vibrant energy.

On Monday, which would've been the first day of classes for them had they enrolled in school, they also didn't get up and run. He found her in the kitchen, same as always, but today, she wore her pajamas—a silky set which consisted of a long-sleeved shirt and pants in a dark, rich purple.

"Nervous?" he asked, coming up behind her and wrapping his arms around her. She swayed with him, and Skyler took a deep breath of her skin.

"How'd you know?"

"Number one, I know you a lot better now," he said, falling back. He liked holding her. He liked talking with her. And since Skyler had fallen in love before, he knew very well that his feelings were morphing into love.

"Number two, you've made enough food for my whole

family and it's not even seven yet." He took in the bacon, the hash browns, the perfectly over-easy eggs. "Not that I'm complaining." He picked up a plate and held it toward her. "I'll take two of those eggs."

"You don't even eat breakfast," she said. But she scooped the eggs out of the pan and put them on his plate anyway.

"And see how you know that about me?" Skyler grinned at her and moved over to the dining room table. She brought him juice and a plate of bacon, which he would eat too. She nursed a cup of coffee, both hands wrapped around the ceramic as she looked at him.

"He's going to tell us everything we need to know," Skyler said. "That's why we hired him." He cut into his yolks, his mouth watering.

"I'm just nervous to talk to him."

"You just need to file the right paperwork," he said. "And do the hearing. They're not going to send you back because you forgot to send in the paperwork."

"That's exactly what they said they'd do."

"But John isn't going to let them." Skyler had to hold onto that hope, or there wouldn't be anything to cling to. "You'll see." He finished eating, said, "I'm going to get in the shower," and left her in the kitchen.

He knew she was bored out of her mind. He was too, especially now that he didn't have classes or homework to occupy his time. Moving to Three Rivers sounded like a great solution for him, because then he could work on the ranch. He'd be able to spend time with his brothers, their families, and his parents. Mal could too, and he knew she liked his family.

He couldn't believe it, but she'd said she thrived on the noise and busyness of all of them coming and going, babies crying, toddlers spilling milk, and Momma hovering around everyone. He'd never introduced Shayla to anyone in his family except for Micah, and Skyler let his thoughts dwell on his brother for a few minutes.

"Today's the day, Lord," he said. "If it be Thy will, Mal and I would love a good meeting with John Castle about the hearing this week. If there's anything we need to get ready, bless us that we'll have the time and means to do so."

He turned his face into the hot spray and let some of his own nervous energy flow down the drain with the water. After shutting off the shower, he added, "And help Micah. I don't know what he needs, but Thou does, and I'm sure he could use some help today."

After toweling off, shaving, and getting dressed, Skyler sat on the edge of his unmade bed and texted Micah.

Thinking about you this morning. How are things?

It was still early enough that Micah should still be at the homestead. Sure enough, the three little dots started to flash next to his name, indicating that he too was typing a text.

Things are good, Micah said. *I met someone at church yesterday, and we've been talking.*

A smile and a bit of surprise lifted Skyler's spirits. *A woman?* he asked.

Yeah, Micah said. *A woman. I'm thinking I'm going to ask her to dinner tonight.*

Wow, bold.

Micah sent a laughing emoji, and Skyler looked up from his phone. He knew Micah and Simone Foster had been seeing each other last year. For some reason, Simone hadn't wanted to take their relationship out of the shadows, and Micah's self-confidence and self-esteem had taken a big hit.

He'd claimed Simone was embarrassed of him, but Skyler couldn't imagine why. As far as he knew, Micah hadn't had any trouble with the law. His last girlfriend hadn't stolen from him, lied to him, and caused him to lose everything in Temple.

No, Micah had closed down his woodworking shop voluntarily.

"Stephanie did give him a lot of trouble," Skyler reminded himself, because Micah had had a bit of a problem with his girlfriend in Temple. She hadn't accepted his decision to break-up, and he'd had a hard time saying and doing what needed to be said and done to truly end the relationship.

A knock sounded on his door, and Skyler's gaze flew to

it. Mal had never come to his room before, and a second or two passed before she said, "Skyler?"

He jumped to his feet and strode across the room, taking in everything at once. Did it smell bad in here? He never made the bed, and usually tossed his clothes over the arm of a recliner in the corner. What would she think of that?

They were married, but they didn't share a bedroom, and there were still things about him she didn't know.

He pulled open the door to find her standing there, her hands pressed together in front of her. "Hey."

"I think it's time to go."

"Is it?" He looked at his phone, and sure enough, it was time to go. "Shoot, I lost track of time." He lifted his eyes to hers, and time seemed to still. He reached for her and cradled her face in one palm. "It really is going to be okay."

She closed her eyes and nodded, and Skyler found her so beautiful in that moment. She had such a kind spirit, and such a good soul, and he closed his eyes too. He basked in the warmth of her body and soul, and he knew then that he was in love with her.

"Okay." He opened his eyes and dropped his hand. "I just need to grab my jacket and my keys." He felt his back pocket. "And my wallet...where's my wallet?" He turned back to his dresser, where he kept that kind of stuff. It was either there or in the kitchen, as they had a drawer in the island where he put keys, spare change, and his wallet sometimes.

But it was sitting on the dresser, and he crossed over to it, stuffed the wallet in his back pocket, and swept the cowboy hat onto his head too. "Okay, let's go."

Mal kept her hand in his down to the parking garage. Across town to the law office. All the way into John Castle's office. "So good to finally meet you," John said, a tall, thin African-American man that looked like he'd blow away with the slightest of Texas's breezes. "I've got everything here for you." He sat down behind his desk, his smile wide and comforting. He opened the folder on his desk, which had files stacked as high as a human probably dared to stack them covering the entire left side of it.

Skyler sat just after Mal, his stomach tying itself into a knot.

"We have all the appropriate paperwork ready," John said, looking up. "Thursday will be really simple, Mal. We'll go to a hearing with a judge, and it'll just be us and them. It's not a jury. It's not a trial. We'll provide the proper paperwork, and express that you want to keep going to school and having a job. I one-hundred-percent expect that we'll leave with your conditional green card. So it's not the permanent one you meant to apply for, so you'll be set back a couple of years in your process."

"Yeah?" she asked. "You think I'll get the conditional one?"

"Yes," John said. "We'll have to resubmit the application. You'll have to pay the fee again, and the time won't start back in August, like it would have. But it shouldn't be a problem."

"And then?" She cleared her throat, as her voice had come out scratchy. "Then what happens?"

He flipped a page. "You've only ever been here on a visitor's visa, and you recently got married." He glanced at Skyler and then focused on Mal. "Is that right?"

"That's right," she said.

"So they'll probably give you a probationary time of two years, while they determine if the marriage is real."

Skyler worked very hard not to move. Not to even breathe. Everything in the room grew hot, including his face, but he just kept looking at John.

He said, "You'll have a conditional green card, which after the two years, if everything is good, they'll move to a permanent green card. And after five years, you can apply to be a naturalized citizen. That's when they'd do the background check, the fingerprints, all of that." He leaned forward, his personality still jovial and happy, but he was serious too. "You won't be able to get a passport until all of that is done, Mal. You won't be able to go visit your family for probably eight more years."

Eight more years.

Skyler looked at Mal, and she swiped quickly at her face.

"Is that what you want to do?" John asked. "That process?"

"Yes," she said, lifting her chin. "That's what I want to do."

Satisfaction moved through Skyler. She wanted to stay in the US, and he'd married her to help that process. It was the right thing to do.

"All right." John stood up, the meeting apparently over. "See you on Thursday morning, then."

Skyler and Mal shook his hand and they left the building. Mal crumpled into Skyler's arms at the truck, and he just held her, whispering, "It's okay. It's going to be okay."

Eight years.

He couldn't help but wonder where he'd be in eight years, and if he'd have the opportunity to still be at Mal's side.

―――――

The next morning, Skyler got up early again. He found Mal in the living room, ready to run. "Be safe," he said, leaning down to kiss her.

"Good luck in Three Rivers," she said. "Call me on the way back."

"Okay."

She smiled and headed out the door while Skyler wished he could ask her if she'd ever think of this apartment as her home.

His thoughts went round and round and round as he

showered and dressed and drove to the counseling office in Three Rivers.

"I'm here for Doctor Haskell," he said ninety minutes later, and twenty after that, he was called back into an office with plenty of light, beautiful furniture, and a blonde woman at least a decade older than him.

"I'm Michelle Haskell. So nice to meet you," she said, smiling as she shook his hand. "I can see the Walker blood in you. You look a lot like Jeremiah."

"I guess there are worse things," he joked.

Dr. Haskell kept her smile on her face as she sat down in an armchair. Skyler took a spot on the nearby couch, taking a moment to settle in and lean against the armrest. He'd never been to counseling before, and he had no idea how to start.

Thankfully, Dr. Haskell said, "Tell me why you're here."

Skyler drew in a deep breath. How did he even start? Did she need a history? Should he mention Mal? His brothers? What did she already know about his family from her sessions with Jeremiah?

"Uh," he said, clearing his throat. He ducked his head, glad he wore his cowboy hat so he could hide his face. "I feel like I get unreasonably annoyed with simple things."

"What kind of things?"

"Texts from my family. The fact that my wife won't call our place home."

She went on to ask him more questions about that, and

he ended up talking a lot about his family, as well as his new marriage with Mal.

"Why do you think you're frustrated with those things?" she asked.

"I guess...I don't know." But Skyler had just had a thought. A dangerous thought he didn't want to say out loud.

"Oh, something just happened." Dr. Haskell, who'd been scribbling on a clipboard on her lap, had completely paused.

"What?" he asked.

"You shut down."

"Did I?"

"Completely." She cocked her head, her eyes narrowing for a moment. "What's going through your mind?"

"I think." He shifted, leaning forward like he'd run from this office. "I mean...I have things I don't want to tell people. I think that might be why I get a little annoyed with them."

"Things you don't want to tell people."

"Right."

"Like what?"

"Like...I don't know." But he did. He knew that too. The embezzlement accusations. The fraud charges. The lying and stealing. The fake marriage....

"I just feel like I'm the black sheep in the family," he said. "I have...things I'm dealing with no one else does. So they don't understand. And their perfect lives are annoying."

"Have you told them these things?"

"No."

"Do you think that's lying?"

Skyler's defenses shot right up. "Lying?"

"Yeah, not telling them things. Have you told your wife these...things?"

"Not all of them." He blinked at the doctor. "And it's not lying. I just haven't told her."

"Is that misleading though?"

Skyler didn't know what she was trying to get him to say. "No."

"So someone has to specifically say, 'Hey, Skyler. How was your weekend? Did you go rock climbing?' for you to answer?"

"I'm not lying to them about anything." And he wasn't. No one had asked him why he and Mal had gotten married. He could see what Dr. Haskell was getting at though, and he wondered if he was deceiving his family by not telling them. And Mal, by not cluing her in about the things in his past.

"You just haven't told them."

"I didn't realize I'd have to defend myself here." Skyler folded his arms, about ready to bolt. He didn't want to feel like he was a liar, someone who couldn't be trusted.

But maybe that's why you don't fit, he told himself.

"You don't," Dr. Haskell said. "I'm merely trying to

find your baseline, where you're operating from in all things, including your morals. That's all."

"You make it sound like I don't have any morals."

"Not at all." She wasn't agitated in the least, and Skyler worked to keep himself from moving on the couch.

"There are some things I haven't told my family," he said. "Or my wife. Everyone has secrets."

She nodded, made a note on her clipboard and said, "I'd really like you to think about something before we meet again."

Skyler didn't think they'd be meeting again at all, but he just nodded.

"Take some time to write it out, too, if you can."

"Okay," he said.

"Think about how you'd feel if you found out your wife had been keeping something secret from you. Something big. Something important. How would you feel? Would you feel lied to? Betrayed? Deceived? Or would it be okay, because everyone has secrets?"

Skyler's jaw clenched, but he nodded.

"There's no wrong answer," Dr. Haskell said, clicking her pen. "And we'll talk about it next time."

Skyler stood up, shook her hand and left the office. Anger and irritation accompanied him to his truck, making his steps more like stomps and his strides long. He didn't want to feel like he'd been lying to his family—or to Mal.

But by not telling them everything, had he been?

He got behind the wheel of his truck, Mal's words from earlier that day in his mind. *Call me on the way back.*

He didn't want to call her, not while he felt so out of sorts. Not when he didn't know if he'd been doing the right thing or not.

So he started the truck, locked the doors, and bowed his head to pray.

12

Mal had just finished setting up the sewing machine in the spare bedroom in Skyler's apartment when her phone rang. He actually had two extra bedrooms, so he still had plenty of room should he want to take up a hobby too.

"Hey," she said after connecting his call. "Tell me about it."

But Skyler didn't say anything. She could hear that he was definitely in the truck, though, so the line between them was good. "Skyler?"

"I need to tell you some things," he said, his voice flat. She didn't like flat. Flat meant Skyler had hidden behind one of his masks, and she had no idea who she'd be talking to.

"Okay," she said. She pulled out the rolling chair she'd bought and sat down. She hadn't specifically discussed setting up a sewing studio in the house, but she needed something to do all day, and she loved to sew. Cooking could only take her so far, and she'd gone through a lot of recipes already.

"I mentioned Shayla in the past," Skyler started. "She was the last girlfriend I had before coming north, right?"

"Right," Mal said.

"Well, we broke up, obviously, and I left Dallas, obviously. But there's a whole lot more to that story."

Mal said nothing, because it wasn't her story to tell. Skyler could have all the time he needed, but thankfully, he launched right in with, "She stole a lot of money from me. Over fifty thousand dollars. She'd been stockpiling it through the business, and she skipped town in my truck, which she also stole from me."

He took a deep breath and sighed. "I was brought in for questioning with federal authorities for embezzlement. They thought I'd committed tax fraud by hiding the money she'd stolen. They thought I was going to run for the border."

Mal sat there and stared out the window, trying to make sense of everything.

"They held me for three days while they investigated. I wasn't allowed to leave town. I had to bankrupt the business and abandon it. I lost a lot, and I've never felt...."

"Good enough," Mal said, finishing for him.

"Yes," he said. "My brothers are all successful, and I just feel like a complete failure."

Mal's first instinct was to tell him he wasn't a failure because his ex-girlfriend had stolen from him. But she knew him well enough to know by now that he didn't want her reassurance. At least not in that way.

"Do they know this?" she asked him.

"No," he said. "You're the first person I've ever told. Well, I mentioned it to my father last week while we were there for New Year's. But not as much detail as what I just told you."

"Thank you for telling me," she said. "I don't think you're a failure because someone took advantage of your trust."

"I should've known," he said, and an angry vibe came through the line now. "I was in love with her. I was going to ask her to marry me. I should've known."

"Some people are really good liars."

"Okay," Skyler said. "I'm going to go see my parents while I'm here in town. Momma invited me to lunch."

"Okay," Mal said, wondering what response he wanted from her. If she couldn't tell him that some people were liars, what should she have said? "When do you think you'll be home?"

"I don't know. What are you doing today?"

"Well, I sort of bought a sewing machine, and set up a table in the bedroom next to mine...." She waited for Skyler's reaction, and when his laughter came pouring through the line, Mal smiled too.

"I didn't know you sewed."

"Well, now you do," she said. "I bought all the stuff I need to make a quilt for your mother. She told me she loves to sew, and we really talked about it a lot. I got excited to get back to it." She hoped he heard what she didn't say. Then she decided to just say it. "I feel like it's going to give me something to do."

"That's great, Mal," he said, and she heard how genuine he was. "I'll tell Momma."

"Okay." Mal leaned back in the chair. "Text me when you leave Three Rivers, okay? I'll make dinner or call for something."

"Sounds good."

The call ended, and Mal took a few moments to just soak in the silence. She examined how she felt about Skyler, and she knew he was easily the most important person in her life right now. Probably ever.

She had other people she'd been friends with before their fake marriage, but she hadn't spent as much time with them since quitting her job and retreating to the top floor of this apartment building. She didn't want to lie to them, and she didn't want to tell them she'd married Skyler. So it was easier to simply stay away.

It had been fine, because she had Skyler, and they'd been relying on each other, especially since Christmas. Mal was used to being on her own, and she didn't mind spending time with herself, her projects, and the things that were important to her.

But Skyler had given her the space she wanted—and

some she didn't. They were still getting to know one another, she rationalized, and then she went to get the fabric that she'd bought and left in the kitchen as she carried the sewing machine down the hall and around the corner.

As she measured and cut and started to sew, she thought about Skyler and the embarrassment he'd been shouldering all alone. She understood on a deep level, because she'd come to this country to make something of herself, and she hadn't quite done it yet.

Soon, she promised herself. She leaned back and looked up at the ceiling, imagining she could look through it all the way to heaven. "Soon," she promised the Lord.

Hours later, Skyler walked in the apartment a few minutes after Mal had started a movie. She immediately paused the show and got up off the couch. She rounded it and met him at the door, stepping easily into his arms.

"I missed you," she said, holding onto the width of his shoulders. He was strong, and steady, and sturdy, and she sure did like that. She sure did like *him*.

She tilted back and looked up at him. "Skyler, I think you're an amazing man."

He gazed back at her, and Mal smiled, tipped up on her toes to take off his cowboy hat, and kissed him. Skyler kissed her back, and he moved with a bit of that wild, unbridled passion that had existed in their first kiss.

"I'm trying to do the right thing," he said. "I'm trying to be smart."

"I know that," she said. "I feel the same."

"Do you think we're doing the right thing?"

"I can't even imagine doing this by myself," she said. "You've been such a big help." She knew a lot of that came from his money, but she only felt a blip of guilt steal through her.

"How do you—I mean, how do you feel about us?"

"Honestly?"

"I thought we'd decided to be completely honest with each other."

They had, that was true. But he'd just barely revealed a lot about his past. Mal reasoned that she didn't need to know everything up front with her other boyfriends. Of course, Skyler had never really been her boyfriend.

He'd gone straight to husband.

Mal looked into his eyes and employed her bravery. "I'm falling in love with you."

Skyler smiled slowly, and he was the most handsome man Mal had ever laid eyes on.

"I'm falling in love with you too." Skyler dipped down and kissed her too, and pure hope filled her, because maybe they had a chance of making it through this hearing.

But more importantly, she suddenly felt like she had a real opportunity of spending her life with someone she loved.

"I love coming home to you," he said, sliding his lips along her neck.

"I like that too," she said, clinging to those strong shoulders. But really, she loved being that sense of home for him. And she wanted him to be her idea of home too.

———

THURSDAY MORNING, Mal stood in front of the mirror in her bedroom, and she hardly recognized herself. She wore a classy navy blue dress with a white collar and white cuffs on the sleeves. She'd bought a pair of blue pumps, and she'd spent an hour on her hair and makeup. She was amazed at what money could do, and she tipped her head back.

"Thank you, Lord," she said, glad Skyler had brought up the topic of religion a couple of weeks ago. "Bless us that today will go well."

She didn't know what else to say. She'd been praying steadily all week, and she knew Skyler had too.

"Bless Skyler that this will not cause any more problems for him." He'd confessed to her on Tuesday after he'd returned that he was worried as the immigration authorities looked into their marriage that they'd go back to the issues he'd dealt with in Dallas.

Mal hadn't known how to reassure him, because there was no reassurance. She couldn't control what someone looked into, or what they thought about it. They had John coming with their files. He'd texted last night, and he was very good at reassuring them that all would go well. She was so glad to have someone in her corner who knew what to expect at the hearing, and she couldn't wait to meet up with John.

She turned away from her reflection and went into the kitchen. Skyler stood there, wearing his shirt and tie that he wore to church. "Hey," he said, smiling at her. He did a double-take and then his gaze slid down to her heels and back to her face. "Wow."

"Wow?" She grinned at him and cocked her hip, putting her hand there. "You like this dress?"

"I super like that dress." He stepped over to her and took her into his arms, smiling at her as his eyes broadcasted his desire for her. Mal liked that she could make him want to touch her, and she ran her hands up his chest.

"Well, I *super like* your tie."

He leaned down and kissed her, and there was definitely some charged energy between them. Mal felt the anxiety, and she tried to get rid of it by keeping up with him stroke for stroke.

He finally broke their connection, but he kept his forehead against hers. "I'm wondering...." His eyelashes brushed his cheeks as he kept his eyes closed. "I'm wondering if you've thought about sharing—" He cleared his throat. "Moving into my bedroom."

Fear and joy, worry and excitement, filled her. She stepped away from him, her heart pounding, pounding, pounding in her chest. "I've thought about it," she said.

She'd have to be a robot not to think about doing more than just kissing Skyler Walker.

"Okay," he said simply. He opened the drawer in the island and picked up his keys. "We better get going. John said to be there thirty minutes early."

She nodded and followed him out, and it felt like a new companion had joined them. She wanted to talk more about what sharing his bedroom would be like, but she didn't. She'd slept in the same bed with him before, and thinking about anything else only increased her anxiety.

John waited in a chair on the third floor of the federal building downtown, his phone stuck to his ear. He spoke in rapid Spanish, and while Mal didn't speak the language daily like she'd used to, she still understood everything he said.

And he was telling someone that he'd put in the proper paperwork, and that he was supposed to have heard on a naturalization ceremony on Monday and hadn't. He wrapped up the call fairly quickly, stood, and shook their hands.

"They're on schedule," he said. "Which is pretty much a miracle. We'll wait here until they call us in. There are four cases, including ours. I'm going to try to go first, since I have to be in court at noon."

"Sounds good," Skyler said, sitting down next to John. Mal sat next to Skyler, and silence ensued. He was deep inside his mind, and Mal didn't blame him. She really didn't. She just wanted this hearing to go well.

Please, please, she thought.

The minutes passed slowly, and she watched more people gather in the waiting area, all of them with lawyers like John. Finally, someone opened the door, and a man dressed in a uniform stood there, welcoming people in. John got to his feet like a shot and approached him. They exchanged a few words, but Mal was still trying to catch up so she didn't hear what they said.

Inside the room, a couple of tables sat between rows that looked very much like the pews they sat on at church. Up front, raised up, was where the judge would sit.

John went all the way to the front row and sat down, Skyler following. Mal managed to get though the other people entering the room, and she sat beside the two men that felt like her only lifeline at the moment.

Only minutes later, the door in the corner opened, and a woman came through, followed by another in judge's robes. The first woman took a spot in the box to the side, and the judge climbed a couple of steps and sat behind a microphone.

Mal watched her, feeling like this woman with an outdated hairstyle held her very future in her hands.

"Are we all here?" the judge asked. Her name plate in front of her read Judge Andrea Andreas. Mal found it humorous that she only had one letter different between her first and last name, and she wished she could text Skyler. He'd like it too.

"All four have checked in," the man who'd stood at the

door said, moving through the room toward her. He handed her the clipboard, and she looked through the bottom of her glasses to read the paper.

"Mister Castle? Let's start with Mallery Viera and her improper filing status." She looked up. "Are you both here?"

"Yes, your honor," John said, standing. He motioned for Mal to join him, which she did. She drew a deep breath, though her head spun slightly. The room rotated, and she blinked, trying to get her bearings."

The woman in the box read something, and the proceeding started. John spoke about how Mal had simply filed the wrong form, with the wrong supporting document. "She was a student at West Texas A&M, working two jobs, one of them in a managerial position. She didn't realize her ten-year green card would take so long to process, and she applied for an extension on August eleventh when she realized. The wrong paperwork was given to Miss Viera, who has since been married to Skyler Walker, also a student at West Texas A&M and businessman with strong family ties in nearby Three Rivers."

He looked down at his papers. "We have the correct paperwork here, and request that Miss Viera be permitted to have a conditional green card, which can be updated to a permanent green card, and eventual naturalization, which is her goal. She wants to work and go to school, and she wants to participate in her new life with Mister Walker."

"You have the paperwork?" the judge asked.

"Right here." He handed it to the uniformed officer, who walked it up to Judge Andreas. She studied the paperwork, and the silence in the courtroom felt like it had been hooked to a live wire.

"Is Mister Walker present?" She looked up over the top of her glasses.

"Yes, your honor," John said, gesturing for Skyler to stand. He did, tugging on the ends of his sleeves. He stepped up to the table, and Mal slipped her hand into his.

"Mister Walker, you and Miss Viera got married on November eighteenth?"

"That's right, your honor," he said, and he sounded strong and sure. This was nothing like what Mal had envisioned, and she was so glad. She'd thought she might be taken into a white room without windows, where she'd be questioned ruthlessly by two officers, one Good Cop and one Bad Cop.

She wasn't even talking, and she didn't think she'd need to. Having John Castle in her corner had been invaluable, and she squeezed Skyler's hand. He didn't look at her, but maintained eye contact with the judge.

"And this is a real, nurturing marriage?"

"Yes, your honor," Skyler said.

"She didn't coerce you into the marriage so she could stay in the country?"

"Your honor," John said. "Miss Viera and Mister Walker have known each other for two years. They are happily and legally married, and it has nothing to do with Miss Viera's green card status. She simply filed the wrong paperwork. She didn't get married to stay in the country."

Mal wondered if she could've hired John and gotten the results she wanted without having to marry Skyler. She didn't know—and she'd never know. Because she didn't have the money required to hire someone like John Castle. She'd have gone to the immigration office and begged to know what to do.

Skyler had taken control, and the first thing he'd done was marry her. Then he'd hired John.

The judge leafed through a couple of papers. "Her conditional status has been renewed for the time period of one year." She handed the paperwork to the woman in the box. "And Mister and Mrs. Walker, be prepared to visit with immigration officers in the next twelve months to determine whether or not this marriage is real. Your next hearing will determine if you can receive a permanent green card, which will then lead you to naturalization."

"Thank you, your honor," John said, and the judge didn't even look at him. He herded Skyler and Mal away from the table in the front and someone else stood up to take their place as the judge called their names.

Mal left the room, barely able to feel her legs. Out in the hall, the air went down into her lungs in huge gulps. She'd been granted another year. Conditional, yes, but so much could happen in a year. And she had John now.

And Skyler, she thought, watching him shake John's hand, both of them made of smiles.

"Let's go celebrate," Skyler said, facing her. And he looked so full of joy that Mal finally realized what had just happened.

She wouldn't have to leave the country.

"Yes," she said, feeling that same joy. "Let's go celebrate."

13

Marcy barely had time to cut the engine before she bolted from the cockpit and bent over, not even trying to get to the bathroom before she threw up. Her morning sickness had been particularly bad the past few weeks, and she'd take a hose to the dirt after she finished her flights.

She'd been working longer than normal, because she had to come down and throw up a couple of times each morning. She put her hand on her stomach, which still hadn't started to get bigger, and said, "You're causing Momma a lot of trouble."

But she wouldn't trade the baby for anything. She already felt a terribly great connection to the life growing inside her. Wyatt's surgery was only four days away. Their anniversary was only four weeks away. Skyler and Mal were moving into the house in Church Ranches that afternoon.

In fact, they might have already left Amarillo. Marcy wasn't sure, as Wyatt had been handling all of those details.

Drawing a deep breath, Marcy turned back to the plane. She climbed into the cockpit and took off again, stealing comfort and strength from the same place she'd always gotten it—the sky.

She flew south and west toward Shiloh Ridge and got one field dusted before she saw someone on the ground, waving her down. At this rate, she'd never get her day's work done, and she tried not to think about the mountains of paperwork, maintenance, and cleaning to do back at the hangar.

As she landed on the long, wide, dirt road that led up to the ranch, she remembered that she'd hired two people to help her. Agnes was the new office manager, and she worked around the hangar full-time now. She'd have the place clean, and she'd do all the paperwork. Marcy liked the business side of Payne's, but really, she just wanted to fly. She'd hired Joel Barlow to help her dust the fields, and he was handy with a wrench too. So she'd definitely have time to stop and talk to Bear, who was walking toward her plane.

Marcy took a moment to let the propeller slow, and then she got out of the cockpit for the second time that morning. "What's goin' on, Bear?" she asked. Usually when the tall, burly cowboy bachelor wanted to talk to her, he set something up in her office. He had been known to wave her down once before, when he'd had a large infestation of grasshoppers.

"Mornin', Marcy," he said, ducking under the propeller. He wore a smile today, and that gave her a good hint that he wasn't upset with her. Or anything much, really. Bear seemed to have two sides—well-fed or grizzly.

Marcy shook his hand, definitely thinking he was on the well-fed side of the bear today. "What can I do for you?"

"I've decided to cultivate fifty more acres this season." He turned and looked over his shoulder. "Out on the west side. The dormant fields out there."

"Okay," she said. "You want pre-treatment?"

"Yeah." He looked at her again. "And we're putting corn out there for my herd, so I want the completely organic mix."

"You got it. I'll tell my new office manager when I get back to the hangar. I think she'll probably call you, and she can email over the new contracts."

"All right." Bear didn't ask how much it would be. He had new fields that needed work, and Marcy did the work. Besides, Bear Glover seemed to have a bank account like Wyatt's—deep and never-ending.

"I also wanted to say thanks for the recommendation on Sammy. She's been doin' great."

"Oh, I'm glad," Marcy said, smiling. "She's great."

"Yeah." Bear nearly transformed into a grizzly right in front of her. "Anyway, that was all. I saw you, and I thought you might have a second to land."

"I do." She smiled at him, shook his hand again, and got back in the cockpit. She finished dusting Shiloh Ridge, got over to Wade Rhinehart's, and returned back to the hangar.

Embarrassment funneled through her as she taxied to a stop, because Agnes stood outside with the hose, cleaning up after Marcy. She cut the engine, gathered her clipboard, and climbed down.

"Agnes, I was going to do that," she said. "I'm sorry." She approached her new manager, and the dark-haired woman waved away her apology.

"It's fine, Marcy. I've had three kids. I get it." She turned off the hose and reached for the clipboard. "Your husband stopped by and brought breakfast for everyone. Joel radioed in and said he's on his way back."

"Great," Marcy said. "I need to look at his plane when he gets back. Oh, and Bear Glover has an additional fifty acres with organic pre-treatment."

"He's Shiloh Ridge, right?"

"Yes, ma'am." They went into the building together, and sure enough, Agnes had the place as clean as an airplane mechanic hangar could be. The familiar scent of motor oil and metal mixed with maple syrup, and Marcy's stomach growled and lurched at the same time.

She knew she should eat before she left the house, but she was even more tired now that she was pregnant. She barely got out of bed in time to get dressed and get to the hangar on time, and she didn't want to set an example for her new employees that she wasn't as dedicated to this business as she'd always been.

She found the plastic bag of food in the office, and she sat at the desk and pulled out a plastic plate of pancakes. Wyatt knew what she loved, and he took good care of her. A smile filled her soul as she ate, and she texted him to tell him *thank you. I love you.*

Hours later, she stepped out of her blue coveralls and stepped into her office to say good-bye to Agnes. "Joel is doing all the flights tomorrow," she said.

"Yep," Agnes said. "And we got another call from a small family farm."

"We have room," Marcy said.

"Right," Agnes said. "I got them set up."

"Great." Marcy smiled at her, an overwhelming sense of gratitude filling her. "Thank you so much, Agnes. You're a life-saver." A Godsend.

"Oh, I love it," Agnes said. "Ooh, I got you something." She jumped up from the desk and stepped over to the counter. A light green bag sat there with a pastel rocking horse on it. How Marcy had missed it, she wasn't sure. She felt like half of her brain had taken a vacation since she'd found out she was pregnant.

"Agnes," she said, tears springing to her eyes. "We haven't even told our families yet."

"Well, no one throws up every morning if they're not expecting." Agnes grinned at her with the force of gravity as she extended the bag toward her. "I'm sure you don't know if it's a boy or a girl, but you'll need this no matter what."

Marcy took the bag, trying to tame her emotions. Those had been out of control the last couple of months too, but at least she had an excuse now. She took out the yellow tissue paper at the top of the bag and peered inside. A beautiful receiving blanket sat there, with a crocheted edge.

"I make them," Agnes said. "None of my kids are old enough for babies yet, but I have more than enough when they are."

"Thank you, Agnes." Marcy took out the blanket, which was orange and yellow and covered in baby lion cubs. She hugged it close to her chest and then hugged Agnes, the blanket between them.

"And don't worry," she said. "I won't tell anyone your news."

Marcy nodded, repacked the blanket, and headed outside to her car. She drove through town and up into the hills, her commute to the hangar much longer since she and Wyatt had moved.

A truck and trailer sat in the driveway, and Wyatt and Skyler came down the front steps, both of them smiling as

Marcy rounded the corner and her house came into view. She instantly worried that Wyatt would overextend himself, though he claimed he knew his limits and he'd stop when he reached them.

The man didn't stop, though. Marcy knew that. He was still working at Bowman's Breeds, though they didn't need the money. He wasn't one to sit around and do nothing, though, and this back surgery might be the death of all of them.

She'd suggested he ask Skyler and Mal to come, because Skyler would tell it to Wyatt straight. He'd make him stay in bed if that was necessary. And Skyler seemed like he could use a friend, and there was no one better than Wyatt to help someone through a hard time. The man had a heart of gold, and he genuinely loved everyone he came in contact with. Marcy had sensed somehow that Skyler just needed a little more tender loving care.

She pulled into the driveway and got out of the car. "Hey," she said as Wyatt immediately detoured toward her. He always greeted her with happiness, a hug, and a kiss that left her toes tingling. And it didn't matter that Skyler and Mal stood at the back of the trailer, watching. Wyatt took her into his arms and said, "Did you like your pancakes?"

"Always."

He grinned at her, kissed her, and pulled back just an inch or so. "How's the baby?"

"Good," she whispered.

"And you?"

She fell more in love with him every time he asked her about their baby, and then wanted to know if she was okay too. "I'm good," she said. "Hungry. But good. I got two new contracts today."

"Wow, baby, that's great." He turned back toward Skyler and Mal. "Who wants pizza? Marcy's starving."

"I never say no to pizza," Skyler said, hefting another box. Wyatt went to get a box too, but Marcy just followed them inside, hoping Mal wouldn't think her rude.

"This is all you brought?" she asked, pausing to look inside the trailer.

"We kept the apartment in Amarillo," Mal said.

"Oh, of course," Marcy said. "Because Skyler owns the building."

Mal whipped her head toward Marcy, who knew immediately that she'd said something she shouldn't have. Horror moved through her, and she watched the pure shock and surprise cover Mal's face.

"He owns that building?" she asked.

"I shouldn't have said anything," she said. "I'm sorry." She backed up a couple of steps, mentally kicking herself. But Skyler had plenty of money too, and their situation here in Three Rivers was temporary. He didn't need furniture here, as she and Wyatt had put a fantastic king-sized bed in the room where Mal and Skyler were going to sleep. Marcy had made sure they had fancy, fluffy towels in their bathroom, and sweet-smelling body gels and shampoos for Mal's gorgeous hair.

Mal turned and stared at Marcy, who spun and scurried into the house. "Skyler," she hissed, and he turned from the stairs. "You didn't tell Mal you owned that apartment building?"

"You told her?" Skyler looked like Marcy had declared another world war. His face paled, and he looked over Marcy's shoulder toward the front door.

"I'm sorry," Marcy said. "I didn't think it was a secret." She looked helplessly at Wyatt, who watched Skyler and then Marcy.

"I'm sure it'll be fine," Wyatt said. "She knows you have money, right?"

"Yeah," Skyler said, sighing. "I'll go talk to her."

"I'm sorry, Skyler," Marcy said as he went past her. He didn't glare, but his irritation was like a scent on the air, and it smacked her in the face as he walked out of the house. She looked at Wyatt, feeling all shades of stupid. "I didn't know."

"They'll work it out," Wyatt said.

"Are you working too hard?" Marcy asked.

"Nope." He pulled out his phone, clearly not interested in talking about how he felt. "Double pepperoni?" he asked.

"Yes, please." Marcy felt like she'd just committed two strikes, and the tears gathered in her eyes. "I'm going to go shower."

Wyatt looked up, because he'd obviously heard something in her voice. But she was already moving, and she kept her head down as she went into the living room and around the corner to the master suite. Her husband didn't follow her, and Marcy closed the door, glad for the peace and quiet.

She wasn't worried about having Mal and Skyler here. They were two people, and the house was nearly eight thousand square feet. But she felt like she needed a cheat sheet with acceptable conversation topics. She didn't know Skyler that well, and she'd met Mal three times. She was excited for the opportunity to get to know them better, but she felt like she'd taken a massive step backward in only five seconds. With one sentence.

She sighed, got in the shower, and put on a black sweat suit before heading back into the main part of the house. Wyatt sat on the couch in his swim trunks, clearly ready to get in the hot tub. He glanced up as she entered the living room. "Pizza will be here in ten minutes or so."

"Did I ruin everything with Skyler and Mal?" The front door was closed, as if they'd brought in everything they needed.

"Oh, they're fine," Wyatt said, lifting his arm as Marcy sat beside him. She sighed as she sank into his side. "They went upstairs to unpack."

"Did they look happy?"

"Not particularly," Wyatt said. "But Sky said he'd come down and sit in the hot tub with me."

Marcy couldn't get in the hot tub in her delicate condition, but she almost always sat on the side and dipped her legs in the hot water. "We're going to have to make the announcement soon," she said. "They'll wonder why I never get in the hot tub."

"Will they?" he asked.

"I would. And Mal's smart." Marcy closed her eyes and breathed with Wyatt. "I'm nervous about the surgery, Wyatt."

"I know, sugar." His hand moved up and down her arm. "It's going to be okay."

Marcy wanted to believe him, but she hadn't been around during his last recovery, and she didn't know what to expect.

Footsteps sounded, and Marcy opened her eyes to find Skyler and Mal coming down into the living room. They didn't look like they were having an argument, and Skyler said, "We found a dog, Wyatt."

Marcy barely had time to look at him before he got up. "You did?"

"You're getting a dog? Now?"

"Not now, sugar," Wyatt said with a smile, but Marcy had the very real feeling he'd just fibbed. "We're going to *look* at a dog."

"Now?"

"After dinner and a soak," Wyatt said. "You wanna come along?"

Marcy always wanted to go along with Wyatt, so she said, "Yeah, if you don't keep me up too late."

"That's a promise I can keep, sugar." He extended his hand to help her up, and Marcy put hers in his to let him. They could order pizza, and go look at puppies, and sit in the hot tub. But really, all Marcy wanted to do was get through the surgery.

Soon, she told herself. It would all be over soon.

14

Micah looked up as the front door of the homestead opened. "In here," he said as Skyler started to walk past the office. His brother paused, turned to look at him, and changed direction. A grin burst onto Skyler's face, and Micah couldn't help noticing how much happier he looked.

The smile was like a two-edged knife. Micah was, of course, happy for his brother. Of course he was. He *was*.

Skyler had been distant and continually withdrawing from the family since he'd left Dallas, over two years ago. So he deserved some healing, some peace, some happiness.

Micah simply wanted it for himself too. He wanted to be able to throw a genuine smile on his face at a moment's notice.

"Hey, brother." Skyler took his hand and bumped his shoulder to Micah's. "How are you?" He sat down in the chair across from Micah, who had taken over the front office for himself. Jeremiah kept one out in the barn, and Micah had started making plans to open a general contracting firm here in Three Rivers.

Miles separated him and the actual opening of such an enterprise, but Micah had already been talking to various people around Three Rivers in the plumbing, electrical, and HVAC worlds to see if he could simply contract through them for jobs. They had to have licenses; he did not.

He wanted to build custom ranch homes, like Seven Sons, and he wanted to spend the most time on all of the carpentry inside such a home. Design porches. Guest houses. Custom cabinets, and not just for the kitchen.

He wanted to get back to what he'd loved so much as a woodworker, and that was creating and carving something so unique and so personal that the recipient couldn't help but smile every time they saw it.

"What's going on here?" Skyler said, leaning forward and examining the papers Micah had spread across the desk.

"I'm good," Micah said, letting Skyler look. A buzz of nervousness moved through him, but he wasn't going to be embarrassed about what he wanted. Simone had made him second-guess everything about himself, and he had to fight actively against that. "And I'm putting together a business plan for a general contracting firm that will specialize in custom-built farm houses."

Skyler looked up from the papers, surprise in his eyes. "Wow, Micah." A slow smile spread his mouth. "That's so great."

"Is it?" Micah wasn't sure why he wanted someone else's approval. But Skyler was a good friend, and the two of them had spent the most time together growing up.

"Yeah, totally." Skyler leaned back in his chair. "And it happens to be perfect. I have your first project."

Micah's surprise now mirrored Skyler's. "Is that right?" He leaned back too, and while they both wore Wyatt's custom hat and looked at one another, they could almost be twins.

In that moment, Micah was glad to be a Walker, to have somewhere to belong when the rest of the world didn't seem to have a use for him. His thoughts wandered to Stephanie, the woman he'd been dating in Temple. She hadn't wanted him to leave.

That had more to do with your money than with you, he told himself.

"That's right," Skyler finally said. "I just got off the phone with Jeremiah. He'll be in in a little bit, but he said I could tell you."

"Tell me what?"

"I need a house here, at Seven Sons."

A sound came out of Micah's mouth, coated in surprise. "You're going to live here?"

"Yeah." Skyler shrugged like this was no big deal. But in Micah's eyes, having Skyler at Seven Sons permanently was a huge, massive deal. He wanted to ask Skyler what had happened to drive him away from the rest of the family. And then he wanted to know what had brought him back.

He thought of Mal, and Micah knew she had a lot to do with it, even if Skyler's relationship with her was obviously still fairly new.

"I mean, I'm going to take over almost all of the behind-the-scenes dealings of the ranch," Skyler said. "All the finances, all the budgeting, all the bills, all the paperwork." His gaze cooled. "I'm definitely not looking forward to that part. But Jeremiah said he won't trap me behind a desk all the time, and I haven't had a horse for a while."

"We can go riding in a few minutes," Micah said. "I have a phone call with a plumber first. She's going to fill me in on how she works with general contractors. Then I'd love to get in the saddle."

"Me too," Skyler said. "So what's the process? You design the house? Or do I need to find floor plans or an architect or...?"

It was obvious Skyler didn't know how to go about building a house. Micah's excitement mounted, and he was surprised by that more than anything else that had happened in the past ten minutes. "I design the houses," he said. "And I'd love to do yours as my first. It would be a good learning experience too."

"Are you ready to get started?" Skyler asked, eyeing

the papers. "Looks like you're still in the research phase of all this."

"Time to get in the fire," Micah said. "I'll probably make mistakes, but I'll learn, and you'll forgive me."

Skyler grinned at him and nodded. "All right then. Tell me what you need."

"I'll have you fill out a paper." Micah started shuffling things around on the desk until he found the intake forms he'd printed off the Internet. He hadn't quite had time to merge them into a document of his own yet. "This will tell me size, number of bedrooms, bathrooms, and other things you really want."

Skyler took the paper but didn't look at it. "Are you still talking to the woman you met at church? What happened with that? You've never said."

Ophelia's pretty face popped into Micah's mind. "Did I mention that to you?"

"You sure did," Skyler drawled. "You haven't told anyone else?"

"No." Micah shifted in his seat, clearing his throat. "It's still fairly new. I sneak off the ranch to see her every weekend."

"Sneak off?"

"I mean—" But Micah cut himself off. He *was* sneaking off to see Ophelia. And wasn't that what he'd hated most about his relationship with Simone?

Yes, yes, it was.

"I just haven't told anyone here," Micah said. "We don't sneak around."

"What do you do?" Skyler grinned at Micah, who just shook his head, his own smile taking up his face.

"Take her to dinner. She has a huge sheepdog-poodle mix and a small apartment. We go to the dog park and have toured the apple orchards. That kind of stuff."

"So you go out in public."

"Right." And Micah thought that was infinitely better than confining a relationship to a she-shed on a ranch miles from town, behind a locked door, in a room that often smelled like varnish.

Still, thoughts of Simone plagued him. He missed her more than anything, and his relationship with Ophelia hadn't replaced the strong friendship Micah had developed with Simone...yet.

"I'm seeing her tonight, actually," Micah said. "So let's maybe sit down in the morning and go over your sheet."

"Yeah, sure. What are—?" The front door opened again, and Jeremiah appeared in the doorway. Micah and Skyler exchanged a glance, and Micah knew that was the end of the conversation about his new girlfriend. Warmth filled him that he even had a new girlfriend, and he kind of wanted to climb up on the roof of the homestead and shout it to the world.

"He talked to you?" Jeremiah asked, clearly not knowing—or maybe not caring—that he'd just interrupted a sensitive conversation.

"Yep." Micah stood up. "Give me an idea of where this second homestead will be."

Jeremiah looked at Skyler. "I have no idea."

"You know the ranch," Skyler said, standing too.

"Maybe we should go out to Three Rivers and see how they have their dual homesteads set up." Micah looked between his two brothers.

"I know how they have it," Jeremiah said. "I've been out there lots of times."

"Three Rivers?" Skyler asked. "Isn't that the name of the town?"

"There's a ranch north of town," Jeremiah said. "Huge operation, probably three times as big as what we've got here. They have two homesteads."

"Brothers?" Skyler asked.

"Army brothers," Jeremiah said. "Squire Ackerman owns the ranch. His buddy Pete Marshall runs an equine therapy unit there."

Skyler stepped next to Jeremiah and said, "I want to do that. Do you do that?"

"I have, a few times," Jeremiah said. "How's—?" His eyes cut to Micah, and he realized everyone had a little secret. And they weren't really secrets. Everyone had their own life, and they were living it. The family texts could get out of control, but not every little detail of everyone's life was included. That would be complete overkill, that was for sure.

"It's fine," Skyler said. "I haven't specifically told

Micah that I'm seeing a counselor." He looked at Micah. "But I'm seeing a counselor. Jeremiah's counselor."

"Do you like her?" Jeremiah asked.

"She's blunt," Skyler said. "But I kinda need that." He left the office and opened the front door, going out onto the porch. Jeremiah followed him, and Micah brought up the rear, bringing the door closed behind him.

"What about in that field right there?" Skyler asked. "The driveway already comes up this way. We could branch it to the right too, around the oak tree, and have my place right there."

"Are you thinking a place as big as this?" Jeremiah asked.

Skyler looked at Micah, who thought his idea for the house placement was sound. Jeremiah never planted that field, though he did sometimes put horses in it. "Probably not as big as the main homestead," he said. "But decent. You'll want something you can raise your family in."

"Yeah, of course," Skyler said, but his voice held a hint of falsehood.

"It'd be easy to put the driveway over there," Micah said, seeing the second homestead come to life in his mind's eye.

"Let's do it," Jeremiah said. "What are you guys doing now?"

"Goin' riding," Skyler said. "Can you come with?"

"Yeah," Jeremiah said. "Let me go check on Whit and

JJ, and I'll be out to the stable." He walked back into the house, and Micah kept leaning against the railing.

"Should we call Liam?" Skyler said. "Is that how things work here?"

"How things work?" Micah looked at Skyler. "What do you mean?"

"I mean, do you have to invite everyone to do everything?"

"Not at all," Micah said. "Liam's busy with his Marvel project. He'll just feel bad if we invite him."

"What does Tripp do these days?" Skyler asked.

"He works part-time too," Micah said. "He comes out here a few days a week, but usually not until the afternoon so he can bring Oliver with him. They love to ride, and Ollie has his own horse and everything."

"Maybe we should wait until then."

"What else is on your schedule for today?" Micah asked.

Skyler burst out laughing. "Absolutely nothing."

"Then you can ride this morning *and* this afternoon." He knocked on the railing and straightened. "C'mon, let's go saddle up." Micah led the way down the steps and around the house, itching to get atop his horse. He could think more clearly when he rode, and he hoped inspiration for Skyler's new home would hit him as Memory took him out into the Texas countryside.

———

"You want this one?" Micah asked, holding up the blue and white ceramic pot he'd been carrying for the past twenty minutes. Ophelia looked up from the armoire she'd been studying, her light green eyes bright. She was exotic to Micah, with darker skin and hair and those light, light eyes. She was new to town too, having come to Three Rivers as an interior designer as the town had started growing and expanding in the past few years.

"I think so," she said, coming toward him. "I think it'll look nice on my table."

"What are you going to do with it?" He handed it to her, the scent of her perfume teasing his nose. He still hadn't kissed her, but technically, this was only their fifth date. Shopping wasn't his favorite thing to do, especially not at a home goods store where everything was made from corrugated metal, burlap, and had colors like "shiplap cream."

But he did like spending time with Ophelia, and she said she'd needed something from Homelife, the largest store in Three Rivers to find rugs, textiles, furniture, throw pillows, and more. Micah had even seen a whole wall of paint in the back corner, so people could match their throw rugs with their walls.

All at once, he wanted to talk to the manager. He should be using a place like this in his luxury ranch homes, and he looked around for the customer service desk. "Do you know who owns this place?" he asked Ophelia.

"Yeah," she said. "A woman named Ashley Rivers."

Ophelia looked around too. "She's usually here during the day."

"Ashley Rivers," Micah repeated, wondering if he could hold the name in his head. Probably not, so he took out his phone and started tapping in the information. There were plenty of people in the store for a Friday night, most of them couples like him and Ophelia.

He looked up, realizing she'd wandered off to look at something else, and Micah caught up to her, slipping his hand into hers. "You ready to go eat, sweetheart? I'm starving."

Ophelia lifted those beautiful eyes from the picture frame she'd been looking at to his, a smile lighting up her whole face. "Yeah, let's get this, and then we'll go."

"Great." Micah squeezed her hand, and she squeezed back. He felt like he'd just taken a giant step forward in their relationship, and he turned to step back onto the main aisle of the store.

"Oh."

He pulled up before he rammed into the woman standing there. His brain misfired several times while he stared into the deep, dark depths of eyes he knew very well.

"Simone," he finally said, every part of his body rioting. He looked at Ophelia, who was clearly waiting for him to introduce her.

15

Simone stared at Micah Walker. He didn't really belong in a place like Homelife, but at the same time, he did. She scanned him, her eyes catching on the way he clutched the hand of the woman he was with.

He was dating someone else.

Sharp pains jabbed through Simone's chest, her back, her throat.

Micah cleared his throat and dropped the woman's hand. He took a step away from her as he said, "This is Ophelia Montgomery. Ophelia, this is my neighbor, Simone Foster." He gestured between the two of them.

Ophelia was beautiful in a classic way, with high cheekbones, and a perfectly symmetrical smile. Nothing sat out of place—not even an errant eyebrow hair, and Simone thought of her messy bun and how she hadn't groomed her face in weeks.

No need now that every man in her life had left.

"Nice to meet you," Ophelia said with a smile. "I've heard about your sisters. They're married to Micah's brothers, right?"

"That's right," Simone said, her voice like a rusty pipe. She could barely swallow, and she couldn't stand seeing Micah with someone else. At the same time, she knew she was to blame for their failed relationship. She wasn't really keeping track, but he'd kept her in the friend zone for a while the first time, and she wouldn't go out with him the second time, and she'd refused to take their relationship public the third.

Could there be a fourth time?

Simone's thoughts turned to dust when Micah stepped back to Ophelia's side, took her hand in his again, and leaned into to say something quietly in her ear. She nodded at him and said, "Well, I'm going to go buy this. It was lovely meeting you, Simone."

"Good to meet you," she blurted out as the woman walked away. She pressed her eyes closed. The sexy cowboy in front of her had kissed her many times. Made her knees weak. She'd lain awake in bed thinking about him, both before they'd dated, during, and after.

Regret lanced through her, and she hated that her own misgivings and worries may have robbed her of a future with him.

"How are you?" he asked, and annoyance sang

through her. She didn't want his friendship. She didn't want his pity. She didn't want his kindness.

"I have to go," she said, turning away from him.

"Simone," he said, plenty of frustration in his voice too.

"I'm fine, Micah." She walked away from him, the self-consciousness almost tripping her. Was she walking funny? Did her bun wobble?

His footsteps came behind her, and Simone almost broke into a run. "Where are you going?" he asked.

Her mind spun. She'd just arrived at Homelife, because they had their candles on sale this weekend, and she'd wanted to get one for Callie's birthday. And her shop. The grease and sawdust scent had started to bother her. But she could come back when the place was Walker-free.

And it wasn't even all the Walkers she didn't want to see.

Just Micah.

Which made no sense. Her feelings whiplashed around inside her body, and she just needed to get out. Get away.

"I have my theater company class," she tossed over her shoulder, pushing through the door and escaping into the Texas night.

"Simone," he called after her, but she kept on striding away. Thankfully, he didn't follow her through the parking lot, and she managed to get behind the wheel of her car without talking to him again.

Her pulse sprinted through her veins, and she gulped greedily at the air. She'd made it to safety.

But she'd had to lie to do it. Her theater company classes were on Thursdays, and the cast for the next play hadn't been put up since last weekend's auditions.

She groaned as she leaned her head against the steering wheel, her prayer starting down in her stomach. "I don't know how to deal with him," she whispered. "What do all these feelings mean?"

He'd accused her of being embarrassed of him, but the man clearly had nothing to be embarrassed about. No, Simone was the one with the issues. She felt stupid for being interested in Micah Walker when both of her sisters now bore that last name. It was ridiculous that she couldn't get a boyfriend other than the closest cowboy, and the brother of her brother-in-law.

She pulled out her phone and dialed Evelyn, hoping she hadn't gone to bed yet. It wasn't that late, but Evelyn rarely stayed up past eight-thirty or nine. "Still plenty of time," Simone muttered to herself as Evelyn's phone rang and rang.

"Hey," her sister said, out of breath. "Sorry, I was out on the deck."

Simone took a deep breath. "I need you to match me with someone."

A beat of silence passed before Evelyn said, "What?"

"I need you to match me with someone," Simone said again, setting her jaw as she stared at the cheerily lit home store she normally loved. But if she had the possibility of running into Micah here, she wasn't sure she could ever come back.

"I don't do that anymore," Evelyn said. "It's been years, Simone."

"You can still do it," Simone said. "It's like riding a bike."

Evelyn sighed, but Simone wasn't taking no for an answer on this.

"Please," she said, her voice breaking.

"Simone, what's going on?" Evelyn asked.

Simone didn't want to cry, not over Micah. So she laced everything tight, tight, and said, "I need a girl's night."

"Tomorrow?" Evelyn asked, too much hope in her voice. Simone knew she loved being a mom, and she spent all of her time with Conrad, who would turn two in a couple of months. But Evelyn craved adult conversation too, and she, Simone, and Callie had started having girl's nights at the Shining Star every month. Sometimes twice a month.

"Tomorrow," Simone said.

"I'll call Callie," Evelyn said, too much excitement in her voice. The call ended, and Simone sighed. What was she going to do with her Friday night now? She'd been planning to waste a couple of hours in her favorite store, gathering ideas and inspiration, and then grab her favorite chicken salad, head home, and watch a movie.

It sounded lame now that those had been her plans.

"Stupid Micah Walker," she muttered, though she knew nothing that had happened between them was his fault.

No, all the blame landed squarely on Simone, and she honestly didn't know how to shoulder it.

———

"I HAVE THE GUACAMOLE," Simone said the following evening as she went in the back door of the house where she'd grown up and used to live. She now had her own cabin out in the row with all the cowboys and cowgirls who worked the ranch.

The place smelled like smoked meat and cheese, and happiness kicked through Simone. There were no crying babies or fussy toddlers. No cologne, cowboy-hatted men. When they held girl's night, Callie and Evelyn left their kids with their husbands.

"Where's Liam tonight?" she asked Callie, who stood at the counter stirring a pitcher of sweet tea.

"He took the girls to see his mother." She smiled at Simone, and something wise lived in her sister's eyes now. Sometimes Liam went next door with Jeremiah and Whitney. Sometimes he took the kids out to his twin's house. Sometimes he went to Rhett's, and they let their kids spend time together. And obviously, sometimes he went to his mother's. He had plenty of options, that was for sure, and Simone didn't feel bad about misplacing him for a few hours once or twice a month.

Callie came around the counter and hugged her. "How are you, Simone?"

Simone's first reaction was to push Callie away. Lie. Deny everything. Instead, she clung to her sister and said, "I'm hanging in there."

Callie stepped back and held her at arm's length. "Micah?"

Simone pressed her lips together and nodded. She didn't want to say anything bad about him. She didn't want to comment on how the Walker brothers had moved in next door and blown up her whole world.

The truth was, she missed her sisters. She missed living with them. She missed how the three of them had relied on each other—and only each other—for so long. They'd gone out into the tornado to mark all the live-stock. They'd gotten by on very little over the years, combining their money to make ends meet. They'd had a strong bond since the day their mother died, and even now, they all took care of their father and grandmother as a trio.

But Simone felt like the odd woman out. She didn't have a best friend anymore. She didn't have a husband to confide her deepest fears and worries to. She didn't have children looking to her for their care, their every need.

Both Callie and Evelyn had that, and Simone didn't know her place in her own family anymore.

And among the Walkers?

She didn't belong at all.

"I'm here," Evelyn said from the front of the house, and Callie's attention got diverted. Evelyn came into the kitchen carrying a huge chocolate cake, which caused Simone's mouth to water.

"I'm eating that first," she said.

"I have seasoned beef," Callie said. "One of our own cows. Chips. Cheese. Salsa. Everything for nachos."

Evelyn set the cake on the counter and looked at the other two. "Did I miss anything?"

"Simone just said it was about Micah," Callie said, almost like an off-hand comment. Like the topic of Micah Walker could be thrown around for a minute or two and then they'd move on.

"That's why you want me to match you with someone," Evelyn said. "You found out Micah's seeing Ophelia Montgomery."

"How did you know?" Simone said.

"Oh, someone saw them at the steak house a couple of weeks ago." Evelyn waved her hand like it was no big deal. But she was obviously still in the gossip circles around Three Rivers.

"Why didn't you tell me?"

"I didn't know I needed to," Evelyn said. "You two are

friends. I figured you knew." She looked at Callie, who said nothing.

"He's...I just need someone else too," Simone said. "I don't know how to meet men. Everyone I've gone out with in the past few years has come from right next door—literally."

"What about one of your theater friends?" Callie asked. She arranged some chips on a plate and handed it to Simone. But she didn't want nachos; she wanted cake. Still, she dressed up her chips with all the fixings and let Callie put the plate under the broiler while Evelyn cut the cake.

"Yeah, a theater friend," Evelyn said.

"I'm not interested in any of them," Simone said. "A lot of them are married or in relationships. And the ones that aren't...I'm not interested in any of them." She didn't want to call them weird. She loved the little bit of singing and acting she did, and she loved the people in the company with her. But the men that were single...there were reasons for that.

Maybe there's a reason you're still single too, she thought, and the idea cut deeply. She felt like she was falling, and then she hit a huge, dark lake of water. With the air knocked out of her, she couldn't breathe, and even when she did, she only got a lung full of water.

"There's that masquerade ball coming up," Evelyn suggested. "Part of the Valentine's Day thing in town."

"And do you really think there will be someone there?" Simone asked. "Looking for someone like me?"

"What does that mean?" Callie asked. "Someone like you?" She paused in her own assembly of her food to stare at Simone.

"Oh, come on," Simone said, not amused. She bent to get her plate out of the oven. "I'm at least twenty pounds overweight." Thirty, if she were being honest. "I'm not in my twenties, and I don't have a real job."

"You do too have a real job," Evelyn said. "And any man who looks at you and only sees weight isn't worth having anyway." She stepped over to Simone, who had never felt so much like an ugly duckling as she did in that moment. "Now, stop it. What did Micah do to make you feel like this?"

Tears filled Simone's eyes. "Nothing," she whispered. "He was wonderful, and kind, and *I'm* the one that ruined things between us."

Evelyn wrapped her in a hug, and Callie came over and did the same from the back. "I'm sorry," Simone said. "I don't mean to be a baby."

"Cry away," Evelyn said. "It's fine."

Several seconds later, the sisters backed up, and Simone swiped at her eyes. "I just need to meet someone else," she said. "He did. If he did, I can too."

"Okay," Evelyn said, carrying her plate to the table. "Let's start with a wishlist."

"You're going to do it?" Callie asked, joining her.

Simone sliced herself a piece of cake and sat down with them.

"I have the skills," Evelyn said. "They might be a bit rusty, but I think they're still there. And who better to use them with?" She beamed at Simone. "So start with your absolute must-haves, and we'll go from there."

A giddy excitement filled Simone, something she hadn't experienced for a while. She thought for a few moments, trying to gather her thoughts. "I like a man in a cowboy hat." She went on to describe her perfect man, and Evelyn took notes on her phone while she scooped up sour cream, guacamole, and salsa with her beef-topped chips.

Twenty minutes later, with their plates empty and their stomachs full, the sisters moved over to the couch.

"Okay," Evelyn said, setting her coffee cup on the side table. "I think I can work with this. Give me a week or so to come up with some names, and we'll meet to talk about who we want to approach."

"Okay," Simone said. Her spirits weren't hovering on the floor anymore, and as Callie put on a movie they'd all seen a thousand times, she felt like she'd gotten her sisters back. She had found one piece of her life before the Walkers had bought Seven Sons and moved in, and it sure felt good to have even a couple of hours of peace and calm again.

16

Skyler pulled up to Wyatt's house and peered at the upper level of windows. He still didn't know what was in that first bedroom off the loft, but he'd only been living in the house for a couple of days.

"And not forever," he told himself.

What else are you hiding? rang in his ears, as it had been since Marcy had accidentally told Mal Skyler actually owned the whole building where they'd been living on the top floor.

"I honestly didn't even think of telling you," he'd told Mal. "I wasn't specifically hiding it."

He had not gone back to Dr. Haskell, but her words had been gonging in his ears for days too.

No, Mal had not specifically asked, "Skyler, do you own this building?"

So he hadn't told her. He hadn't deliberately hidden it

from her. He honestly hadn't thought about it. He'd bought the building a few years ago, and all the rent was paid through a management company. He didn't show any apartments, and he didn't even know everyone who lived there.

He made money on their rent, sure. He owned real estate in downtown Amarillo, because it held its value really well. And in fact, last time he'd checked with his real estate agent, he could make almost half a million dollars if he sold the building now. He knew that was because he'd invested almost a hundred grand into the building, including the management service and improving the amenities.

An on-site gym and pool was important to him, and apparently, to other tenants.

Though he'd spoken to Jeremiah and Micah about living out at Seven Sons, he hadn't exactly discussed it with Mal.

"Your *wife*," he muttered again, wondering why he was feeling so negative about the situation today. He'd told her he was falling in love with her weeks ago. Mal had said the same to him.

He hadn't lied then.

He did love coming home to her. He liked that she was the first person he wanted to tell about the conversation with Micah and Jeremiah. He wanted to take her out to the ranch and show her the field where their house would eventually stand.

They'd talked about moving to Three Rivers permanently. She hadn't wanted to, but in the end, she knew that was the goal. She'd agreed to come so Skyler could help with Wyatt.

"So just go tell her," he told himself. He also needed to get another appointment with Dr. Haskell, because he didn't want to live his life in fear of what Mal might discover next about him.

But it was Saturday, and the office wouldn't be open today. So he got out of the car, the scent of something sugary and something browning hanging in the air. Mal was in the kitchen again, and Skyler's spirits lifted as he went down the sidewalk and up the steps to the front door. Wyatt had said he could park in the RV bay and come in the back door, but Skyler usually forgot, as he had today.

"Hello," he called as he walked in. Wyatt and Marcy had left for the weekend—their last one before Wyatt's surgery—for a quick getaway to the Gulf Coast in Florida. Wyatt claimed to have a bit of their mother's beach blood in him, and Skyler didn't understand it. In that regard, he was exactly like his father. Give him a big, Texas sky, a thunderstorm, and a pasture full of horses, and he was happy.

And a problem to fix, he added, which was why he'd loved running the mechanic shop so much. It was also why numbers and finances had interested him. As he rounded the corner and the expansive kitchen spread before him, another problem he needed to fix appeared in front of him.

"Hey, sweetheart." Seeing her in the kitchen, that bright pink apron cinched around her waist, did make Skyler unreasonably happy. Only a bit of tension stretched in his smile, and she grinned back at him. So things between them weren't completely broken.

"Hey, come try this." She picked up a spoon and scooped up what looked like peach pie filling.

"What is it?"

"I'm making peach empanadas, and I couldn't find Mami's recipe. So I'm doing it from memory."

"What am I looking for?" He came to stand beside her in the kitchen.

"Just taste, and tell me what you think." She held the spoon as if she'd feed him, so Skyler opened his mouth and let her.

Soft, sweet peaches, with sugar and lemon and cinnamon, burst to life in his mouth. His automatic response was the same as every other time he'd tasted Mal's cooking —a groan way down deep in his gut.

"That's great," he said around the fruit.

"Is it too lemony?"

"Nope."

"Too much cinnamon?"

"Nope."

Mal looked down into the bowl, clearly not satisfied with the answers he gave.

"It's great," he said. "I wasn't kidding when I said you should apply to work at the bakery." He watched her, but

Mal kept frowning at the peaches like they were trying to pull the wool over her eyes. "I'll take some to Heidi Ackerman. See what she thinks."

That got Mal to look up, her eyes wide. "You can't just take someone else's baked goods into a bakery."

"You can if you're applying for a job," Skyler said.

Mal just gaped at him, and in the next moment, the timer on the oven shrieked that whatever was inside was done. She turned away from him, collected the oven mitts, and pulled open the top oven. "Here's the first batch. I guess we'll know about the peaches when we taste these."

Skyler had never had an empanada before, and when he told Mal, she said, "They're hand pies. Street desserts." She put a spoonful of powdered sugar in the tiniest sieve Skyler had ever seen, carefully dusting the hot empanadas. "You can serve them with an icing, or without. They usually don't have anything, because you eat them as you walk. Less mess."

His mouth watered, and he wanted to taste one right now. She transferred the eight on the tray to a cooling rack and started rolling more dough. He retreated to the other side of the island and sat down to watch her work, the muscles in her arms impressive as she formed a flat disc of dough into a beautiful pie, with the peaches between the thin layers of dough. When eight more were ready and formed, she slid the tray into the oven.

"Want to try?"

"Yes, please," he said.

She put one on a plate and slid it toward him. "I just pick it up?"

"That's right." She'd already picked one up, and she took a bite as Skyler watched. She gave no indication of how it was though, and he took his own bite.

The crust wasn't too sweet, because the peaches were. It was light and flaky, and exactly the right ratio between bread and filling, and Skyler enjoyed every last bite before he said, "Those are dynamite."

"Dynamite." Mal shook her head, but her grin sure was pretty to look at.

Skyler had spent the morning at the ranch, first meeting with Micah and Jeremiah and then horseback riding. He had no plans for the rest of the day, and he had the thought that he better enjoy such a luxury while he could.

Wyatt wasn't a terribly difficult man, but anyone in a lot of pain, with limited mobility, wouldn't be pleasant to be around.

"Want to go to a movie today?" he asked Mal. "I could call Tripp and see what he's doing."

"Sure," Mal said. He left her in the kitchen and took up a spot on the couch while he started texting. But Tripp and Liam were already together, their families having gone to the mall and then lunch, and they couldn't do anything that night.

My wife has girl's night, Liam said.

Oliver has a school thing, Tripp said.

Skyler tapped out, *Okay, no problem. Another time,* and left it at that. He couldn't be upset his brothers had lives and couldn't drop everything to spend time with him on a weekend. It wasn't personal, he knew that.

He knew it, but somehow, it still felt like a pinch against his heart.

"That's it," she said. "Twenty-four big ones, and I made several little bites you can take to the bakery." Mal sat on the couch beside him, and Skyler automatically lifted his arm so she could curl into his side. But when she did...Skyler felt like he was coming home.

"That's great, Mal," he said. "The twins are busy today."

"Okay." She wasn't upset by it, but Skyler wasn't sure he could just lay around all day.

"The sun is out," he said. "What do you want to do?"

"I didn't sleep well last night," she said. "Maybe I can take a nap, and then we can go to that movie you suggested?" She looked up at him, and Skyler fell, fell, fell.

"Thanks for coming to Three Rivers with me," he said.

Surprise danced through Mal's eyes, as he'd rapidly changed the subject. "Yeah, of course."

"I went out to the ranch this morning and talked to Jeremiah about building a house for us out there."

That surprise increased as Mal searched his face. "So we won't go back to Amarillo?"

"We can, sure," he said. "We have the apartment

there. It can be like a getaway when we need it. Or we'll live there sometimes and here sometimes."

"Two houses."

"Lots of people have two houses," Skyler said lightly.

Mal laughed, the sound truly happy. "No, Skyler, I don't think they do."

"Well, we do," he said. "We will. It's not a big deal." At least he didn't want it to be a big deal.

"My life is just...I can hardly believe it," Mal said. "I mean, three months ago, I'd just taken a second job so I could get my car fixed."

Skyler thought for a few seconds. "It's definitely different now."

"It's not even close to the same," she said. "It's night-and-day different."

"And why do you think that is?" Skyler asked.

"Why is my life different? That's easy. It's different because of you."

"No, I don't think so," he said slowly, his mind really whirring now. They'd been going to church every week, and this week, they'd go to the same little white brick building where his brothers went. His parents. The whole Walker clan.

"I think it's different because God needed it to be different."

"What do you mean?" Mal asked.

"I think...." Skyler swallowed, hoping this didn't sound utterly ridiculous. "God knew I needed a purpose for my life. And he put me in your life to help." He realized how that sounded, and he knew Mal wouldn't like it.

Sure enough, she said, "I'm not a project."

"I know that, Mal. I didn't mean it like that. I meant, the Lord knows I have money. He knows you don't. He knows my heart, and he knows yours, and I think He put us in each other's lives for a reason."

He looked down at her, desperate for her to understand. "And one of the reasons *for me* is so that I can feel like I'm doing something good. I haven't felt like that for a long, long time."

"What's another reason?" she asked, gazing up at him with those soft, chocolatey eyes.

"To bring me back to Three Rivers." He didn't particularly enjoy saying so, but he knew he needed to be here. "I know I'm supposed to be here," he said out loud, just to give weight and power to the prompting.

"Yeah, I know that too," Mal said with a sigh. "I'm still working on coming to terms with it, but I know it."

"And I think God knew I needed a good, kind, beautiful woman to show me that I'm...." He cleared his throat. "Worth loving." He looked at Mal again, and she kissed him, her mouth sweet and firm against his.

He kissed her back, his arms going all the way around her. As he kissed his wife, he knew he was in love with her, and he was fairly certain she loved him too. He'd said he was falling before, but he knew he'd arrived.

"I love you, Mal," he whispered against her lips.

And the best words in the world were, "I love you too, Sky."

———

Skyler lay in bed and watched his wife sleep. He wanted her to have a nap if she needed one—or even if she just wanted one. He didn't know everything about Mal's life, but at this point, he knew a lot. And he knew her life had not been easy, not in Mexico, and not once she'd come to the US.

Somehow, without speaking, they'd agreed to take their relationship to the next level, and Skyler hadn't known how beautiful a marriage relationship could be until he'd made love to Mal. Now, it seemed that love covered his entire heart and soul with a warm blanket, and he didn't dare move for fear of breaking it.

He wasn't tired, and he didn't want to wake Mal, so he showered quickly and went back downstairs. Her mini peach empanadas sat on the cooling rack, the beautiful white snow of powdered sugar along the tops of them.

He carefully put all sixteen empanadas in a plastic container and went out to his truck. Perhaps the right person wouldn't even be at the bakery. It wasn't like Skyler knew who to talk to about a job for Mal. But he wasn't afraid to ask questions, and he knew Mal would love something to occupy her time here in Three Rivers.

She was a good worker, and she didn't like to sit idle and do nothing.

The drive to town happened quickly, and before Skyler knew it, he'd stepped into the warm interior of the bakery. In the middle of the afternoon, it wasn't terribly busy, and a short, silver-haired woman sat at one of the tables while several other customers had formed a line.

He held the plastic container with Mal's creations in it, wondering if he should join the line or try to get the attention of someone behind the counter first.

"Can I help you?" the woman asked, and he turned to find her standing. She wore a warm smile and a T-shirt that had the bakery's logo across the front of it. "You look like a Walker, and I haven't seen you around before, so I'm guessing you're the brother who's off at college in Amarillo."

She smiled at him with all the charm and warmth that his mother would, and Skyler felt safe in her care. He didn't even mind that she seemed to know his business, a fact that would've normally annoyed him.

"That's right, ma'am," he said, reaching up to touch the brim of his cowboy hat. "I'm Skyler Walker." He glanced at the counter and back to her. "My wife and I just moved back here to help my brother with his back surgery."

"Oh, yes," she said. "We've had Wyatt in our prayers for a few weeks now."

Surprise darted through Skyler, though he wasn't sure

why. Small towns were a hotbed for gossip, especially if people attended the same church.

"I'm mighty thankful for that," Skyler said with a smile. See, Wyatt wasn't the only person who could turn on the charm when necessary. "My wife is an excellent baker, and I wanted to bring in some of her peach empanadas for the manager...or someone to taste."

"Ooh, empanadas," the woman said. "I can never get that dough just right." Her eyes dropped to the container in his hands.

"Do you work here?" he asked.

"Oh, my goodness, I'm so sorry," she said with a laugh. "Yes, I own this bakery, Mister Walker. I'm Heidi Ackerman."

Joy and gratitude filled his heart, and Skyler put a big smile on his face. "Perfect." He extended the container toward her. "My wife's name is Mal, and she's from Mexico. She makes authentic Mexican desserts."

Heidi plucked a peach empanada from the container and took a bite. Skyler knew the moment she tasted the treat how much she liked it. "Oh, dear," she said once she'd swallowed, immediately taking another bite.

"Right?" Skyler tilted the container toward her as she put the third and last bite of the empanada in her mouth. "Another one?"

"You know what? Let's hand them out as samples and see what the customers think."

"Deal." Skyler turned toward the door as someone opened it.

"You go on now, Mister Walker. I'll take notes." Heidi smiled at him encouragingly, and Skyler didn't waste another moment.

He stepped over to the couple who'd just come in and said, "We have peach empanada samples today. Would you like one?"

17

Mal woke on Monday morning, a heaviness in her stomach she hadn't felt before. Nerves, for sure, because Wyatt was going in for surgery that morning.

The shower connected to the bedroom was already running, which meant Skyler couldn't sleep. Mal knew how he felt, and it wasn't even her brother going in for surgery. She wondered what her brothers were doing, and she determined to call them later to find out what was going on south of the border.

She got up at the same time the shower turned off, and her heartbeat accelerated. She and Skyler had consummated their marriage on Saturday—and yesterday morning, and last night, though she'd been worried about Marcy and Wyatt now being home. She wasn't sure why that had bothered her; she'd never heard a peep from downstairs once they'd come up to their bedroom.

She waited until Skyler stood in front of the mirror, a towel around his waist, and started shaving before she went into the bathroom. Their eyes met, and he paused to smile at her. "Morning, peaches."

She shook her head though a smile crept across her face too. He'd started calling her peaches after returning from the bakery with Heidi Ackerman's phone number. "And I gave her your number too," he said, absolutely giddy. "She loved the empanadas, baby."

Mal was glad he'd taken the initiative, because she knew she never would have. And she did want the job at the bakery. Heidi hadn't called on Saturday or Sunday, and Mal had already decided that she'd find a time to talk to Heidi that day, hopefully after they got Wyatt back into surgery.

By the time she came out of the bathroom, Skyler was in the bedroom. "I'm gonna go start breakfast," he said, leaning back into the bathroom to kiss her. Though he was on his way out, he still took the time to tell her he loved her without words, and Mal sure did like that.

"We leave in an hour," he said when he pulled back, and Mal nodded. He left, and Mal finished getting ready, finally going downstairs to discover she was the last one to arrive. The tension in the house was palpable, though both Marcy and Wyatt smiled at her and said good morning.

Wyatt was very good at making coffee, and Skyler said, "Wyatt made the coffee, baby. We heated up your cinnamon rolls from yesterday."

"I see that," she said. "I'm glad. They're not too stale?"

"Wyatt has a trick where he puts a whole stick of butter on them and puts them in the microwave." Skyler grinned at his brother, and Wyatt chuckled as he shook his head.

"It's not a *whole* stick of butter."

"Marcy?" Skyler asked.

"It was a whole stick," she said. "Sorry, sugar, but it was."

"And it's good," Skyler said.

"Wish I could have some," Wyatt said.

"I'll make you whatever you want after the surgery," Mal said. "We're doing meatloaf the first night you're home, right?"

"Yes, please," Wyatt said.

"He won't make it on hospital food," Marcy said.

"We'll sneak him something in," Skyler said.

"No," Marcy said. "Not if we want him to heal right."

"Marce, a hamburger instead of a disgusting muffuletta sandwich isn't going to matter," Wyatt said, exchanging a glance with Skyler. The brothers would definitely sneak whatever they had to sneak, and Mal poured herself a cup of coffee and added cream and sugar to it. She too ate a buttery cinnamon roll, and it was good with all that extra fat.

Soon enough, they arrived at the hospital—and they weren't the first ones there. Rhett, Liam, and Tripp all stood the moment Wyatt went through the door, and a major hugging and well-wishing episode ensued. Before that had finished, Jeremiah and his family arrived, with Penny and Gideon.

Penny had a pan of breakfast casserole with her, and Mal was impressed as she started serving it to everyone in the waiting room in paper cups with plastic forks in them. Mal glanced around as if someone would come over and tell her she couldn't host a family breakfast in the waiting room at the hospital. No one did, but Mal really wanted to see what Penny Walker would do if they did.

She accepted her cup of eggs and sausage, with a layer of cheese and breadcrumbs on top, the scent of it making her stomach roar as if she hadn't eaten in days. The food was hot, surprisingly, and Mal took a bite.

"This is good," she said.

"It's my grandmother's recipe," Skyler said. "Momma made it on Christmas morning growing up." He finished his cup and went to get more. Micah arrived alone, and he hugged Wyatt and got his breakfast all within a few minutes.

Wyatt was unusually quiet, but that didn't mean the rest of the Walker family was. Mal thrived on their energy, and she missed her big, loud family so keenly when she was with Skyler's. She realized as she watched Penny get around to talk with every person that she loved this family.

She reached for Skyler's hand and squeezed his fingers. He looked at her with questions in her eyes, but she just smiled at him.

"Wyatt Walker?" a nurse asked, arriving in the waiting area with a clipboard.

The whole family stood, including Wyatt, and the nurse looked like someone had thrown ice water in her face. Mal knew the feeling, because she'd experienced the same stunned, incredulous feeling the first time she'd met the whole Walker clan.

"I'm Wyatt," he said, moving through the crowd.

"We're ready for you," she said, still glancing around at the others. "You'll be able to bring one person back with you who can stay while you change and the doctor goes over a few things. You'll have to go into the operating room with just me, I'm afraid." She smiled at Wyatt, who gave her a mega-watt smile in return.

"Oh," she said. "You're *the* Wyatt Walker."

"That's right, ma'am," he said instead of denying it. "You're my date for the operating room today?"

"That's right." She beamed at him like they really would be going on a date. "I'm Stacey, and you'll be in great hands with me. Who's coming back with you?"

Marcy stepped to Wyatt's side, and they locked hands.

"Give everyone another hug," Stacey said. "And we'll head back."

That got everyone moving again, and all the in-laws and the Walkers hugged both Marcy and Wyatt. When it was Mal's turn, she held Marcy tight and said, "You're awesome, Marcy. You've got this."

Their eyes met, and Mal felt a connection to the

blonde that made her feel like a genuine part of the family. She hugged Wyatt quickly, all the embracing finished, and he and Marcy followed Stacey through the doors.

The group seemed to take a visible breath, and then Gideon turned toward everyone. "I'd like to have a family prayer for Wyatt."

Everyone stepped in together automatically, as if they'd practiced the move in the past. Skyler made room for Mal in front of him, and everyone joined hands and bowed their heads. Gideon acted as voice, and he prayed with all the tenderness and heartfelt love a father could have for his son.

"Bless him, Dear Lord," he said, his voice tight. "Bless Marcy that she'll be strong, and bless Skyler and Mal as they assist with Wyatt's recovery that they'll have the patience and kindness needed to deal with him."

He continued to ask for health and safety for everyone else, and the prayer ended. Mal lifted her head and started to step back, but everyone stayed in the tighter circle, just breathing together. Rhett finally said, "All right, guys. We don't all need to stay here."

"I'm staying until Marcy comes out," Penny said. "And probably for a while with her."

"I have a shift paper here," Evelyn said, stepping into the middle of the circle. "Everyone can take a turn until Wyatt's out of surgery."

Mal didn't know she'd need to abide by a schedule, but no one said anything as they took the half-sheet with the schedule on it. Mal found her and Skyler near the end of the rotation, because they'd be staying after that to see how the surgery went, get instructions for after-care, and move with Wyatt to his recovery room.

In fact, next to Skyler's name, instructions detailed that he should text everyone what room Wyatt was in and a complete update. He said nothing as he looked at the paper, and the group finally broke up.

Penny and Gideon sat back down, and Jeremiah took the casserole pan and his family and left. Rhett and Evelyn wandered out too, as did Liam, Callie, and their girls. Tripp stuck around for a bit, and Skyler sat next to one of the twins.

Marcy came out about a half an hour later, and she hugged Penny tightly as tears streamed down her face.

"Now don't you worry so," Penny said, stroking her hair. "He's done this before, and he's going to be fine. I just know it."

Marcy nodded, stepped back, and wiped her face. "I broke up with him before last time," she said. "I didn't know what it would be like, watching them take him back. He looked so small in that bed."

"Wyatt is not small," Penny said. "Are you sure?" She gave a light laugh, but she did not let go of Marcy's hand. "Now, what do you need?"

"I'm thirsty," Marcy admitted, and Gideon got to his feet.

"Diet Coke?"

"Just water, please," she said. "The baby doesn't like cola."

"Okay," Gideon said, taking one step away.

"Baby?" Penny said, her voice mostly made of air.

Marcy sucked in a breath, and Mal suddenly knew what she and Wyatt were hiding in that first bedroom at the top of the steps.

"Oh, no," Marcy said. "Wyatt's going to be so mad at me." She put one hand on her stomach, which wasn't showing a baby bump at all.

"You're having a baby?" Penny took Marcy's face in both of her hands and wept. Marcy did too, and it was clear these two women had a special relationship Mal couldn't even begin to understand. A relationship between a mother and daughter, though they weren't blood relatives. A relationship Mal wanted with every fiber of her whole soul.

In fact, she found her own tears filling her eyes as she watched and listened to Marcy swear them all to secrecy and say she was due at the end of July or beginning of August. "Wyatt will still want to do a big announcement," she said. "I promised him we could do it after the surgery at our place." She looked around at Skyler and Mal, Tripp and Ivory, and Gideon and Penny. "So act surprised when he invites you, okay?"

"I'll be so surprised," Skyler said, grinning. He got up and hugged Marcy, said something to her, and added, "I'm going for drinks. Who else wants something?"

"I'll walk with you," Mal said.

"Ollie will want chocolate milk," Ivory said, glancing over to where her son played with a toy several years too young for him. But his baby brother seemed to be enjoying it, and Mal liked watching the two of them. The rest of the drink orders were put in, and Skyler and Mal left with Gideon to go find something to drink.

Before they reached a vending machine or the cafeteria, Mal's phone rang. She didn't recognize the number, but it had a Texas area code, so she answered it.

"Is this Mallery Walker?" a woman asked.

"Yes, ma'am," she said, the last name still a bit foreign to her.

"It's Heidi Ackerman, dear. I met your husband on Saturday, and your peach empanadas were a huge hit. I'm wondering when you'd like to come into the bakery and talk."

She glanced at Skyler. "I think tomorrow would be best, ma'am. We're kind of tied up at the hospital today."

"Of course," Heidi said. "I'll bring dinner up to your place for y'all tonight."

"Oh, that's not necessary," Mal said.

"It sure isn't. You're staying with Wyatt and Marcy up at Church Ranches, right?"

"That's right," Mal said, realizing there was no denying Heidi Ackerman. And she liked that.

"Great. I'll just bring something you can heat up

easily. You'll be able to keep all the containers and all that."

"Okay," Mal said. "Thank you, Heidi. What time should I come by tomorrow?"

"Oh, whenever works for you," she said. "I'll be there in the morning, and I usually leave for a few hours in the middle of the day and come back in the afternoon."

"Okay," Mal said, trying to decide what time would be best. "Mornings seem like they'd be busier, so I'll come in the afternoon."

"Okay, see you then." Heidi ended the call, and Mal smiled as she stuck her phone in her back pocket. "That was Heidi," she told Skyler. "She's bringing us dinner tonight, and I'm going to go see her tomorrow afternoon."

"That's great," he said.

"What are you doing with Heidi?" Gideon asked.

"I think I'm going to work at the bakery," Mal said, and she couldn't believe it. Joy chased the disbelief, making her heart light and her soul rejoice. She'd spoken true when she'd said her life was completely different than it had been only three months ago. So different she didn't even recognize it.

She let Skyler buy her a soda, and she carried it and Marcy's water and Oliver's chocolate milk back to the waiting room. After all the drinks had been handed out, she said, "I'm going to go call my sister," and she excused herself to make the call.

She ducked around the corner and pressed her back

into the brick, taking a deep breath to steady herself. Things with Skyler had evened out, though she'd been shocked to find out he owned the building where they'd been living. She wasn't sure what else she'd learn about him, but she didn't believe he deliberately kept secrets from her.

He just didn't even think to tell her. The things in his life were second-nature to him, and Mal realized the man didn't have a deceptive bone in his body. He had some trust issues, yes. He'd gone to a counselor to get some help with his irritation.

"But he only went that one time," she whispered to herself. He hadn't said much about it either. Mal hadn't wanted to pry, but she wondered if, as his wife, she had prying privileges.

Sighing, she took out her phone and dialed her sister. It was time to tell her family she was married, and she hoped she'd be able to get the words out without too much backlash from Julia.

18

Skyler waited in the truck for fifteen minutes before Mal came hustling around the back of the house and got in the passenger seat.

"Sorry," she said. "Your mother asks a *lot* of questions."

He chuckled and put the truck in reverse. "She sure does." Momma had come up to Wyatt's house for the morning, claiming she missed seeing Wyatt recover last time, and she wanted to help as much as she could.

A month had passed since Wyatt's surgery, and those first few days home from the hospital had nearly sent Skyler back to Amarillo. Daddy's prayer about treating Wyatt with kindness had come in handy, as Skyler had uttered it a few times himself.

Wyatt was a good man, and he was generally jovial and fun-loving and kind. But he'd been in terrible pain for a few days there, and he hadn't left his bed for more than the walks Skyler forced on him for five solid days.

He'd been getting better with every passing day now, and he walked around the neighborhood with Skyler and Mal in the morning, and they left him to make breakfast and soak in the hot tub while they ran.

At least on days Mal wasn't working at the bakery. She worked four mornings a week now, going into work while the sun was still asleep, and coming home by ten or eleven in the morning. She wore a smile almost all the time now, and Skyler loved kissing her curved lips, watching TV with her in the upstairs loft after Marcy and Wyatt went to bed, and making love to her in the bedroom down the hall.

Micah had been working on the blueprints for the second homestead at Seven Sons, but Skyler was still waiting for a date for the groundbreaking.

"What was Momma wanting to know?" Skyler asked.

"Oh, you know." Mal grinned and shook her head. "Stuff that's impossible for me to answer."

Over the past few weeks, Mal had been spending more time with Marcy and Momma, and Skyler liked that she'd found some friends in Three Rivers, even if they were family members.

"Like what?" Skyler pressed.

"If we're going to have kids," Mal said, looking over at him.

"Oh, well, yeah." Skyler shifted in his seat. "I guess we've never really talked about that."

"It's not like we're preventing it," Mal said, matter-of-factly. "So I told her I could be pregnant at any time."

Shock moved through Skyler. "You told her that?"

"She seemed delighted," Mal said.

"Would you be?" he asked. "Delighted if you got pregnant?"

Mal's gaze on the side of his face was plenty heavy, but Skyler focused on the winding road that went down toward town. Even when it straightened, he kept watching the dark grey rope of cement in front of him.

"Would you be delighted?" Mal asked instead of answering the question.

Skyler felt like he'd just walked out onto thin ice. He was sleeping with his wife, and he sure did like that. He loved Mal. And he'd always wanted kids. So what was he afraid of?

"Yes," he said. "I think I'd be delighted to find out you were pregnant." He looked at her. "Are you?"

"No," she said, looking out her window. "I think we should start with this puppy and see how we do."

"You don't think you'll be a good mom?"

"I think...I've taken care of myself—and only myself—for a long time," she said. "It was a little hard to let you into my personal routines."

Relief flooded Skyler. "Me too," he said. "But you're happy, right?"

"Yeah," she said. "I'm happy. I don't want to be your wanna-be wife. I want to be your real wife." She coughed, and Skyler's heartbeat leaped.

He pulled to the side of the road and stopped, reaching for Mal in the next moment. He kissed her, letting some of his unbridled passion come through in the kiss. Mal didn't seem to mind, and he pulled away once he'd gotten control of himself. "I want that, too."

"All right," Mal said. "Let's go get this dog and see how we do."

Skyler got the truck moving again, and he reached for the radio to turn it up. A moment later, he remembered he wanted to talk to Mal about Seven Sons. He still hadn't brought it up with her, and he and Jeremiah had been having a lot of conversations over the past few weeks.

So he turned the radio back down, drawing Mal's attention toward him. He took a deep breath and said, "Jeremiah and I have been talking."

"Oh, here we go," Mal teased.

Skyler supposed he did start a lot of conversations with "I've been talking to...."

"It's about the ranch," he said. "And where we'll live down there."

Mal just waited for him to continue, and Skyler wished he could open his mind and let her see his thoughts. He still wasn't great at conversing, despite visiting with Dr. Haskell a couple more times this past month.

"I talked to Jeremiah," he said again, because he felt great about the things he'd been doing with his brothers since he'd come back to Three Rivers. "I've been praying about these things, and I feel good about them."

"Okay," she said.

"Jeremiah and I want to buy the ranch from Rhett. Jeremiah is going to call a brothers meeting to talk about it. See, Rhett bought the ranch and moved here first. The twins and Jeremiah came at the same time, but the twins don't really work the ranch. Liam has one of his own now and everything. It's always been Jeremiah who works the ranch, and now I'm going to be doing the finances, and some other stuff too. So we thought now was a good time to talk to everyone about it—especially Rhett—and see if he'd sell it to us."

Mal said, "That's a good idea, Sky."

"Yeah?" Her opinion meant so much to Skyler, and he looked at her.

"Yeah," she said. "It makes sense."

"Good." A sense of pride filled him, and Skyler couldn't remember the last time he felt so good about himself. "Which leads me to my next thing: The house will be ready before their baby comes."

"That's great."

"Yeah. I'm excited to be down at the ranch instead of so far up here."

Again, Mal just smiled. "It'll be quicker to the bakery than it is now," she said.

"That it will," Skyler said, grinning too. He wasn't sure why he hadn't brought these topics up earlier. Only that he liked to have time to think things through, get down on his knees and ask the Lord what he should do, and then go from there.

He pulled up to the house where he and Mal had visited the puppies a couple of times while they waited for them to reach the eight-week mark when they could be adopted out. "Ready?"

"So ready."

"What have you decided on for the name?" He opened his door and slid out of the truck. Mal met him at the hood, and he put his hand in hers. "Ribbon or Rosie?"

"I haven't decided yet." Mal looked up at him, and she seemed so happy to him. Four months ago, she might have laughed at something he said, but she didn't wear the easy happiness on her face that she did now.

The front door opened before they got there, and the sixteen-year-old girl they'd been dealing with, Holly, stood there. "Hey, y'all, c'mon in." She held open the door, and Skyler guided Mal to go in front of her.

The mother dog stood there, a pretty, doe-eyed cattle dog. Skyler had always wanted a dog that could run and run, and there was nothing better than a cattle dog for that. He wanted to train it to work with the cattle at Seven Sons too, and he couldn't wait for Micah to get the house done.

"Here she is," Holly said, stooping to pick up one of

the puppies from the pen in the kitchen. She handed it to Mal, who giggled as the black and white pup licked her face.

"She's got the food we've been feeding her," Holly said. "Her blanket, and her papers." She smiled at Skyler. "If you have any trouble with her, let me know. I'll help any way I can."

"Thank you," Skyler said, watching Mal as she cuddled the dog, pure love in her eyes. She'd looked at him like that too, and he'd never felt more loved by anyone in his life.

And he knew one thing—she'd be a great mother.

Their eyes met, and grinning, she said, "Definitely Rosie."

"All right, Rosie," he said. "Time to go to your new home." He wasn't nearly as nervous loading up the ten-pound dog as he would be loading up a baby and taking it home with him. He knew how to deal with a dog. He knew she would cry that night, and he knew how to train her to sit, and shake, and fetch, and come when he wanted her to.

Mal cuddled the dog the whole way home, and back at Wyatt's, the dog tiptoed around like she wasn't sure about all the tile. Wyatt accepted the pup from Mal, chuckling as she licked his face too.

"You're just the cutest thing ever," he said to her, settling her on his chest. Skyler worked around the house, getting her blanket in the kennel he'd bought, and setting out food and water bowls.

Mal busied herself in the kitchen, and an hour later, Wyatt took the puppy into his bedroom, where a yelp came out a few moments later as he used the dog to wake Marcy from her afternoon nap.

Skyler breathed in the life and love in this place, and he once again thanked the Lord for guiding him back to Three Rivers. Back to Wyatt, where Mal could befriend Marcy—and his Momma. Where they could truly start a real life together, filled with real love, and a real marriage.

No one from the immigration office had called him, and he'd almost forgotten about their investigation. Almost. Every once in a while, the thought lingered with him through the day, while he took Wyatt on walks, or drove him down to Momma's for lunch, or as he enjoyed a sermon on Sunday with his family.

But he really felt that even if he did have to go in for an interview, he wouldn't have to lie about the legitimacy of his marriage.

Nope, he thought. *Nothing wanna-be about this.*

———

"Do they know why you called the meeting?" Skyler asked as Jeremiah continued setting out plates, forks, and knives.

"Nope," Jeremiah said. "They know what I sent on the

text. Family meeting. Brothers only. Tuesday night." He looked up, obviously seeing Skyler's nerves. "It's going to be fine."

"I just haven't done many of these," he said. "You don't think Rhett will feel...ambushed?"

"I can't remember the last time Rhett worked here," Jeremiah said. "He works a few days a week next door, if that. For the most part, he's taking care of his land, house, and family. And I know he just picked up a new case for the state, and the prep work for those takes a lot of time."

"Why did he buy this place then?" Skyler took the salt and pepper shakers over to the table and returned to the counter for the two plates of butter Jeremiah had prepared.

"He needed a fresh start," Jeremiah said. "That's what we all need when we come here." Jeremiah paused and looked at Skyler. "You seem to be doing a lot better, Sky. Are you?"

Skyler looked right into Jeremiah's eyes, the way Dr. Haskell had asked him to do. "Yeah," he said. "I'm doing a lot better."

"You don't have to tell me if you don't want to," Jeremiah said. "But what was it that drove you away?"

Skyler's first instinct was to shrug and bury the true reason behind an excuse. Or an "I don't know." Heaven knew he'd said that dozens of times when he didn't want to truly answer a question.

He pushed back that instinct, and said, "I had some hard things happen in Dallas. Really hard things."

"Yeah?"

"Yeah," Skyler said. "Not as public as yours, and you know, Jeremiah, you've been a good example for me." His emotions surged, and Skyler's mouth felt too sticky. "My girlfriend stole money from me over a period of two years, finally loading up my brand-new truck and leaving town in the middle of the night."

Jeremiah opened his mouth to say something, but promptly closed it again.

"Yeah, that's how I felt," Skyler said. "And when the federal agents showed up and accused me of embezzlement? That wasn't fun either." He turned away from his brother, unsure of what reaction he'd get from Jeremiah. His older brother was so perfect in so many ways. Sure, he'd had a few years there that were dictated by anger, but that was understandable.

Your situation is understandable too, he thought as he set the two pitchers of sweet tea on the table and turned back to Jeremiah.

His brother stood right there, around the other side of the island from where he'd been working. "I'm so sorry." Jeremiah took Skyler into an impromptu hug, right there in the homestead.

Skyler gave a nervous chuckle, though it wasn't the first time he'd hugged his brothers. But Jeremiah didn't laugh, and the awkwardness quickly passed. Jeremiah stepped back a few seconds later and looked at Skyler. "You thought you weren't good enough for us, is that it?"

"Maybe a little," Skyler said, though he'd been nearly overcome with inadequacy.

"Maybe a lot." Jeremiah smiled at him. "But the real change happened when you married Mal."

"Yeah," Skyler agreed. "She's great." He ducked his head, and thankfully, the back door opened and Liam came in. A new kind of nervous energy inflicted Skyler, and soon enough all the brothers had arrived.

The noise level increased with each one that came through the door, and Tripp seemed to be starving to death as he tried to eat everything in sight, despite Jeremiah's protests that he wait.

Finally, Jeremiah nodded at Micah, who went down the hall and returned with a rolled-up blueprint. Skyler's pulse skipped and leaped, and he made his way to Micah's side. "I want to see that."

"I'll reveal it after we see how they handle the ranch transfer," Micah said out of the corner of his mouth.

"All right," Jeremiah said over the din. The brothers quieted down, and everyone looked to him. He clearly ran the ranch, and Skyler sent one more prayer heavenward that Rhett wouldn't get his feelings hurt by this proposal Skyler and Jeremiah had come up with.

19

Jeremiah wiped his hands on a paper towel while everyone calmed down. They all looked at him expectantly, and a flash of love for each of his brothers individually passed through him.

For Rhett, who had always been the best example of how to be a leader, how to work hard, and how to be a good man.

For Liam, who had shown Jeremiah what it was like to truly forgive, how to get out of the way when he wasn't needed, and how to follow any and all promptings from the Lord that he received.

For Tripp, who'd taught Jeremiah how to love unconditionally, that emotions didn't make a man weak, and that there were multiple paths to happiness.

For Wyatt, who had demonstrated absolute faith in a tough career choice, shown Jeremiah what it was like to suffer and still be happy, and who brought life and joy to everything he touched.

For Skyler, who had more depth than Jeremiah even knew, who thought he didn't fit when he was the glue that held them all together, and that he could change his circumstances no matter how old he was.

And for Micah, who had been Jeremiah's best friend for the past year, who loved Whitney as much as Jeremiah did, and who had big dreams and plans he would surely accomplish.

Jeremiah cleared his throat and looked at Skyler for strength. He nodded, and Jeremiah's gaze went back to Rhett. "Skyler is going to be moving here permanently," Jeremiah said. "And working the ranch more fully with me." He cleared his throat again. "I know Rhett originally bought the ranch and opened it up to anyone who wanted it."

He looked around at each of his brothers, noticing the twins exchanging a glance. Surely they knew this was coming. Everyone had to know.

"I want to buy the ranch from Rhett," Jeremiah said, being as bold as he dared. "Well, Skyler and I do. We don't want anyone to feel like they're not welcome here, or they can't buy-in too, if they'd like to. Heck, Rhett might not even want to sell it to us."

Rhett wore an expression of shock, that was for sure. Maybe he hadn't thought about selling the ranch. But honestly, he worked more on the Shining Star than he did Seven Sons.

"I haven't had my lawyer draft up anything yet," Jeremiah said. "I thought we'd eat and talk about it and see where everyone was."

Micah raised his hand, and Jeremiah nodded at him, feeling a bit foolish that he had to call on him.

"I'm going to be opening my general contracting business soon. I'm working with someone to come up with a good name, and then we'll license the business, get cards, all of that. But my first design will be Skyler's homestead, which will sit right across the driveway in that field where Jeremiah sometimes puts his pregnant mares."

Everyone looked at Skyler, and Liam even said, "Wow, Sky. You're moving here."

Skyler shifted next to Jeremiah and said, "Yeah, as soon as the house is done. I'm not going to finish school. I know enough to be able to run the ranch finances, and I'm tired of being trapped in a desk."

Skyler was a lot like Jeremiah in that he craved the outdoors, and he adored dogs, and he wanted an honest day's work to feel like his life meant something good.

"I don't want part of the ranch," Tripp said. "I mean, I was thrilled to come here, and live here with y'all for a while. But I've got my place in town, and Ivory and I are happy there."

"Same," Liam said. "I've got Callie's place to deal with,

and my contract with Marvel doesn't end for another two years."

Jeremiah nodded; he'd fully expected the twins to bow out quickly. They had never really worked the ranch, except for help during calving, haying, or branding season.

"I've got a place too," Wyatt said. "And my job at Bowman's. I'm happy to come help here any time you need it, Jeremiah, but I don't really need to have ownership in the ranch."

"I figured," Jeremiah said. He looked at Micah.

His youngest brother drew in a deep breath. "I'd like to have some ownership, mostly because I'm not sure how much business I'll have with the general contracting. I'd like to be able to say I'm a real cowboy." He smiled around at everyone. "And I'm going to find out about the land across the lane there, and see if I can buy that. Then I'll build my own luxury dream ranch house, be close, and be able to help Seven Sons and the Shining Star when they need it."

And there were those dreams and big plans. Jeremiah grinned at Micah. "That sounds great. How much of a buy-in?"

"What were you and Skyler thinking?"

"Well, we haven't heard from Rhett yet, but I think Sky and I were thinking like sixty-forty, with me having the majority."

"Something like that," Skyler said. "I don't need full ownership. I want to be able to work here, have some say in things, run the finances, and all of that. But I don't need to be equal to Jeremiah, who's built this place into what it is."

Everyone looked at Rhett now, who had his head down, the brim of his cowboy hat obscuring his face.

"Rhett?" Jeremiah prompted.

His oldest brother exhaled as he lifted his head. "Well, I haven't really thought about selling the ranch." He looked around the homestead, as if he could see the memories of the last few years here. He probably could. Jeremiah could see them, hear them, smell them, trapped right in the walls of this huge room where he'd cooked, cleaned, entertained, heard and given multiple announcements, found forgiveness, and built his family.

"I'm happy to sell it to you and Skyler," Rhett said next. "But I think I want a small piece, like Micah."

Jeremiah's relief was instant. He didn't want Rhett to feel like he was being shoved aside. His relationship with Rhett had been through ups and downs, that was for sure, but Jeremiah owed a huge part of himself to Rhett. That also couldn't be denied. He'd provided respite and relief for Jeremiah in the most trying of times, and Jeremiah wouldn't be here without Rhett.

"How small is a small piece?" he asked, looking from Rhett to Micah.

"Ten percent?" Rhett guessed.

"I'd take ten percent," Micah said.

"That leaves eighty for us," Jeremiah said, looking at Skyler. "Forty-five, thirty-five split?"

"Sure," Skyler said. "That puts four of us on the board for Seven Sons. When we have major things come up, we'll have to meet and discuss them."

Jeremiah nodded. "That's fine. I can have Tim get the papers together. Rhett, what would you sell the ranch for? Micah, Sky, and I will put our money together to equal ninety percent of that."

A timer went off, and Jeremiah bent to get the heat-and-eat rolls out of the oven.

"I'll sell it for what I bought it for," Rhett said.

Jeremiah looked up even as he reached for the pastry brush to wipe butter across the tops of the rolls. "Really? It's surely worth more than that now."

"Only because of the work you've done on it," Rhett said. "I'm not going to gain from that."

Jeremiah quickly brushed butter over the rolls. "Okay, well, name the price, and I'll get the papers drawn up. We'll get our money together."

"I bought the place for four million," Rhett said. "Minus ten percent, I need three-point-six million to be bought out."

"Deal," Micah said, because his share was only four hundred thousand.

Jeremiah put the rolls in a basket and set it beside the slow cooker, doing the math in his head. Forty-five percent of three-point-six million was almost two million dollars. One-point-six? One-point-seven? Somewhere in there.

He had the money. That wasn't the problem at all.

And he wanted the ranch.

A sense of excitement built within him, and he looked around at his brothers. "Okay, let's eat."

"And after," Micah said before they could burst into noise again. "I want to show everyone Skyler's design. Even he hasn't seen it yet."

"Do we have to wait to eat to see it?" Skyler asked, eyeing the rolled up blueprint papers.

"Yes," Tripp said. "I'm starving."

"Ditto."

"We'll eat fast."

Jeremiah looked at Skyler, and he was clearly outvoted. A grin sat on his face, and Micah moved over to the long counter leading toward the garage and put the plans down there so they wouldn't get buttered and barbecued while the brothers ate.

Happiness spread through Jeremiah as his brothers started talking and loading up their plates. He loved feeding people, and he loved this ranch. And now it was going to be his, for the most part.

He couldn't wait for Skyler's house to be finished so he could move here, if only so Jeremiah didn't have to deal with the paperwork of the ranch anymore. He hated the budgeting and finances, so he was grateful Sky would be handling all of that.

"Let's pray," Rhett said once they'd all sat at the table. They reached for one another's hands, and Jeremiah shared a long look with Rhett, the man who'd been his best friend for so long.

"Dear Lord," Rhett said, closing his eyes. "Thank you for family." He paused, and Jeremiah's chest tightened with emotion. What a blessing family was.

"Thank you for good men in our family," Rhett continued. "Bless us to always be able to get together and talk things out in a respectful way. Bless our wives who put up with us. Bless Momma and Daddy, who raised us."

He paused again, and Skyler's hand in Jeremiah's tightened. He opened his eyes to see Skyler looking right at him, his dark eyes a bit glassy. So at least Jeremiah wasn't the only one currently in a battle with his emotions.

"We thank Thee for all our blessings, especially this good food. Amen."

Rhett drew in a breath and hurried to wipe his eyes. "Wow, that was a tough one." The tension broke, and Jeremiah gave a light chuckle. Glancing around, he saw the same love and brotherly bond on each face he looked at.

"I love you guys," he said while reaching for the butter knife in front of him.

"Same."

"Love you guys too."

"Brothers are the best."

"Love you all."

"Ditto."

Skyler

Amid the chorus of voices, Wyatt just took off his hat and waved it at everyone at the table.

Then they ate.

20

Mal carefully spread the melted chocolate over the cold marble at the back of the bakery. She loved working here more than any other job she'd held over the past fifteen years. Heidi was a good taskmaster, but she was kind. She realized sometimes things happened in a kitchen that were unpredictable. She showed up every morning, ready to work. And she worked hard, so she expected everyone else to do the same.

Not only that, but she expected nothing but kindness and friendly faces. During Mal's first staff meeting, Heidi had said, "I know we can't all have a perfect day every day. So if you need to be left alone, just let me know. I'll spread the word."

And that word got spread through a group chat. Skyler hated those, but Mal loved her work group chat, and she checked it even when she wasn't at the bakery.

She worked four days a week, and Heidi had hired her specifically to make Mexican desserts. So she'd been perfecting her flan, her empanadas, and her churros. The first time she'd made churros, they'd sold out in less than an hour.

Heidi had deemed Thursday churro day, and the lines had started forming before the bakery even opened at six a.m. Mal went into work at three, and all of her hard work over those three hours were gone within one.

Heidi was thrilled, and Mal could hardly believe churros were that popular. But she did make dulce de leche to go with them, and Heidi sold a chocolate sauce with them as well. It was something new and delicious, and Heidi claimed that was what every resident of Three Rivers wanted.

Something new and delicious.

Mal smiled as she rolled up the now-cooled chocolate into perfect tubes. The two cakes she was making today had to be perfect, because they were for Marcy and Wyatt.

They were hosting the entire Walker family at their house in Church Ranches tonight, and Marcy would be telling everyone the news about their baby. And of course, such an announcement required beautiful cakes.

Rhett's wife, Evelyn, had also ordered a cake for their son's second birthday. That was still a couple of weeks away, but Mal would be making that one too. After the bakery opened and she'd made her Mexican treats for the day, she worked on special orders. She'd mastered the ice cream cake within a week of starting at the bakery, and Heidi simply gave her the order sheets now. Mal made whatever the intake form said, and she hadn't had a single complaint.

With the pretty cakes done for Marcy, she put them in the fridge and turned her attention to the next item. Doughnuts—and a lot of them. Twelve dozen doughnuts, for pick-up at one p.m.

"Here we go," Mal said, reaching for the recipe book. Heidi had tested, cultivated, and refined every recipe the bakery used. Everyone in the bakery used the same recipes; that way, everyone who bought doughnuts got the same experience.

So she measured, mixed, and fried for the next few hours, finally washing up and taking the two cakes with her when it was time to go home.

Working at the bakery was physically exhausting, as she was on her feet all morning, had to get up early, and did a lot of lifting and bending. But she loved it with every fiber of her being. And she only worked four days a week, so she still got to sleep in sometimes.

Not that getting up at six to run with Skyler could really be considered sleeping in.

"Hello," she called as she entered the house through the back door. She and Skyler parked over on the RV pad and came in through the back, leaving the garage for Wyatt and Marcy. That way, the driveway was accessible for anyone to get in and out, and she'd seen Wyatt's truck in the garage.

He didn't answer her though. Skyler had probably taken him somewhere in his truck, and Marcy should be home soon. Mal slid the cakes into the fridge and went upstairs to shower.

She'd just stepped out when her phone rang. With dripping wet hair, she reached for her phone and found her sister's name on it. "Julia," she said. "I need just a sec, okay?"

"Okay," her sister said.

Mal quickly put her hair in a towel and stepped into her bathrobe so she wouldn't have to hold a towel around herself while she chatted. "All right." She moved back into the bedroom and climbed into bed. "What's up?"

"Just wondering how the fake marriage is going."

Mal sighed in a very exaggerated way. "I told you last week, it's not fake anymore."

Julia just laughed, and Mal regretted that she'd confessed about the marriage to Julia. She'd done it the day Wyatt had gone into the hospital for surgery, and she shouldn't have said anything at all.

There had just been so much on her mind, and she'd needed someone to talk things through with. But all Julia had done was tease her, and Mal hadn't been able to have a real conversation about it anyway. She was left with annoyance with her sister, a ton of irritation with herself, and the familiar regret that she'd made the wrong decision.

And worse, she hadn't told Skyler that she'd told her family about their marriage.

"You haven't told anyone else, have you?" Mal asked.

"Only Jorge, but I had to," Julia said, her voice moving into a whine. "He wanted you to come home for his wedding, and I had to tell him why you couldn't."

"Julia," Mal said. "You could've just said I didn't file my paperwork right, so I don't have a visa or green card to use."

"Oh, well, yeah, I guess."

"He's not great at keeping secrets."

"He honestly didn't care."

"If you say so." Mal wanted to go home for her brother's wedding, but she wasn't even sure Mexico would feel like home anymore. She hadn't been back in years, and the more time she spent in Three Rivers, this magical small town was starting to feel like home. Way more than Amarillo ever had, which was surprising to her.

"Tell me about the wedding plans."

"Oh, you're never going to believe this...." Julia launched into the story, and all Mal had to do was sit back and listen. Every once in a while, she'd hum or say "Okay," or "Wow," but she didn't have to truly participate.

She got the scoop on everyone in the family, told her sister she loved her, and hung up. She felt drained from the long conversation, and now her hair was probably half dry and half wet, which would make it that much harder to get to lay right. Or even brush through.

She sighed and closed her eyes, intending to just rest for a moment.

The next thing she knew, Skyler said her name. Her eyes flew open to find him just a few inches from her and the room nearly dark.

"Hey." He grinned down at her with the sweetest expression of love on his face. "How long have you been asleep?"

"What time is it?"

"Almost six," he said. "Everyone's here, and we're getting ready to eat in a few minutes."

Horror filled Mal. She wasn't even dressed, and she couldn't imagine what state she'd find her hair in, it having been encased in the towel for hours. A groan came out of her mouth, and she hurried to get up. "Can you ask them to wait ten minutes? I don't want to miss the announcement."

"Sure." Skyler picked up her phone while she flew into motion.

"I just fell asleep after talking to Julia. She wore me right out."

Skyler chuckled. "I think it's the getting up at two a.m. that wears you right out, Mal."

"Maybe." She pulled a sweater over her head and darted into the bathroom to assess the hair situation. It would be better to get it all the way wet again and go from there, so she did.

Ten minutes later, she went downstairs behind Skyler,

humiliation spilling from every pore. Several people looked their way as they joined the party in progress, but no one made a big deal about it.

"There you are," Penny said, coming over to Mal and giving her a hug. "Skyler thought you might have fallen asleep."

"I did," Mal admitted. "Sorry about that."

"Oh, please," Penny said. "Wyatt's not even back with the food yet."

"I told them I would cook," Jeremiah said from one of the barstools.

"They like to cater," Penny said. "Not everything has to be a home cooked meal, son."

"It's better, though," he said.

"I made the cakes," Mal said. "So they're homemade." That seemed to appease Jeremiah slightly, and in the next moment, Wyatt came in through the garage, carrying two long trays of food.

"We're back," he said. "Everyone go grab something out of the truck."

To Mal's surprise, the men got up and did just that, bringing in salad, rolls, and more trays. They were uncovered to reveal smoked turkey, brisket, macaroni and cheese, mashed potatoes, and coleslaw.

"And the cakes," Mal said, getting them out of the fridge. They probably should've been taken out an hour ago to get to room temperature. The chocolate would likely sweat, but there wasn't anything she could do about it now.

"Where's Marcy?" Momma asked.

"I'm starving," Liam said. "Are you doing an announcement?"

"She's comin'," Wyatt said. "And yes, we have an announcement." He stepped over to the door and opened it, and Marcy walked in. A moment of silence ensued while everyone looked at her, and then Mal burst out laughing along with everyone else.

Marcy wasn't a terribly tall or big woman, and tonight she wore a pair of tight jeans and a bright blue T-shirt that stretched across her baby bump—which was now very prominent. Mal had seen it before, because Marcy didn't try to hide it around the house. When they went to church though, Marcy wore sweaters and baggy maxi dresses to keep everyone out of the loop.

But this bright blue T-shirt had IT'S A BOY right across the baby bump, making the announcement to everyone.

Wyatt put his arm around Marcy and kissed her temple. "We're due at the end of July."

Congratulations went around, along with plenty of hugs. Mal basked in the vibrancy of the family, so glad she got to be part of them. Ivory came to stand next to her, her baby in her arms.

"Can I?" Mal asked, reaching for the little boy. He had Ivory's shock of blonde hair, and he willingly came to Mal.

"I know what you like," she said to the baby. She swiped her finger through the very corner of the mashed potatoes and gave the bite to Isaac, who did seem quite happy for it.

Mal stayed out of the way while grace was said and while people started getting food. It felt like organized chaos, and the party spilled out the back door onto the huge patio in the backyard. Parents got food for their kids first, and Mal moved through the line with baby Isaac on her hip as if she'd been doing such a thing for years.

She hadn't, but she had been fourteen when her youngest sibling was born, and she had helped her mom a lot with the younger kids. Ivory eventually took Isaac from her and put him in a highchair, where she fed him bits of noodles and bread.

Mal filled her plate with food and found Skyler on the patio with Wyatt, Marcy, Liam, and Callie, and their kids. She sat next to him and sighed happily.

"Okay?" he asked, putting his hand on her knee under the table.

"Okay," she said, because she was okay. More than okay. Happier than she'd been in a long, long time.

21

Rhett and Evelyn pulled up to the ranch, and Rhett put the truck in park but didn't get out.

"Are you sad?" she asked.

"Not really," he said. "I'm not really sure how I feel about it." He looked at the homestead. The first time he'd come here to look at the house and land, he'd known immediately that this ranch would be his home. But things in his life had changed after only a year in Three Rivers.

He loved the life he had with Evelyn and their son, Conrad. He loved the white house on Quail Creek Lane, and he didn't want to move back here.

Jeremiah had acted quickly with the lawyers, and only a couple of weeks had passed before his brother had texted to say everything was ready to sign. He and Evvy didn't need the money, and he thought about what they both wanted—another child.

Money could help them with the adoption process, that was for sure, but it wasn't like they didn't already have enough.

He'd been trained to see things no one else saw in his work for the state. He could examine dirt and find prints that no one else had noticed. He'd taken more impressions in sand and clay than anyone.

And he'd known this ranch was the perfect place for him.

"We still own ten percent," Evelyn said. "I know how much you love this place."

Rhett looked at his wife. *She* was the perfect place for him. Wherever she was, he wanted to be. "Remember when we met in the cellar?"

A soft smile adorned her face. "Yes." She ducked her head and tucked her hair behind her ear. "I thought you were the most handsome man I'd ever met."

"You stared at me," he said, chuckling. "And I felt an instant pull to you."

Evelyn looked at him, and he'd never been happier than the day the tornado had forced him into the cellar, only for him to find the three Foster sisters already there. They'd taken care of his animals, because they weren't sure when he'd be arriving. And they'd been caught and couldn't get back to their own place.

"We were only down there for a couple of hours," he said. "And it took me a whole year to figure out how to ask you out. But here we are."

Evelyn reached over and took his hand in hers. In the back seat of the truck, Conrad babbled happily to himself.

"This is the right thing," Rhett said. He took a deep breath. "Let's go sign the papers." He squeezed his wife's hand and got out of the truck, immediately turning to get Conrad out of the back. He set the boy down so he could toddle his way into the house, something the boy loved to do.

Evelyn stood right behind him as he navigated the steps up to the porch, and Rhett waited for them both by the front door. "I love you, Evvy." He put one arm around her while Conrad leaned into the door like he could open it that way.

"I love you too, Rhett." She kissed him, and Rhett sure did like the shape of her lips against his.

"Maybe we should look into adoption," he whispered.

"I think we will," she said, leaning her forehead against his chest. "If this last round of fertility drugs doesn't work." She pulled back and looked up at him. "Okay?"

He nodded, because he certainly couldn't argue with her. "Okay." They'd been trying for another baby since the day Conrad was born. Rhett would go to any lengths, any end of the Earth, to give Evelyn what she wanted, and what she wanted was another baby.

They'd only done one round of Evelyn taking drugs to help her body be healthier and more susceptible to getting pregnant, and they hadn't mentioned it to anyone. That way, if the treatment failed, Evelyn didn't have to tell anyone. Rhett's heart hurt for her, because he didn't quite understand the quest for another child.

He loved Conrad with his whole heart and soul, and the boy was enough for Rhett. He liked taking him outside with Penny to throw a ball or walk back to the trees that lined the fence in the backyard.

He'd brought him out to the ranch whenever he could, and next year, Conrad could ride a horse by himself, as long as it was tethered to Rhett.

Yes, Rhett was looking forward to teaching and raising his son on Seven Sons Ranch, and if he were being honest, that was why he couldn't give it up. Of course, Evelyn had the Shining Star too, and even if Rhett did sell Seven Sons outright, he still had access to a ranch.

He opened the door, and they stepped inside. Breathing had always been easier inside this house, and Rhett swooped Conrad off his feet as they went down the hall to the kitchen.

"Cookie," Conrad said, and Rhett set him on the counter while he opened the cupboard where Uncle Jeremiah kept all the cookies for the nieces and nephews. He handed one to Conrad, who tried to shove the whole thing in his mouth.

"Small bites, bud," he said, setting the boy on the floor. "Go say hi to the doggies."

Conrad waddled over to the back door, where Jeremiah's dogs pressed their noses to the glass. Winston and

Willow were good dogs, and Jeremiah had trained them to herd cattle. He'd just gotten three more dogs too, and he loved moving cattle from horseback.

The ranch used quads too, but Jeremiah sure did like the traditional way of doing things. He'd been doing them more and more, and he'd even started talking about using a more traditional way of harvesting hay this summer. "No bales," he'd said. "You use a beaver slide, and push the hay onto it. Then it lifts it up and creates a haystack for you. Right there in the field."

"Okay," Rhett had said, because he didn't care how Jeremiah harvested hay for the ranch.

They were the first to arrive, but Rhett didn't worry. Skyler ran late most of the time, and Jeremiah had work to do on the ranch. He'd come in when it was time, and not a moment before. He was right in the middle of calving season, and that kept a cowboy up day and night. Rhett knew; he'd done it a time or two.

Or twenty, he thought with a smile.

Evelyn curled into the couch with a sigh, and Rhett knew she'd be asleep within minutes. "I'm going to take Conrad out back," he said.

"Okay."

He stepped over to the door with his son and opened it. Winston and Willow started licking and sniffing, but Conrad just laughed and pushed them back. Rhett often brought Penny to the ranch and let her run too, but she'd been getting older and slower the past few months. So he'd left the dog he'd named after his mother home today, and the hound hadn't even gotten off the couch when they'd left.

"Hey guys." Rhett bent down and patted the dogs. They trotted to the end of the deck and looked back, almost like they were asking Rhett if he wanted to follow them. "Lead on." He picked up Conrad and added, "Should we go see the horses?"

"Horse."

Rhett let the dogs lead him across the lawn and past the first barn. The stables spread before him, and Jeremiah did have the horses out in the greening pasture.

"Daddy, horse."

"Yeah," Rhett said, moving right up to the fence and putting Conrad on the top rung. "You want to ride, bud?" He grinned down at his son, who looked so much like a Walker, with that strong jaw and sloped nose. He did have Evvy's eyes, and a softness in his eyelashes that was not characteristic for the Walkers.

"Ride Daddy."

"Yeah," Rhett said again. "We'll go after the meeting, okay, bud?" Rhett wasn't working today, and he could take his son on a horseback ride for a few minutes. "It's kind of windy today."

He looked up to see his rich, dark horse coming toward him earnestly. Rhett put his fingers in his mouth and whistled, and Ebony kept on coming. "Hey, girl," he said as she arrived. She huffed and nickered, and Rhett realized he hadn't been out to see her in far too long.

"Conrad, that's Ebony," he said as the little boy reached up to pat the horse's cheeks. "She's Daddy's horse."

"Daddy horse."

"That's right." Rhett gazed at Ebony, sheer love moving through him. "Jeremiah takes good care of you, doesn't he?" He stroked the horse, who closed her eyes in bliss. "I'm sure he does. You look good. Nice and big. Shiny coat." He grinned at Ebony, who leaned into every touch he gave her.

His phone rang, and Rhett pulled it out to check it. Skyler's name sat there, and Rhett swiped on the call. "Hey, I'm out with Ebony. I'm comin'."

"Okay," Skyler said. "Jeremiah just came in from the barn and he's getting the papers."

"We'll be in in a jiff." Rhett hung up and looked back at Ebony. "Okay, girl. Here we go." He picked up Conrad and put the boy on his shoulders, and they walked back toward the house, three dogs with them now.

When he went inside, he realized just how cold the wind was. "How's the calving going?" he asked Jeremiah who had just sat at the big dining room table.

"Good," he said. He looked utterly exhausted though, and it was Whitney who said, "He didn't come home last night."

"Three calves came after midnight," Jeremiah said. "I

was sitting with the mothers before they came, because I knew they'd deliver in the night. And one needed help."

Rhett nodded, because that was the side of ranch life he did not miss. Staying up all night, catching swatches of sleep in a barn, hoping you knew when to pull for the newborn calf, and that they wouldn't be born dead.

"I've got another in labor," Jeremiah said, wiping a hand down his face. "But Orion can handle it. And we're doing a C-section later today."

"Good luck," Rhett said, taking Conrad into the living room, where JJ played with a couple of toys on the floor. Whitney sat on the couch watching them, and Evvy was still asleep. Maybe she was pregnant, and Rhett watched her for a moment, trying to decide just by looking.

They'd just gone through round two of their drug treatment, and Evvy had to wait another eight days before Rhett would drive her back to the clinic for a pregnancy test. But the way she rested with her hands over her stomach like that....

He finally turned back to the table and picked up one of the pens. "All right," he said a little too gruffly. "Let's get this done."

RHETT CLICKED around on the computer, reading about adoption centers. He'd found one right there in Three Rivers, but he hadn't mentioned it to Evelyn yet.

She prayed every morning, noon, and night that this third round of drugs would do something. Their second back in March, when Rhett had sold the majority of the ranch and then celebrated his son's second birthday, had resulted in a false positive. Evelyn had cried then, and Rhett could admit to getting teary himself.

But only a week later, the test was negative, and Evelyn had had to go through an ultrasound to find out that there was, in fact, no baby. No pregnancy.

So she'd gone back on the fertility drugs and they'd waited the three months to try one last time. They'd gone in for a blood test three days ago.

Evelyn had an appointment at the clinic in a couple of hours to find out if she was pregnant or not, and Rhett needed a back-up plan in case the test was negative.

They'd already decided that if this third time wasn't the charm, they would start looking at other ways to have a bigger family. Neither of them felt good about going a step past the drugs to something like in vitro fertilization, though they'd met with the pastor, and he'd said such decisions were personal, and that he would support them in whatever they chose.

Liam and Callie had gotten foster kids, both of whom they'd adopted in the past year. There were other options, and Rhett had been praying that Evelyn's mind would be open to them.

"Ready?" she asked, and Rhett practically knocked his

monitor to the floor in his haste to turn it off. "Or do you need a couple more minutes with your case?"

"I'm ready," he said, standing up and blocking the computer with his body. He had been working on his case before he'd turned to the Internet for more research about adoption. "I'm almost done with it." He joined her in the doorway of his office.

"Good," she said. "You're due in court in four days." She smiled up at him, and he loved the bravery she put on for him. It wasn't necessary, but he liked it anyway. He wanted to be the absolute anchor for her, and she laced her arms around him and leaned into him.

"Evvy," he said. "No matter what the test is today, it's going to be okay."

"I know," she whispered, her voice tortured. "I'm trying not to be too hopeful, but I don't want to not hope either."

Rhett understood. He wanted another baby too, and Evelyn probably didn't even know how deep his pain ran. He'd tried to hide it from her, because she could barely shoulder her own disappointment, and he didn't want to add to it.

"Conrad," he called. "Time to go to Gramma's."

"He's on the front porch with Penny," Evelyn said. "He's ready." She stepped away and wiped her eyes. Rhett reached out and tucked her hair behind her ear.

"Love you, baby."

She smiled at him, and together, they got their son

loaded up. Evelyn ran inside to take Conrad to Rhett's mother, because if Rhett did it, he'd be stuck in there answering questions for fifteen minutes. And not just Momma's.

Evelyn came back out in just a couple of minutes, and as she climbed into the truck, she asked, "Did you know your dad now has over thirty miniature horses?"

Frustration built inside Rhett, but he also found his father's new habit somewhat comical. He burst out laughing as he backed out of the driveway. "I'm not surprised. Daddy grabs onto something and holds on tight."

"I guess he's going down to some farmer in a couple of weeks to get some equipment or something. Your mother wanted to know if you could find out more details. I guess he's been shifty with telling her everything."

"Sure, I can spy on my father for my mother." Rhett's words only carried sarcasm, and he gave Evvy a grin. "Honestly, I don't think getting in the middle of that is wise."

Evelyn giggled and shook her head. "You're so right."

After that, they both fell quiet as he drove them to the clinic in town. They checked in, waited, and waited, and finally it was their turn.

Rhett sat with his wife, both of them on the edge of their seats, nothing to say. Nothing to do.

Ten minutes later, the doctor came in. "Rhett," he

boomed. "Evelyn." He hugged them both, and pleasantries were exchanged. "Are you going to lunch after this?"

"Yep," Rhett said.

"But not that Chinese place," Evelyn said. "It really wasn't good, Dr. Johnson."

"No?" Dr. Johnson shook his head. "Well, my wife swears by it."

"The twins love it too," Rhett said, looking at Evelyn.

"Maybe try one of those new places that went in on the west side," Dr. Johnson said. "I hear there's a really good grilled cheese sandwich place there. You can get pulled pork on it, or a pizza grilled cheese. That kind of thing."

"Sounds good to me," Rhett said, but he knew Evelyn wouldn't go there. She was a sandwich purist, and she didn't want pork on a grilled cheese sandwich. And if the test was positive...she'd want to celebrate, and not with grilled cheese sandwiches.

Rhett pushed against the hope, because he didn't want to break down in the doctor's office.

Dr. Johnson looked at his charts. "Everything looked good going into last month." He looked up. "How are you feeling?"

"Hopeful," Evelyn said.

The doctor looked at Rhett, and he decided he had to be honest. "Tired."

Dr. Johnson nodded. "That sounds about right." He seemed to be able to see more than a normal person. "I think you're both about to be even more tired." He grinned, and hope sparked in Rhett's heart.

"Because Evelyn, you're pregnant."

She gave a little shriek and turned to Rhett, tears streaming down her face. Rhett held her so tight, so tight, trying to use the pressure to keep his own chest from collapsing.

"Congratulations," Dr. Johnson said. "Now, Evelyn, I want to get you on some hormones in these early stages to make sure we don't lose this pregnancy."

"Okay." She drew in a deep breath and wiped her face. "Okay."

"And guys," the doctor said. "There was a *lot* of hCG in the blood. We might have more than one baby."

Rhett nodded like he was totally on board with that. He was actually scared out of his mind. "When will we know?"

"Not for a while," Dr. Johnson said. "We can sometimes tell at the first ultrasound, but that won't be for another six weeks."

"We're not telling anyone until then either," Evelyn said with a pointed look.

Rhett lifted his hand in agreement and looked back at the doctor. "Are we talking twins?"

"There's no way to know," Dr. Johnson said. "The fertility drugs can be a tad unpredictable, and of course, every woman is different. I once had a patient who had five babies using the same medicines Evelyn took."

Five babies.

Rhett almost passed out, but he managed to nod and listen as Evelyn asked him about what the next steps were.

When they left the office, he hugged Evelyn tight and said, "We did it, baby."

"Praise the Lord," Evelyn said, and Rhett echoed her. God was good, and even if He hadn't given Rhett and Evelyn another chance to be parents, Rhett knew that.

22

Skyler pulled up to Seven Sons Ranch, his truck full of boxes, and the trailer he towed full of new furniture he'd picked up on his way through town.

The landscape had changed over the past five months as the house Micah had designed for him and Mal had taken shape. First the foundation had been poured, then the frame had gone up. The roof, the walls, the front door, the windows. The sidewalks and driveway had been poured, the landscaping done, the pieces put together inside, from trim to appliances to fixtures.

Skyler and Mal had come out every few days and documented the process. If he put together all his cell-phone photos, he could make a time-lapse video that took the ranch from field to two-story home with six bedrooms, three and a half bathrooms, two laundry rooms, one office, and the biggest kitchen in the world.

Fine, Wyatt and Marcy probably had the biggest kitchen in the world, but Mal would definitely have enough room to cook and bake. She'd already started making meals for Wyatt and Marcy, whose baby was due in only five days.

"Okay," he said, forking right at the oak tree they decorated for Christmas every year, and pulling into the driveway. "Here we are. It's done, sweetheart."

"It's beautiful," Mal said. She hadn't been out to the house in a few days, and all the finishing touches were now in place. The upper half of the house was a cool robin's egg blue, and Skyler loved it.

Whitney walked out from the garage, her camera around her neck, accompanied by Micah. They'd been taking pictures every step of the way too, and Micah wanted to put the floor plan and finished product on his website.

Skyler slid from the truck and lifted his hand in a wave. "Hey, guys."

"It's so gorgeous in there," Whitney said. "I want everything I see." She beamed at him. "And the pictures are going to be *amazing* with all that light coming through the huge windows."

Skyler took off his cowboy hat and wiped his forehead, as he was already sweating in this July heat. "Thanks, Whitney. I can't wait to see them."

"You've got everyone coming, right?" Micah asked. "Because your truck from Amarillo just arrived."

Skyler turned to see the eighteen-wheeler pausing out on the road instead of trying to turn into the gate. "Yes," he said. "Everyone is coming. All the ranch hands from Seven Sons and Shining Star too. We start in twenty minutes."

Mal looked at him, her hands full of the cinnamon rolls she'd made last night. He started helping her carry in the churros and more cinnamon rolls, and they got out plastic cups for juice, milk, and water too.

"I hate moving," he said.

"We didn't even have to go to Amarillo and pack anything," she said. "They did it all." The front door opened, and a man stood there with a clipboard.

"Skyler Walker?" he asked.

"Yep." Skyler jogged through the house to him and signed the clipboard.

"We'll get it unloaded," the man said, and he left. Skyler watched him walk down the few front steps, and then he turned back around. They didn't have a giant lobby like Wyatt and Marcy did, but a little entryway with a bench where someone could sit to put their shoes on. Above that sat some hooks, and then Skyler's office was right around the corner. The living room opened up beyond that, which bled into the dining room and the kitchen. The master suite forked to the right off the living room, with its large master bath and closet. A guest bathroom sat in the hall, with the guest bedroom right beside it.

Upstairs, they had four more bedrooms and two more bathrooms. A half-bath sat off the kitchen, along with the laundry room. The house was filled with light, and the dark gray furniture Mal had picked out would look great in here.

The kitchen counters were quartz, done in a dark brown, and they popped against the white cabinetry. Micah had painted the kitchen the same color as the outdoor siding, and it was bright, cheerful, and beautiful.

"The rugs will look good," Skyler said as the moving men brought in the first box. They'd labeled everything too, and he directed them where to go.

Only minutes later, the help he'd procured arrived, and Skyler grinned around at everyone as they started eating breakfast.

The truck and trailer got unloaded. Laughter rang through the house and the countryside. Furniture filled the house, and soon enough, everyone had left again.

Skyler stood in the living room, having just put a throw pillow in the corner of the couch. "This is amazing, don't you think?"

Mal came to stand beside him, and she finally smiled. She'd seemed so nervous up until now. "This is great, Skyler."

"You want to live here, right?" he asked.

She shrugged as she leaned into him. "We'll have the apartment for weekend getaways." She laughed, and Skyler joined her, beyond glad the house was finally done. He was tired of sharing his living space with Wyatt and Marcy, and Wyatt didn't need his help anymore.

"Okay," he said. "Let's go get groceries and your car. Then we can settle in."

"I'm going to take a nap in our new bed," she said.

"Perfect," he said. "Maybe I'll join you." But first, he had to make the long drive back to Church Ranches for Mal's car. They didn't speak, because they'd both been up since dawn. Skyler thought about how much his life had changed since finding Mal in her apartment that day, almost eight months ago.

He wouldn't be in Three Rivers. He wouldn't be married. He wouldn't be thinking about the future or a family. This house at Seven Sons wouldn't exist. Not only that, but he now *owned* thirty-five percent of Seven Sons Ranch, which was crazy every time he thought about it.

None of the things that had happened since last November had been on his agenda.

But he was eternally grateful for them, and he thanked the Lord that Mal had filed the wrong paperwork to extend her green card.

He mused on these things while they walked through Wyatt's house one last time. While he drove behind Mal to the grocery store. While they shopped.

Back at the ranch, they got all the food put away and put new sheets on the bed. Mal collapsed onto the bed with a huge grin on her face, a big sigh coming from her mouth.

Skyler jumped onto the bed with her, causing her to

laugh. He laughed with her, relief flowing through him now that all the work was done for the day.

"Watch, Jeremiah will call in a minute, saying there's a cow I need to go round up somewhere." Skyler grinned at her, drowning in Mal's beauty.

"Hey, you're the one who wanted the ranch," she teased.

Skyler chuckled just before he leaned down and kissed her. She kissed him back with a passion that spoke of married things, and Skyler's heart raced.

The doorbell rang, and Skyler groaned as he pulled away from Mal.

"Your turn to get it," she said, smiling at him.

"My turn?" He shook his head, but he got up, his feet protesting slightly for making them work again. He went down the hall and to the front door, wondering why one of his brothers didn't just walk in.

Then he was grateful they didn't just walk in. He wouldn't want to be kissing Mal—or more—with an audience. But he and Micah had discussed easy access to the ranch for Skyler, and for others to get into his ranch house, and there was a back door that faced the ranch and would be easier for someone to come in from the homestead too, as it sat back further on the road than Skyler's new house.

He opened the door, but it wasn't a family member who stood there. A woman wearing a sharp skirt suit waited on the front porch, and she did not look happy.

"Mister Walker?" She glanced down at a notebook in her hand. "Skyler Walker?"

"Yes, ma'am," he said, wishing he wasn't sweaty and dusty from the day's move. This woman looked like someone he should be wearing a white shirt and tie to converse with.

"I finally found you," she said. "You know you're supposed to keep your address updated with the immigration office, don't you?"

"We just moved today," Skyler said, though that wasn't entirely true. He thought about his sessions with Dr. Haskell, and he didn't want to be caught even one step on the wrong side of the truth. "I mean, we've been living here in Three Rivers to help my brother with his back surgery. But we just moved into this house today."

The woman's expression softened, and she said, "Yes, I've been out to Church Ranches already."

"I'm so sorry," he said. "Why don't you come in? You're from immigration?"

"Yes," she said, stepping up and into the house. "I'm Madison Wilkerson, and I'm the case agent assigned to your case."

Skyler closed the door behind her and slicked his palms down the front of his shorts. Immigration had come to Three Rivers. "I'm Skyler Walker. My wife, Mal, is down the hall. Let me grab her."

He'd just rounded the corner when Mal came out of the bedroom. He tried to communicate telepathically with her, and he was sure she could feel his nerves. "Hey, sweetheart," he said, feeling stupid for laying on the endearment so thick. But he'd called her sweetheart before, and it hadn't sounded as fake as it did right now.

He reminded himself that if the doorbell hadn't rung, he and Mal would still be in bed, and he reached for her hand. "There's an immigration agent here. Madison Wilkerson. She's the agent assigned to our case."

"Our case?" Mal wore the anxiety plainly on her face, and she peered over Skyler's shoulder.

They faced the living room together, where Madison had sat on their new couch and put her notebook on the coffee table Skyler had brought from Amarillo. She stood and smiled at Mal. "You must be Mal Walker."

"Yes," Mal said. "Nice to meet you."

"And you." She nodded at Mal and then Skyler. "I just have a few questions for you, and I need to get some names for family interviews."

Skyler focused all his attention on not swallowing. "Sure," he said, moving over to the love seat, practically pushing Mal in front of him. "Anything you need."

"Who would be the best to interview about your marriage?" Madison asked, looking between the two of them.

"Well, we were living with my brother," Skyler said. "The one who had the back surgery. They probably know us and our relationship best."

"Yeah," Mal said. "And your mom and dad."

"Oh, sure, they'd be great." Skyler had slid right into one of his fake persona skins. He hadn't been wearing it as much as he did in Amarillo, and it was tight against his smile. "So Wyatt and Marcy Walker, though they're about to have a baby."

"I met Wyatt today," Madison said. "He's the one out in Church Ranches?"

"Yep."

"The rodeo champion." Madison smiled and made a note in her book."

"Yes." Skyler kept his smile on his face.

"And your parents?"

He looked at Mal. "I mean, sure. I have seven brothers. Jeremiah would be a good choice. Or Micah. He built this house."

"I can talk to your parents," Madison said. "Name and address?"

Skyler gave her the information she wanted, and then Madison sat back and crossed her legs. He felt like he'd just shown up for his therapy appointments, and Madison was going to fire uncomfortable questions at him that he hoped he answered correctly.

"You two have been married for how long?"

"Eight months?" Skyler guessed. "We got married in November, so just over eight months."

"And you left school?"

"Yeah, I'd been studying to be an accountant, but I don't actually need the degree to do the ranch finances, which has always been my goal. And Wyatt needed help after his surgery, and we came here."

"You're not going back to school, Mal?" Madison asked.

Mal swallowed, and Skyler could see her nerves. "I couldn't go for the winter semester," she said. "And now I have an amazing job at the bakery here, so...no. I haven't thought about going back this fall."

Madison nodded, asked a few more questions about their jobs, their new house, and their plans for the next year, five years, and ten years.

She didn't make any notes, and Skyler had no idea what she was looking for. She finally collected her notebook and stood. "Thank you for your time. Be sure to call the immigration office or go online and update your address."

"We won't be moving again," Skyler said.

Madison nodded and started for the front door. "This is a lovely home," she said.

"Thanks." Skyler and Mal both followed her to the door and saw her out. Skyler kept his fake skin and smile on his face as he closed the door. Then he sagged against it with a huge sigh.

Mal stumbled over to the bench. "I sort of thought they'd forgotten about us."

"Apparently not." Skyler stood up and went into the kitchen, his throat parched. "Is it hot in here?"

"A little," Mal said.

Skyler looked out the kitchen window, and he could see the oak tree several yards away. In mid-summer, all the foliage prevented him from seeing the homestead. But the leaves were blowing hard in the wind, and he reached for the window and lifted it to let in the breeze. It hit him in the face, and he closed his eyes and breathed in.

Mal joined him at the sink. "Do you think she believed us?"

"There's nothing to *not* believe," he said. "We're married. It's not wanna-be anymore." He searched her face. "Right?"

"Right." Mal reached for a glass and filled it with water too. "But it *was*, Sky, and what if she finds out?"

"How could she find out?" Skyler leaned back against the counter and folded his arms. "I'm so glad I didn't tell Micah and Wyatt when I went to breakfast with them." And to think, he'd felt bad after his sessions with Dr. Haskell where he'd withheld the information from them.

Mal hung her head and hissed her breath out in a slow leak.

"What?" he asked.

"I told my sister."

"You told your sister what?" he asked, his stomach dropping to the soles of his feet.

Mal lifted her head and looked at him, her eyes glassy. "I told Julia that we'd gotten married so I could stay in the country."

"Are you kidding me right now? When?" Skyler

couldn't believe this. A hole in the ground opened up, threatening to swallow him whole. If he was found aiding an illegal alien...he couldn't be arrested again. Flashes of his life in Dallas, the police questioning, the documents showing all the customers whose accounts had been overpaid, the fact that his girlfriend, his truck, and the money was all gone, assaulted him.

"Way back in January," she said, swiping at her eyes. "I'll call her right now. She won't have told anyone, I swear."

"Mal." Skyler huffed out in irritation and paced away from her.

"They're not going to interview her."

"You don't know that."

"She asked for people in your family."

"That doesn't mean the list is comprehensive." Skyler felt caged, and he needed to get out. Get out now. "Mal, I could get arrested over this. Go to *jail*. We weren't telling anyone that this was fake."

Air felt like the wrong thing to breathe. "Because it's not fake anymore. What are we going to do?"

"I said I'd call her."

"Great, go call her."

Mal looked like she was going to throw up, and Skyler knew exactly what that felt like. He stormed out the back door as she went down the hall to get her phone.

Micah, Jeremiah, and Wyatt stood there, all of them with a strange look on their faces. Skyler wanted to yell into the sky. "What did you hear?" he asked, remembering the open window above the kitchen sink.

"You could get arrested," Micah said, almost in a deadpan.

"You married Mal so she could stay in the country?" Jeremiah at least had the decency to phrase his statement as a question.

"It's not fake anymore," Wyatt said, grinning.

"There is nothing funny about this," Skyler said, his desperation threatening to explode from him. "An immigration agent just stopped by. She's going to be interviewing you and Marcy." He looked at Wyatt. "She can *not* think our marriage isn't real."

"Brother, I've seen you with Mal," Wyatt said. "Never once did I think it wasn't real."

"I don't need you to lie for me," Skyler said. "It's not worth that."

"I won't have to lie," Wyatt said.

"What are you going to do now?" Jeremiah asked.

"Yeah," Micah said. "Where were you going?"

"Just...away," Skyler said. "I needed some space."

"We were coming to see if you wanted to go horseback riding," Jeremiah said. "Well, Wyatt still can't get on a horse. But he's going to watch JJ while I go." Jeremiah bounced his baby in his arms. "Whitney doesn't feel well today."

"Horseback riding sounds great," Skyler said. What really sounded good was an afternoon with his brothers.

Maybe they could reassure him. Maybe he didn't have to jump off the ledge.

"Let's go," Micah said, turning toward the ranch. Skyler fell into step with his brothers, a prayer already filling his mind.

Please, Dear Lord, he prayed. *I don't want Mal to have to leave the country, and I really, really don't want to get arrested. If possible, help this work out for us.*

23

Wyatt glanced at Marcy when she froze, and he knew instantly that something was wrong. "Marce?" He reached across the space between them and took her hand.

She raised her gaze to his, panic in those blue, blue eyes he loved so much. "I think...." She relaxed in the next moment, her grip on his hand loosening. "It was probably just the baby kicking."

"You sure?" Their baby was due tomorrow, and Wyatt hadn't been able to sleep very deeply for the past few nights. He didn't want to miss a single moment of the delivery, and he didn't want Marcy to have to wake him up to take her to the hospital.

She nodded, leaning back in the camp chair Wyatt had carried and set up for her so they could watch the concert in the park. Wyatt loved summertime, and Three

Rivers did a summer concert series, with local bands—and some big names too—every Monday night. He loved the downtown park, and that families brought blankets and chairs, coolers with drinks, bags of licorice and chips, pizzas and burgers and anything else they wanted to eat.

Food trucks filled the west parking lot, and Wyatt and Marcy had bought fried chicken cones and eaten them half an hour ago. Jeremiah and Whitney had just arrived, and Rhett had called to say Evelyn was too tired to make it that night.

Wyatt continued to watch Marcy, but she didn't tense again.

He looked at Jeremiah, but he didn't even know what to ask. According to the stories he'd heard, Jeremiah had been out on the ranch when Whitney had gone into labor, and he'd arrived in their bedroom just before Whitney had delivered their baby at home.

That baby now babbled on Jeremiah's lap as Whitney dug through a diaper bag for something. She handed a wipe to Jeremiah, who used it on his son's face. The baby didn't like that, and jerked away, but Jeremiah got the job done and handed the wipe back to Whitney. "You've got applesauce all over your face, Jay," Jeremiah said. "You're fine." He put the boy over his shoulder and bounced him as he fussed.

"He's just tired," Whitney said. "Let's feed him and see if he'll go to sleep." She dove into the bag again and came up with a peanut butter and jelly sandwich. She'd cut it in half, and she took out one piece and handed it to Jeremiah.

He settled the boy back on his lap and ripped off a small chunk to offer to JJ. He took it happily, stuffing the sandwich in his mouth. "There you go," Jeremiah said. He looked at Whitney. "Did you bring the chips?"

"Yep." She produced those, opening the bag and holding it on her lap. Jeremiah reached across and took several, crunching through them as his son continued to eat his sandwich.

Wyatt marveled at the normalcy of it all. Jeremiah and Whitney were good parents, and Whitney seemed to always have exactly what she needed to satisfy JJ. Wyatt could only hope and pray that he'd know how to be a father, and a familiar vein of worry threaded through him.

Marcy groaned, and Wyatt's attention flew back to her. She had both hands on her very pregnant belly, and her eyes were closed. Not squeezed tight, but definitely not closed in bliss.

"Marcy," he said, stronger now. "You're not okay."

"I think I'm having contractions," she said.

"Really?" Whitney got up, abandoning the chips and the diaper bag. "Let's go." She wore a look of panic on her face.

"Wait a second," Wyatt said. "Don't we have to time them or something?" He himself hadn't read any books about delivering a baby, but Marcy had listened to at least five over the past few months as she flew over the fields of Three Rivers.

"Yeah," Marcy said.

"How close together are they?" Whitney asked.

"I don't know." Marcy looked up at the other woman. "I feel like I can't think."

Whitney crouched down in front of her and put both hands on her knees. "Marcy, look at me."

Marcy did, and Wyatt could see the wide-eyed panic on his wife's face. He stood up too, not a single twinge of pain in his back. Thankfully. "Maybe we should go," he said.

Marcy looked at him next, and he watched the pain slide right off her face. "I'm okay."

"I'm timing," Whitney said. "Because that was just a contraction. How she's in pain and unsure of what to do, and then she's fine? I know what that feels like."

Wyatt looked at Jeremiah, who was watching them with intensity on his face. "Whit," he said.

"What?" she asked. "Do you think she wants to have this baby in the park?"

"I don't want to have the baby in the park," Marcy said.

"Let's just go," Wyatt said. "What's the worst that can happen? They tell us to go home?" He started folding up his camp chair, suddenly glad he and Marcy preferred to buy their food instead of bringing it with them. All he had to carry was the two camp chairs—and possibly his pregnant wife as she went into labor.

"Oh, boy," Marcy said. She sucked in a breath and held it.

"What?" Wyatt asked, ready to go. "What's wrong?"

"I think my water just broke."

"Time to go," Wyatt said, his heartbeat accelerating. He reached for Marcy's arm and helped her to her feet. He didn't care who saw what; he needed to get them to the hospital right now. "Can you walk, sugar?"

"Yes," she said, panting just once. "I can."

"Jeremiah?"

"Leave everything," his brother said. "We'll get it."

Wyatt nodded, patted his back pocket for his wallet and his phone, and started across the grass toward his truck. The very first time Marcy made a noise like she couldn't take another step, he swept her into his arms.

"Wyatt," she said, her voice tight. "You're going to hurt your back."

"I'm fine," he said, able to move faster now that she wasn't delicately stepping like she didn't want to tramp down the grass. "Honestly, baby. I'm fine." He got her into the truck, and she pulled her legs in. That was when Wyatt saw the wet stain on the front of her pants. "You okay?"

She nodded a little too rapidly, and as Wyatt jogged around the front of the truck, gratitude struck him that they were already in town. The drive from Church Ranches would've added twenty minutes to the trip.

As it was, he was able to carry his wife into labor and delivery only twelve minutes later. "Her water broke about twenty minutes ago," he said to the nurse there. "She's had a few contractions."

Being at the hospital brought such a sense of relief, but his worries and fears didn't subside. He'd been there when Ivory had almost died in childbirth. "Please, Dear God," he said as a couple of nurses helped Marcy into a bed.

She reached for him, and he went right to her side. "I'm here, sugar," he said. "It's going to be okay."

Tears streamed down her face. "We're having a baby."

He grinned at her, his own emotions threatening to come out in the form of tears. "We sure are." He looked up as the nurses spoke to each other about which room to take her to. "I'm okay to stay with her?"

"Every step of the way, Mister Walker," the nurse said with a smile. "Who's her doctor?"

"Hoffman," Wyatt said. "Thadeus Hoffman."

"It's *Tyrone* Hoffman," Marcy said. "Wyatt." She gave a strained giggle, and Wyatt looked at her.

"Oh, right," he said with a smile. "Tyrone." He'd been the only one to call the doctor Thadeus, as he'd gone on and on about how he used to be in the MMA during one of their appointments.

"We'll call him," the nurse said, and Marcy started to move. Wyatt kept his hand in hers as they went down the hall and past several empty rooms. They put her in one on the end and one of the nurses started putting on a pair of gloves.

"We'll check her here," the first nurse said. "And see how far along she is. We'll move her to a delivery room once we do the epidural." She moved to Marcy's other side. "You do want an epidural, don't you, ma'am?"

"Can I have one right now?" she asked.

The nurse smiled and shook her head. "Not until you reach a four or a five."

"Shoot," Marcy said, and Wyatt thought she was in pretty good spirits for a woman in labor. He relaxed slightly, and he stood right by her side as they checked her, determined her water had indeed broken, and that she was dilated to a three.

"Looking good," the nurse said. "We'll be back in a few minutes to check on you again. If you have a contraction, don't push."

Surprise wound through Wyatt. "Will she want to push?"

"Definitely," the nurse said. "It's the natural reaction." She nodded to the two of them and left the room with the other nurse.

"Don't push," Wyatt said. "I don't know why, but that surprised me."

Marcy leaned her head back and closed her eyes, but she only got a few minutes of peace before she tensed again. Wyatt watched every muscle in her body coil and tighten, and she squeezed his fingers hard. "Not pushing is hard."

Wyatt didn't know what to say or do, and that was hard on him. Wyatt *always* knew what to say and do. He waited for the contraction to pass, and he pulled his phone out of his back pocket. "I'll text Jeremiah and get him to let everyone know what's going on."

"They'll all be here within minutes," Marcy said, looking at him. "Is that what we want?"

Wyatt did want his whole family there. Not in the room with Marcy as she gave birth, but he'd loved being in the waiting room while his nephews were born. He'd loved holding them while they were mostly made of just a head attached to a tiny body, and he loved the sweet smell of a newborn baby.

"I'll just tell him that you've gone into labor, and that we'll let everyone know when to come."

"Okay." Marcy nodded.

He only had half the message typed out when Marcy groaned again. "Another one?" He moved quickly back to her side. "They're coming fast."

"Are they?" a man asked, and Wyatt looked up to see the gladiator doctor coming into the room. He looked like he'd just come from the gym, as he was wearing a pair of basketball shorts and a T-shirt. He took a pair of gloves from the box affixed to the wall. "How close together?"

"I don't know," Wyatt said. "But she just had one."

"Let's take a look." He sat in front of Marcy while the

nurse adjusted the light. "She's at a five. Where was she before?"

"Eleven minutes ago," the second nurse said. "Three."

"Let's get the epidural going," the doctor said, and the nurses moved around him. They talked and did things, and everything blurred together for Wyatt. He realized he'd never sent his text, and he hurried to do that before they wheeled Marcy out of the room.

Wyatt trailed behind them into the delivery room, where she finally got the epidural. She relaxed quite a bit after that, and she said not pushing was a little easy now that there wasn't so much pressure and pain.

Wyatt wasn't sure how much time had gone by. He wasn't sure if Jeremiah had texted or not. What he knew was that Marcy was suddenly told to push.

"Now?" she asked.

"Yes," Dr. Hoffman said. "Now, Marcy. Push."

Wyatt watched her work and work and work, and still their son would not come out.

"He's a stubborn one," Dr. Hoffman said. He wore a smile, but his frustration was thinly veiled behind it. He looked at Wyatt. "Did you give your momma trouble like this?"

"Oh, he's a barrel of trouble," Marcy said. Her head fell back against the bed behind her, a weary smile on her face.

Wyatt just smiled and stroked Marcy's hair off her

forehead. "You're doing great," he said. "He's going to be here soon."

"Here we go again," the doctor said. "We need to get him out."

"What happens if we don't?" Wyatt asked.

"Push, Marcy," the doctor said, positioning himself again.

She did, her face scrunched up in concentration, her fingers gripping the railings on either side of the bed. A yell came from her throat, and Wyatt had never felt so helpless in his life. Not when he'd been strapped to a bed and said good-bye to his family before being wheeled back into surgery. Not when Marcy had broken up with him and fled the hospital. Not when he'd found her in her father's house after he'd passed away.

"Here he is!" the doctor announced triumphantly, as if he'd been the one pushing for the past few hours. He lifted the baby in both hands, and Wyatt saw his son for the first time.

Pure love moved through him, and he stared at the infant as the doctor passed it to one of the nurses.

"Why isn't he crying?" Wyatt asked, moving away from Marcy.

Three nurses worked over his baby, who lay on a tray under a bright light.

"Wyatt?" Marcy asked, but he didn't turn back.

Worry spiked in him—and then, the baby's voice filled

the air. Relief filled Wyatt, and that brought tears to his eyes.

"Come on over, Dad," one of the nurses said, and he stepped around the doctor, still working with Marcy. Wyatt stepped up to the heat lamps where his son lay, and everything about him was perfect.

"All ten toes and fingers," the nurse said. "He's beautiful."

"He sure is." Wyatt swiped at his eyes as one nurse continued to clean the baby up a little bit. She wrapped him in a white blanket and handed him to Wyatt.

"Go show your wife."

Wyatt turned back to Marcy, this tiny human in his hands entirely too fragile for someone like him. Their eyes met, and if Wyatt thought he'd experienced joy before, he'd been wrong.

"Look, sugar," he said, his voice breaking. "Your son." He gave the baby to Marcy, who wept as she looked down at the life they'd created together.

"Oh," she said, and that summed it up absolutely right.

24

Simone wiped the kitchen counter in her cabin, determined not to call or text Evelyn or Callie about the new baby born to the Walker family.

She wasn't a member of the Walker family. Not really.

Just because her sisters had married Walkers didn't make Simone a close family member. They were her brothers-in-law, and it was fine to go over to Seven Sons for Sunday dinner. But she didn't need to rush off to the hospital to see Wyatt and Marcy's new baby.

Frustration built into a sigh, and Simone let it out. She loved Marcy and Wyatt, and she did want to be there to support them. But Callie had texted an hour ago to say the baby had been born healthy and everyone was doing great. They'd named the boy Warren Wyatt Walker, and Simone smiled at the triple W's.

But she would not be going to the hospital. She could

wait and see the infant in a couple of weeks, when Marcy and Wyatt were out at the ranch or back at church.

She had a hard time swallowing, because she didn't like this solution any more than rushing right over to the hospital. Micah would surely be there, and he'd been dating Ophelia Montgomery for seven months now, and no amount of matchmaking had worked for Simone.

Evelyn had lost her touch, that was for sure.

Even as Simone thought so, she knew she was simply deluding herself. The problem with the three other cowboys her sister had tried to set her up with was that they weren't Micah Walker. Plain and simple.

Simone had humiliated herself at the masquerade ball over Valentine's Day, earning herself a couple of phone numbers. But when she'd called, one man said he already had a girlfriend, and the other said he couldn't remember her.

"Couldn't remember me," Simone muttered to herself. She was a lifelong resident of Three Rivers. People knew who she was, as she attended every boutique, every fair, and every town celebration. She'd sold furniture to hundreds of people in town, and everyone knew that if there was a need for custom, antique furniture, the first phone call should be to Simone.

She should be out in the she-shed right now, as she'd gotten a call for a custom vase a couple of days ago. But she couldn't make herself go out to the hot shed and work. The cost to air condition the she-shed was astronomical during the summer, and Simone tried to get up early and work before the sun heated everything past comfortable.

Instead, she set about making a batch of peppermint chocolate cookies. She normally made them during the holiday season, and never again throughout the year. But she knew they were Marcy's favorite, and she figured she could take a plate of them up to Church Ranches to tell her and Wyatt congratulations.

Simone loved babies, and she couldn't help the sense of longing that pulled through her. She was thrilled to be an aunt, and she loved her nieces and her nephew. She knew Evelyn was trying to get pregnant again, but no announcements had been made. She was usually the last to know anything in the Foster family, as she did spend a lot of time alone, either shopping at estate sales, yard sales, or junkyards, or working on the "trash" she found and turning it into treasure.

She had to drive a lot, as Three Rivers had plenty of yard sales in the summer, but not enough supplies to keep Simone working year-round. Since her sisters had both married billionaires, Simone had been able to keep all the money she made on her restoration projects. She made enough to buy herself a used delivery truck big enough to hold a lot of treasures. She was getting ready to go down to the swap meets in the Hill Country to stock up for the winter, and she liked bumping along in the delivery truck.

It was a very long drive, and Simone almost didn't want to make it—at least not alone. She normally took camping equipment with her, set up a tent in a commercial campground, and saved money on hotels. She was already looking forward to that, as Simone did love getting out and experiencing a little bit of Texas from time to time.

She measured flour and baking soda while the butter and sugars creamed. "You'll be glad to get out of here," she told herself. "And you don't need a friend to go with you."

Besides, she knew perfectly well she didn't want just a friend. She wanted Micah to be her boyfriend again. The missing inside her intensified until she thought for sure that today would be the day that she'd break.

But she simply kept making cookies. She measured. She scraped. She added the dry ingredients. She poured in peppermint chips. She scooped. She bent. She baked.

She steadfastly refused to look at her phone, which sat face-down on the counter next to the fridge. She would not go next door and see if Micah was home.

He had a girlfriend.

Simone simply needed to find someone else.

"You can," she told herself, surveying the three dozen cookies she'd turned out. Leaning both hands into the counter and tipping her head back, she sighed as she looked up at the ceiling. "Please, Lord, help me find someone else. Or know what to do about Micah."

Her house was very quiet, only the hum of the refrigerator behind her and the low rush of the air conditioning keeping the cabin cool.

"What should I do about Micah Walker?" she asked.

She believed God knew exactly how she felt about Micah. He was aware of her, and He'd led her many times to good things in her life.

Why not Micah too? she wondered.

Simone closed her eyes and listened, trying to discover what the Lord wanted her to do. "If I'm supposed to give him up, just let me know," she said. "I'll try to find a way to do it." And she could do it then, because she knew God didn't give her a trial she couldn't handle.

Go visit Daddy and Grams.

Simone didn't see how a visit to her father and her elderly grandmother would do much good, but she also didn't have a habit to question the Lord.

And her father loved peppermint cookies too, so Simone put six on a paper plate, grabbed her keys, and headed out.

———

Twenty minutes later, Simone pulled into Daddy's driveway. He and Grams had lived with Callie and Liam for a couple of months, but they'd been back home for a while now.

His truck hadn't moved since the last time she'd been here, and she wasn't sure if that was comforting or not. She'd brought dinner a little over a week ago, and she'd helped her father order groceries to be delivered. She'd checked with Whitney, whose family owned the store where Daddy had ordered from, and Whitney said he'd set up a recurring order once a week.

So at least they wouldn't starve.

"Grams?" she called as she entered. "Daddy?" She went down the hall past the formal living room that had become a museum for things no one ever touched and found her family in the family room.

"Simone." Grams grinned at her and took several long seconds to push herself out of her armchair. By that time, Simone had put the peppermint cookies on the kitchen counter and turned to steady her grandmother.

She kissed her cheek, feeling the papery, soft texture of her skin. "Grams, you look good." Simone smiled at her and held onto her arms. "Have you been getting out and walking?"

"Heavens, no," Grams said, waving her hand. "But Belinda comes here and makes me do some exercises."

"She does, huh?" Simone released her grandmother as her father came in the back door.

"I thought I heard someone pull up," he said, smiling at her.

"Hey, Daddy, I brought some of those peppermint cookies you love."

"Thanks, sugar." He stepped over to the counter and picked one up, taking a bite. "Mm."

"What were you doing outside?" Simone peered out the window over the dining room table. Callie and Evelyn used to be the sisters who monitored their father and grandmother, but with the additions to their families, the task had fallen to Simone for the past couple of years. She didn't mind it so much, because no one else was relying on her for anything. To be honest, she felt a bit lost among all of the people in her life.

They had lifeboats with spouses and significant others, babies and children. She was in a raft built for one, and it seemed like no matter what she tried to do to get into a bigger boat, she only ended up capsizing her own.

"Oh, just ripping out those old rose bushes," Daddy said.

"The rose bushes?" Alarm pulled through Simone, and she looked at her father. He looked like he'd lost a battle with a whole herd of cats, as he had scratches up and down both arms. "Why don't you just call someone?"

"Who would I call?"

"Rhett," Simone said. "Liam. The two of them could come over and have them out in no time." Simone narrowed her eyes at him. "Why are you taking them out anyway? I thought you liked them."

"I did." Her father picked up another cookie, and at this rate, Grams wouldn't get any if Simone didn't rescue one for her. She'd made her way back to the recliner in the family room, and Simone shot her a glance.

"I'm going to go wash up," her dad said. "Do you want to stay for dinner?"

"What are you making?" Simone asked, watching him shuffle through the dining room and kitchen. The house was cleaner than normal, and he seemed more...spry than she'd seen him in a while. Something was definitely afoot; she just didn't know what. Yet.

"Oh, we're having someone bring burritos," he said when he reached the mouth of the hall that led down to his room.

Simone's eyebrows shot up. "Someone's bringing them? Or delivering them?" There was a difference, Simone knew. She moved into the family room when Daddy didn't answer and perched on the edge of the couch. "What's going on, Grams? Did you call the pastor again for meals? I told you not to do that. Callie, Evvy, and I can bring you dinner if you need it."

"He didn't call the pastor," Grams said, pushing herself in the rocking armchair with the toe of her foot. She kept her focus on the newspaper in front of her, and Simone couldn't remember the last time she'd even touched a newspaper.

"So you ordered dinner and are having it delivered."

Gram looked up from her crossword puzzle. "No," she said. "Belinda is bringing the burritos."

"Who's this Belinda?" Simone asked. She had never heard the woman's name, and now Grams had said it twice. Perhaps Callie or Evelyn had hired a housekeeper of sorts, and the woman had been cleaning up, bringing meals, and getting Grams out of the recliner every now and then.

And apparently, inspiring Daddy to rip out perfectly

good rose bushes. Those would not go without a fight, Simone knew that.

"She's the lady who comes to help with my exercises," Grams said.

"How's Daddy's heart?" she asked. "He's taking his medicine?"

"Every day, sweets." Grams gave her a smile and went back to her puzzle. Simone had barely had time to stand up before the front door opened, and another woman's voice filled the house.

"Dinner's here," she said, and a few moments later, she came around the corner from the front of the house. She wore a wide grin, a bright yellow blouse, and a pair of black shorts. In her hands, she carried a pan of cheesy, steaming burritos, and she hurried into the kitchen like she'd drop them at any moment.

Pushing out her breath, she said, "Whew. Those were hotter than I thought." She took off the oven mitts she'd been using and tossed them on the counter, right on top of the peppermint cookies Simone had brought. "You must be Jerome's daughter. One of 'em, at least." She stuck out her hand, and Simone felt like the world was moving too fast. "I'm Belinda."

Simone looked at Grams and back to Belinda, finally putting her hand in the other woman's. She was easily a couple of decades older than Simone, though not nearly as old as Grams, but she didn't look a day over fifty.

"There you are," Daddy said, and he'd done a lot more

than wash up. He'd scrubbed his hands and face clean, combed his hair, and as the most nauseating smell hit her, Simone realized just how much cologne he'd put on.

Horror combined with shock as she realized her father had a crush on Belinda. Big time. "Looks great," he said, his smile never wavering. "You met Simone? She's my youngest."

"Just did," Belinda said, still as cheerful as ever. "You look like you lost a battle with a tiger." She reached out and ran her fingertips down Daddy's arms, tracing some of the wounds from the thorns. "I told you I'd have my son come take those bushes out." She wore concern in her eyes, and another terrible realization crashed down on Simone.

Her father and Belinda were dating.

Dating.

And Simone couldn't get a man to remember her.

Pure humiliation filled her, and tears sprang to her eyes. Daddy and Belinda conversed around her. Grams got out of the recliner and started pulling down plates. The house had a completely new energy to it, and Simone didn't know what to make of it.

It was good, and she didn't care if her father dated someone. It was just...unexpected. Simone's mother had died when she was very young, and Daddy had never dated. Never remarried, in almost forty years.

"Are you staying, sugar?" Daddy asked.

"No," Simone said, deciding on the spot. "Everything

looks amazing, Belinda." She forced a smile to her mouth. "But I can't stay. I just came to see how you two were and bring you some cookies."

And they were fine without her. Just like everyone else.

Simone's throat closed up as she hugged Grams and Daddy, as she walked toward the front door, as she got behind the wheel of her SUV.

"Is that what you wanted me to see?" she asked the Lord. "What am I supposed to do with that? How does this help me with Micah?"

God didn't inspire any more thoughts in Simone's mind, and she backed out of the driveway, determined not to cry that her father's love life was more active than hers.

As she drove back to the ranch, she only had one thought in her mind. *Go talk to Micah.*

Go talk to him.

Just go talk to him.

Instead of fighting the urge to go see him, Simone turned into Seven Sons Ranch instead of continuing down the lane to the Shining Star.

Her father's bright eyes and Belinda's laugh as she'd left the house drove Simone up the steps. Her own loneliness got her to knock on the door.

And the constant prayer just behind her tongue kept her there while she waited, and waited, and waited for someone to open the door.

25

"What do you mean, it's for me?" Micah stood in his bathroom, his electric razor in his hand. Ophelia never came out to the ranch, because that made no sense. He picked her up from her house in town when they went out—as they were set to do in an hour or so.

"It's for you," Jeremiah repeated. "Could you just come get it, please? I've got a lot to handle in the kitchen as it is." He walked away as another cry filled the air. JJ had been particularly fussy tonight, and Whitney was only a couple of days away from delivering another baby. Then she and Jeremiah would have two kids under fourteen months old.

Micah took his razor with him as he followed Jeremiah down the hall. The chaos to his left probably should've cured him of his own desire to find a wife and have a family, and he turned right, toward the front door. He wanted the crying kids, the messy house, the faintly frantic air of home and family. That *was* home and family to him, as he'd always existed among many others, and life was often more messy than clean in the Walker household.

He hadn't even heard the doorbell ring, and when he pulled open the front door, he knew why.

Simone Foster stood there, and she wouldn't have used the doorbell. "Oh," he said, the first thing that came to his mind.

"Hey," she said, drawing in a big breath. "I was just wondering, I mean, maybe you're busy." Her eyes dropped to the razor, and pure humiliation poured through Micah that he'd answered the door halfway through shaving. But he couldn't stop now.

He also had no idea what to say. Thankfully, Simone kept talking. "I know I might have messed up too badly, Micah. I know that. But I hate...this. I hate that I can't talk to you. I hate that when I go to my father's and find out he's seeing someone, that I can't call you and gossip about it. I hate that I made peppermint cookies, and you're not in my shed, eating them with me." She took another breath, but she seemed a little out of control to Micah.

And everything she was saying.... Micah wasn't sure what to make of it.

"I know you're dating Ophelia." She started nodding. "I know that. And you two are just so...darn cute together." She pushed out all that air. "It's disgusting, really."

She smiled playfully at him, and Micah wasn't sure who he was looking at.

Simone, the woman who wanted to be his friend and talk about his dates with Ophelia? Or Simone, the woman he'd kissed as passionately as he'd ever kissed a woman?

And that wasn't enough, he reminded himself. She still didn't want to take their relationship out of the shadows. Maybe he wasn't a good kisser, though none of the other women he'd dated had ever complained.

Of course, Stephanie hadn't been truly interested in advancing their relationship until she'd learned how much money he had. So maybe he really wasn't boyfriend or husband material.

"Anyway, I just *needed* to talk to someone," she said, falling back a step. She nodded to the razor. "Are you going out tonight?"

He couldn't very well lie about it. "Yes," he said, still moving that blasted razor over his jaw. He wondered if she just needed to talk to *someone*, or if she needed to talk to *him*. He wasn't sure why he was hoping it was *him* and not *someone*. He was dating someone else.

"Your dad is seeing someone?" he asked, pushing away the confusing feelings.

"Yes." Simone's eyes widened and she huffed. "Can you believe it?"

"I kind of can't," Micah said, finally finishing with the razor. He glanced over his shoulder, surprised Jeremiah hadn't yelled at him to close the front door so he didn't have to cool the whole ranch. That just spoke to how overwhelmed his brother was. "Do you want to come in for a minute? It's hot out here."

"Sure." Simone squeezed right past him, putting one hand flat against his chest. She smiled again, and Micah felt like her touch had branded him right through the fabric of his shirt. And he had no idea what he was doing as he looked both ways, as if he couldn't be seen going into the homestead with Simone Foster and stepped back inside. He closed the door behind him and followed Simone into the sitting room off the main hall that led down to the kitchen and the rest of the house.

"How are Wyatt and Marcy?" she asked, turning back to him.

Micah drank her in, everything about her. He had the lines of her beautiful face memorized, and he remembered what the silky strands of her hair felt like between his fingers. He'd sorely missed talking to her too, and the fact that she hadn't come to the hospital to see the new Walker baby hadn't escaped his attention.

Today, she wore a pair of black leggings that called to his male side, along with a white and pink striped blouse. Micah swallowed and worked very hard not to let his gaze drip down the height of her body.

She wasn't his. He had a girlfriend—a girlfriend who wasn't Simone Foster.

"They're good," he managed to say, even if his voice

did carry the quality of frogs. "They named the baby Warren."

Simone nodded and glanced around the room again. Liam and Tripp had once shared it as an office, so it was plenty big enough for two big desks, six monitors, and their two huge bodies, cowboy hats, and egos.

But somehow, it felt microscopically small to Micah in that moment. He cleared his throat. "You said something about peppermint cookies?"

"Yes."

"And you didn't bring me any?" He made a show of looking at her hands, as if he could miss a plate of cookies. He was flirting, and he knew it. Guilt gutted him. What would Ophelia think if she could see him right now?

"I didn't plan on stopping," Simone said.

"Then why did you?" Micah was done playing games with Simone, that was for sure.

"I...I couldn't shake the thought," she finally said. She wore a look of nerves in those dark, deep, delicious eyes, and Micah didn't like that. But he didn't know how to erase it. She'd created the situation between them, and if it made her nervous, so be it.

"So I'll have to come by your place to get the cookies, is that it?" He grinned at her, hoping he could cover his own anxiety with a smile.

"If there are any left by the time you stop by, they'll be yours." She gave him a smile and nodded. "Okay, I should go. Have fun on your date." She stepped past him again, and Micah just watched her move by him.

She'd opened the front door and stepped onto the porch before he called after her, "When's your next play, Simone?" He rounded the corner in time to see her turn back toward him.

"I'm taking a break right now," she said. "I'll audition in October or November for the spring one. I'm still waiting to see what it will be."

He nodded. He couldn't tell her he'd taken Ophelia to her last play, just so he could see her act, and sing, and dance on stage. He couldn't tell her he'd looked up her theater company and learned that anyone could audition for any play. He couldn't tell her how much he missed her, or how glad he was that she'd stopped by, or how beautiful she was with the early evening light haloing her.

Not while he had a girlfriend.

Probably never again, he told himself as Simone lifted her hand in a half-hearted wave and went down the steps.

"Are we cooling the whole world or what?" Jeremiah demanded behind him, and Micah spun back to the homestead.

"Sorry," he said, hurrying back over to the door as Jeremiah stomped down the hall and further into the house. Micah turned back in time to watch Simone climb into her SUV, back up, turn around, and go down the lane toward the Shining Star.

And he suddenly did not want to go out with Ophelia.

He wished the woman he'd been shaving for was none other than Simone Foster, and that he'd be standing on her stoop in an hour, ready to take her to dinner and then to the llama festival.

A sigh filled his soul as he closed the door and walked back into the bathroom to put away his razor. "But what am I supposed to do?" he asked the empty air around him. "Break up with Ophelia and beg Simone for another chance?"

They'd already tried a relationship three times. *Three.* And wasn't that supposed to be the magic number? Third time's the charm and all that?

Micah shook his head and went into the bedroom to find his cowboy hat. Hatted, with cologne on, properly shaved, and with his new Wyatt Walker collection belt securely fastened, Micah left the chaotic homestead and drove into town.

He rang Ophelia's doorbell, and grinned at Ophelia, and kissed Ophelia hello.

This was right. *This* was a good, healthy relationship. *Ophelia* was amazing, and beautiful, and smart.

He and Simone were simply not meant to be.

"Are you ready for this?" she asked.

"A llama festival?" Micah chuckled and offered his arm to his girlfriend, who laced her hand through it. "I was born ready for this."

26

Mal stirred her coffee, wondering what time Skyler had gotten up. In Amarillo, he'd never beaten her into the kitchen to make coffee. But today, only a week after Madison Wilkerson had come by this new house, he'd gotten up super early, slipped away from her, made coffee, and went running by himself.

It was the running that stabbed the deepest. That was something they'd always done together, even when things between them were strained.

"Never been this bad before," Mal mused, watching the leaves and branches on the huge oak tree sway in the morning breeze. Skyler had been sticking close to his brothers, especially Micah and Jeremiah, since they'd moved to the ranch.

Mal couldn't help wondering if that was because the immigration agent had shown up the same day they'd moved in, and Skyler just needed space from what Mal had told him.

She had called her sister, and she'd learned that everyone in her family now knew that her original I-do with Skyler had been simply to keep her in the country. Nothing was so simple anymore, and Mal didn't know what to do.

Julia had assured her that they wouldn't say anything should anyone from the US contact them, and Mal had to live with that reassurance. She couldn't go to Mexico and make sure they said the right things. She didn't believe her family would really be interviewed, but the hole still existed down deep in her stomach.

She'd never wanted to make trouble for Skyler, and she absolutely could not be the reason he got in trouble with the law again. His previous girlfriend had been the cause of that, and Mal couldn't stand the thought of being in the same category as Shayla.

She also didn't want to spend her day off alone. August was right around the corner, and it was too hot to spend much time outside, especially in the middle of the day. Skyler had taken Rosie running with him, and maybe Mal could take her to the dog park later that day. Maybe she should start on the strawberry shortcake she'd promised Wyatt.

He and Marcy had brought their son home a few days ago, and Mal couldn't think of a better way to celebrate a new baby than with strawberry shortcake. It helped that

Wyatt ate everything she made with a huge smile on his face, compliments for her cooking flowing freely the whole time.

Mal had gone to the hospital with Skyler and the rest of the Walker family. With more people around, it was easy to get lost in the energy of seven sons, their wives and families. But here at home...Mal felt like someone had draped the house under a steel blanket, and she was pushing, pushing, pushing against the weight of it.

"So what do I do?" she asked. Since she'd started going to church, she'd started asking questions like this out loud. They weren't for her. But she was hoping God would hear her and tell her what to do.

She had the sudden thought to go get the rest of her things in Amarillo. Skyler had hired a company to bring most of their stuff from the apartment in Amarillo, but there were still beds there. She could buy food and paper plates for a weekend.

She had a storage unit for some things she'd kept from her apartment that she hadn't brought to Skyler's when they'd first gotten married.

Decided, she picked up her phone and called Heidi.

"Mal, dear, how are you?"

"Good," Mal said, hating what she was about to do. "I'm wondering how hard it would be for me to take Saturday and Monday off?" She closed her eyes and waited for Heidi to say something. A prayer ran through her mind as she begged God to soften Heidi's heart. She didn't want to stay in this tense house for another weekend.

"That should be fine," Heidi said. "I'll have Zack come in a couple of extra days."

Relief filled Mal. "Great. Thanks so much, Heidi."

"Are you going somewhere fun?"

"No," Mal said. "I mean, I just need to get back to Amarillo and get a few things. I thought I'd make a weekend of it."

"I need to get to Amarillo too," she said, her voice softening. "I grew up there, you know."

"I didn't know that," Mal said, her heart opening to Heidi. "Are your parents still there?"

"Daddy is," she said. "My mother died a few years ago."

"Oh, I'm sorry."

"She was a lovely woman, and she lived a long, good life," Heidi said. "Nothing to be sorry about. But I should go visit my father."

Mal nodded, but she didn't know what else to say. She wouldn't see her family for another eight years, and the weight of that pressed against her lungs in the most painful way.

"Have fun," Heidi said, her voice brightening. "I better call Zack."

"See you in the morning," Mal said. The call ended, and she immediately went down the hall to the bedroom. Skyler had been sleeping in the bed with her, but he stayed out in the living room for hours after she went to bed, and she only knew he'd been there because his side of the bed wasn't made in the morning when she got up.

She looked at the rumpled sheets, pausing for a moment. How could she fix things between them? She'd apologized. She'd told him that Julia wouldn't say anything if someone came to ask about their marriage.

Nothing was good enough for him.

With the poisonous thought in her mind, she continued into the massive closet and got a bag out of one of the drawers in the shelving unit. She was just going for a few days, and Mal packed quickly.

"You're leaving?"

She spun around, her heartbeat shooting through her whole body.

Skyler stood there, wearing his running clothes and a frown on his sweaty face.

"I'm just going to get my things out of storage," she said. "Tomorrow. After I finish at the bakery."

"When will you be back?" he asked.

"Monday," she said, swallowing. "I have to work on Tuesday."

He nodded, though he still didn't look happy. At all. "Okay."

"Is there anything you need from the apartment?"

"Nope." He walked away, peeling off his shirt and tossing it on the bathroom floor. Mal scampered out of the closet and bathroom so he could shower. She felt like she'd just made the biggest escape of her life, and she hated that.

But the Lord hadn't given her any ideas about what to do, and Skyler didn't seem keen to forgive her. Nothing bad had even happened yet, but Mal understood why he was so agitated. She hated walking on eggshells all the time, and that was how this situation was.

The immigration agents could show up at any time, and Mal felt like she was living in a glass box. One wrong move, and everything would shatter.

———

THE FOLLOWING DAY, Mal made churros for hours, baked and decorated a cake for someone's fiftieth anniversary, and got two dozen loaves of honey wheat bread rising before her shift ended at the bakery.

"Fifty years," Heidi said, gazing down at the cake. "That's an amazing thing."

"How long have you and Frank been married?" Mal asked, looking at the older woman.

"Thirty-nine years," she said fondly. "We've been through a lot, that man and I."

"That's amazing, Heidi," Mal said. "I might not even make it to my first anniversary." The moment the words left her mouth, Mal regretted them.

Heidi's gaze whipped to hers. "Oh, dear. I'm sorry

things aren't going well. Is there anything I can do to help?"

Mal pressed her lips together and shook her head. "What did you do…I mean, surely you and Frank didn't agree about everything."

"Heavens, no," she said with a smile. "There were times when I wondered what I'd gotten myself into. Frank could be a very hard man to crack, that was for sure. He's a cowboy through and through, and it took me years to figure out how he communicated."

Mal nodded like she understood, but she didn't.

"But I love him," Heidi said. "We loved each other, and that always seemed to be enough to get us to forgive, open up, try again." She patted Mal's hand, but didn't tell her that everything would be okay.

Mal sure did appreciate that. She knew better than most that sometimes things weren't okay. *But aren't they?* she wondered. *Aren't they really, in the end?*

It seemed to her that yes, even if something was hard to go through, on the other side, things did turn out okay.

She drew in a deep breath. "Okay, well, I better hit the road. I have a lunch date with an old friend in Amarillo."

"Okay," Heidi said, turning toward her and taking her into a hug. Mal took a deep breath of her scent, thinking her own mother would smell and feel very much like this. She loved Heidi in that moment, and she couldn't help thinking of Skyler's mother too. Penny was a hugger, and she'd never held back with Mal.

"Please be safe," Heidi said. "See you Tuesday."

Mal couldn't speak past the lump in her throat. So she just nodded and headed out to her car, more than a little excited she didn't have to exist on pins and needles for the next few days. She met Karla at the Mexican restaurant, and Mal couldn't help laughing as she hugged the friend she hadn't seen in so long.

"Girl, you look good," Karla said, stepping back and looking at Mal. "I guess married life agrees with you."

"I guess so." Mal didn't want to say anything bad about Skyler. The man hadn't done anything wrong, and he had every right to be upset with her. But she'd told him once that she trusted him, and she would've supported him had he decided the right thing to do was to tell his brothers about their fake marriage.

The familiar feeling of being Skyler's wanna-be wife coursed through her, and she almost started crying. She worked hard to keep the smile on her face, tuck her hair, and say, "I haven't been here for so long, and I'm starving."

"Let's go get you that smothered enchilada then," Karla said, linking her arm with Mal's. They laughed again, and though Mal's heart pinched with every beat it took, she managed to make it through lunch as if she was the happiest Walker in the world.

By the time she got to the apartment where she'd only lived for a couple of months, pure exhaustion filled her. She had been up for over twelve hours, most of them emotional and turbulent.

The apartment felt hollow to her, but the door locked behind her, and she saw that Skyler hadn't brought the furniture at all.

"You bought new stuff," she reminded herself. Everything looked like it had the day they left, if not for some footprints in the carpet from the movers. Her room sat to the left of the kitchen, but she went right, where Skyler's suite had been.

She'd always thought he had a ton of charm and charisma, and without him here, the apartment just felt like a box with different rooms in it. His bedroom sat undisturbed, though there were no family pictures on his bureau anymore. The bed stood there, made and ready for someone to sleep in it.

Part of Mal wanted to, because then she could smell her husband on the sheets. Tears pricked her eyes. Had she really done something so terrible that she couldn't make up for it?

She turned away from the bedroom she'd never entered and went to the one where she'd slept. It too felt like a foreign land, and Mal could only look around at the bed, desk, and dresser she'd used.

Sighing, she took her bag back into the living room and set about making tea. She'd stopped at the grocery store before coming to the apartment, and she ended up heating the water in the microwave, because there was no teapot in the apartment anymore.

With her paper cup of tea, she sank onto the couch

and sipped it, letting her mind move wherever it wanted to.

The thought that she should move back to Amarillo and go back to school entered her mind.

"I can't do that," she said aloud to the apartment. "I have an amazing job in Three Rivers."

And she realized that the thing tying her to Three Rivers was her job at the bakery—and not her husband.

She set the tea on the coffee table, curled into a ball on the couch, and cried.

27

At church on Sunday, Skyler sat by himself through the sermon. He didn't hear a word of it, as his mind had completely been taken over with the idea of calling Mal. She'd left Friday morning for work at two-thirty, same as she always did.

She hadn't come home after her shift, and while Skyler had known she wouldn't, it had still stolen his breath and stung his stomach. Sleeping in the huge ranch house alone for the past two nights had been torture.

He was lonelier than he'd ever been, even surrounded by family. In Amarillo, he'd been sure to surround himself with friends, but they hadn't been the same as family.

And now his family wasn't the same as Mal.

He had no idea what that meant, and he had no idea why he couldn't just apologize to her. Tell her she was the sweetest, smartest, most spiritual woman he'd ever met, and he was just sorry.

Then maybe everything could go back to normal.

His phone buzzed while the pastor was still going strong, and Skyler's hopes soared. Perhaps Mal would reach out to him. But the text was from Momma, and she said, *Dinner at our house tonight. Everyone is invited.*

He wasn't sure why she hadn't put the message on the family text string, where Skyler may or may not have seen it in time to go. But this message had come straight to him.

He didn't want to go, not without Mal. He suddenly understood how Micah had been feeling for all these months, though he'd started bringing Ophelia to family functions as they grew more and more serious.

"Be courageous this week," the pastor said. "I leave God's blessings with you. Go forth and live with His example in your countenance."

Skyler looked up at the pastor's words. *Be courageous.*

How? he wondered.

Go to Momma's. That was one courageous thing he could do. *Tell the whole truth. To everyone.*

That was another.

Fear gripped his insides with an icy fist, but Skyler couldn't shake the thoughts no matter how hard he tried. No matter how long he rode that afternoon. No matter how long he hesitated to leave to get to Momma's on time.

By the time he joined his truck to the fray of them

already outside his mother's house, he knew he was the last one to arrive. Dread filled him with every step, and someone opened the door before he'd even reached the bottom step. Noise spilled out of the house, and Skyler met his mother's eye as he climbed the steps and moved into her embrace.

"Oh, my son," she said as she held him tightly. "What is going on with you?" She stepped back and held him at arm's length, studying him.

Skyler just let her look, and he didn't try to mask the misery streaming through him. "I dunno, Momma."

"Come in," she said. "Let's you and I have a talk with Daddy."

"I don't want to do that, Momma." Skyler went inside with her anyway, and it seemed like the whole family had been primed for his arrival. They all seemed to pause and look his direction, and Skyler sure didn't like that.

Momma closed the door behind him and linked her arm through his. They faced the crowd together, and Daddy poked his head out of the kitchen to see what the silence was all about. "Oh, Sky's home."

Home.

Skyler's emotions soared, and he looked around at these people who made anywhere they were the meaning of home. He did love them, and that they always accepted him, no matter what he'd done.

He still didn't want to tell them the real reason he'd married Mal.

Be courageous.

Skyler cleared his throat. "Mal went back to Amarillo."

"Permanently?" Marcy asked, swaying with her newborn son in her arms.

"I don't honestly know," Skyler said, dropping his eyes to the floor. He took in their sandals and cowboy boots, shame moving through him powerfully. "She said she'd be back tomorrow, but I have my doubts."

"She has a job at the bakery," someone said.

"Yeah," Skyler said. He looked up again, the words pushing against his throat. "I offered to marry her when she got notice that she was going to be deported for not renewing her green card appropriately." He swallowed. "We'd been friends for a couple of years, and I've always liked her."

No one said anything, and Skyler almost wished he'd kept the secret. But he shrugged, thinking of how great of a session he'd have with Dr. Haskell that week. "Somewhere along the way, I fell in love with her."

People moved in front of him, and he watched them all reach for each other. Tripp linked his hand with Ivory and looked at her, something meaningful passing between them.

"She fell in love with me," Skyler said, wiping his nose. "But now...I don't know."

"Well, what happened?" Wyatt asked.

Skyler didn't see how he could explain without giving

details about everything—including the situation in Dallas. He looked at his father, who nodded one time.

"Well, it's a long story," Skyler said. "But I guess I can tell it over dinner."

"Yes, let's eat," Momma said. "Everyone will feel better then."

"You guys all know Marcy and I got married so she could inherit Payne's, right?" Wyatt took a few steps and came to stand right beside Skyler. "Right? It was fake in the beginning too."

"I married Ivory so her ex-husband wouldn't get custody of Oliver," Tripp said. He edged past people and nodded to Skyler.

"Everyone knows I married Callie to save the Shining Star," Liam said.

"And that I married Evelyn to save her matchmaking business," Rhett said.

Momma started crying, and Daddy looked like someone had just told him he'd have to sell all of his miniature horses and go back to Grand Cayman.

"Fine," Jeremiah said, and he sounded pretty upset. "I asked Whitney to marry me to prove to the rest of y'all that I wasn't broken." He gazed at his wife, who simply looked back at him. "And somehow, she said yes."

Skyler couldn't believe what was happening. He'd known some of his brothers' marriages had come out of nowhere, but he hadn't dreamed they'd all started out fake.

"For the record," Micah said. "I have not married anyone, real or fake."

Skyler blinked at his youngest brother and started laughing. That got everyone chuckling, and then laughing, and the tension in the farmhouse broke. He stepped away from Tripp and Wyatt and over to Micah, who had brought Ophelia to dinner.

"Bet you're wondering what you got into, aren't you?" he asked.

Ophelia too looked like she'd just been struck with a two-by-four. "A little, yeah." She looked around at everyone and how they went right back to their conversations or tending to their kids. "You guys seem so normal. Happy. And they obviously all love each other."

"Yeah," Micah said, also surveying the lot of Walkers crowded into the space. "They do. We do. We're not perfect, but we do love each other."

His words struck something inside Skyler, and he couldn't believe he hadn't thought of them before.

No, he wasn't perfect, he knew that.

But Mal wasn't either, and it wasn't fair of him to expect her to be. So she'd made a mistake in telling her sister about their fake marriage. But she hadn't done it to hurt him. She'd trusted him, and he hadn't done the same for her.

Guilt filled him even as Daddy said, "All right, boys, settle down. It's time to say grace."

Skyler swiped his cowboy hat from his head as all of his brothers did too.

"Dear Lord," Daddy started. "I honestly don't even know what to say. Bless these boys that they'll be the kind of men Momma and I raised them to be. Thank You for the food. Amen."

A beat of silence passed, and then, as if the brothers had practiced it, they all burst out laughing again.

"Daddy, come on," someone said.

"We're good men," another added.

"That's debatable," Daddy said. "Fake marriages, boys? Really?"

"Oh, Gideon, it's kind of sweet." Momma set a huge basket of freshly baked rolls on the table. "Now, let's all try to listen as Skyler tells us what happened with Mal and how he plans to get her back."

"Save me," he muttered to Micah, but his brother just gestured for him to go first into the dining room.

———

Twenty-four hours later, Skyler sat at the kitchen table in his new house, dinner on the table.

Mal had not come home.

No, he had not spoken to her. He hadn't told her he'd gotten her favorite food from her favorite restaurant in town—a huge plate of pork nachos from the diner.

But she'd said she'd be home on Monday night, and she wasn't.

"And she didn't say she'd be home," Skyler said, finally getting up and taking the plate of now-soggy chips with him. He dumped them into the garbage can, at an utter loss as to what to do now.

Call her?

Give her the space she needed?

Send a text of apology?

He honestly felt like getting in his truck and driving until he couldn't keep his eyes open for another minute. Then he'd find a hotel and sleep until he had to face reality again. He wanted to run. He wanted to hide.

He still felt drained from last night's dinner at his parents' place, especially after revealing everything that had happened in Dallas. But no one had judged him. No one had said he should've been able to see through Shayla's schemes. No one suggested that he should've done anything differently than he'd done.

Only Daddy had said, "We'll always love you boys. No matter what, okay? You don't need to be afraid that you'll lose us, ever."

Momma had reached over and threaded her fingers through Daddy's, and just nodded.

Skyler had felt more connected to his parents and brothers than ever before.

But nothing mattered if he didn't have Mal.

He knew the way to Amarillo. Maybe she'd just

needed a few days away, but it hurt that she needed that time away *from him*.

Swiping his keys from the drawer, he left the house in a new kind of hurry. But he wasn't going to drive in any direction until he ran out of gas or couldn't stay awake.

No, he was going to get his wife back.

28

Tripp watched Ivory pace with her phone pressed to her ear. She couldn't seem to stand still and have a conversation on the phone, something he actually adored about her.

But not when the person on the other end of that phone call was her mother.

Ivory had a very strained relationship with her parents. She hadn't told them about their marriage, and the only reason they were talking today was because Ivory had decided she had to do something about the distance between them.

She'd started small, with Christmas cards and birthday cards for her parents. Her mother had called when she'd realized Tripp was now in the picture with Ivory and Oliver.

So when Ivory had gotten pregnant, she'd called her mother and told her. Tripp had still not met the woman, nor her husband, and he and Ivory had been married for over three years now. She'd almost *died* last year giving birth to Isaac, and Tripp focused on the little boy on the floor in front of him.

An instant smile came to his face, because the thirteen-month-old was just so cute. He'd been babbling for months now, and he'd just started walking a couple of weeks ago.

Ivory had refused to let Tripp call her parents and tell them about the trouble she'd had in the hospital. Because of it, she couldn't have more kids, and that made Isaac even more special to Tripp.

He reached down and picked up his son, snuggling him on his lap. The baby grinned up at him, and Tripp pressed a kiss to Isaac's temple as Ivory said, "Okay, Mom, that's fine."

He looked at her, and their eyes met. She wasn't crying...yet. But she definitely wore a look of panic and resignation, and he wondered what she'd just agreed to. Thankfully, the call ended a few minutes later, and Tripp put Isaac back on the floor with his toys and went into the kitchen.

Ivory sighed as she sat at the bar, and Tripp started massaging her shoulders. "What is it?"

"They want us to come for Thanksgiving," she said. "I

couldn't get out of it. They want to see Isaac. They want to meet you."

"Hey, it's okay," he said. "This is what you wanted, right? Reconciliation? You want Isaac to have two sets of grandparents." They'd talked about this for hours. Tripp wanted whatever made Ivory the happiest. And she'd come out of the hospital last year, ready to make changes. She didn't want to leave the world and have bad feelings between her and anyone.

She was the strongest woman he'd ever met, and she'd found a way to let go of her hurt and anger for Daniel, her first husband. Tripp had marveled in the change in her since then, and she carried a new light in her face now that he'd never seen before.

"Yeah, I know." She rolled her neck, and Tripp placed a kiss on her shoulder.

"So we'll go to Tennessee for Thanksgiving. We can handle it."

"They haven't seen Oliver since he was a baby," she whispered. "He's almost twelve, Tripp."

"He sure is." And that eleven-year-old was one of Tripp's absolute favorite people. Today, he was at a birthday party for a friend, and school started—Oliver's last year in elementary school—next week. "It's going to be okay," he said.

Ivory turned toward him, pure anxiety on her face. Tears dripped down her face, and she swiped at them.

"What if it's not? What if it's just as terrible as it always has been?"

"Then we leave," he said, taking her into his arms. She cried against his chest, and Tripp wished with the power of ten suns that he could remove this pain from her life. "We have each other, baby. And Oliver and Isaac, and all of my brothers. My parents. We have the love and support we need."

Ivory nodded against his body, and he released her.

"I know you want to do this, Ivory, and I'm fine with it. But it doesn't seem to be making you happy."

She sniffed and nodded, reaching for a paper towel. "I'm just nervous. Once we go, and we see how it'll be, then I don't know. Then I'll know if it's something I should keep trying to do, or something I have to let go of."

Tripp let a few seconds go by. "You can't control them."

"No, I know."

Their eyes met, and Tripp smiled softly at her. "You're amazing," he whispered. "I love you."

Her eyes watered again, and her smile looked a little crooked and a little pained. "I love you too, Tripp." She leaned toward him, and he leaned toward her until their foreheads rested together.

His phone chimed, and he straightened. "That's probably Daddy."

"Yeah?"

"Yeah, he's on his way back from getting those new horses." Tripp shook his head. "He says eleven more won't even make a difference, and I told him I'd be there to help with unloading and all of that. I guess he got a bunch of equipment too."

He picked up his phone, and sure enough, the text was from Daddy. "He's about an hour out." He pocketed his phone and faced his wife. "So let me heat up some of that soup you like, and then I'll head over there. Okay?"

She gave him a tired smile. "Okay."

"You feeling okay?" He went into the kitchen and opened the fridge while Ivory walked into the living room. Though her brush with death was over a year old, she was still tired sometimes, and Tripp thought she hadn't ever quite been the same.

"Yeah," she said. "Just talking to my mom drains me." She curled into the corner of the couch and smiled at Isaac. She cooed and talked to him while Tripp heated her soup, and she looked up at him with all the heat of his wife when he handed her the soup.

"You're okay to get Ollie from his party?" Tripp asked.

"Yep, two o'clock," she said.

"I'll be back later," Tripp said. "I'm not sure when, since you know how Daddy is. He said he got a few things, and it could be truckloads." Tripp chuckled, his love for his father ironclad.

"Good luck," Ivory said, and Tripp left. He loved their house on the east side of Three Rivers, even if it was isolated from the rest of the family. He thought Ivory needed that, and most of the time, he did too.

His bond with Liam was as strong as ever, and since he only worked part-time, he took Oliver to the ranch several times a week. He never felt left out, and he thought of Skyler's story from Sunday night's dinner.

He'd said he felt like the black sheep in the family, and Tripp couldn't comprehend that. He'd always belonged to the family, and they belonged to him, Skyler included.

His phone rang again, and Daddy's name came up on the screen in Tripp's truck, as his phone had connected to the sound system via Bluetooth. He sighed as he reached out and tapped the green phone icon on the screen. "Hey, Daddy."

Beeping came through the line, and Tripp's pulse accelerated.

"Daddy?"

"Sir," someone said. A woman. "Are you okay? Our system has indicated that your airbag has deployed."

Horror gripped Tripp's heart and lungs. His fingers tightened on the steering wheel. "Daddy?"

A groan came through the line, and Tripp pressed the accelerator all the way to the floor. "Where are you?"

"Sir, I'm dispatching emergency vehicles to your location," the woman said in a tinny voice that crackled over the line.

Tripp realized that he was hearing the On-Star operator talk to his father. His father, who couldn't respond.

His father, who must have somehow dialed Tripp during the accident.

Airbag deployed.

Groaning.

"What's his location?" he yelled into the screen, actually leaning toward it like that would help. "This is his son, and he called me. Where is he?"

The woman didn't answer, and Tripp swung wildly onto the highway that led south out of town. He wanted to stay on the line with Daddy to make sure he knew he wasn't alone. But he needed to call Momma and Rhett. Liam, and Jeremiah, and Skyler, and Wyatt, and Micah. All of them. Everyone.

Everyone needed to start praying. Now.

So with difficulty and indecision still raging through him, he said, "Daddy, hang on, okay? I'm on my way to you. I'm going to hang up now and call everyone. Okay, Daddy?" He waited, but his father didn't answer at all. Not even a groan. The steady beeping coming through the line sounded like a warning from the car to buckle a seatbelt, and Tripp would be haunted by that sound for the rest of his life.

"Hang on, Daddy," he said again, pulling into the opposite lane to pass a slower-moving truck. "I love you. Hang on."

Then he hung up, immediately barking at the truck to "Call Rhett." His oldest brother would know what to do.

He just had to know what to do. Maybe he could even make Tripp's truck go faster.

"Calling Rhett," the cool female voice said, and Tripp pounded one hand against the steering wheel while he waited for the call to connect. "Please, God," he said, fighting with everything he had against the rising panic. "Don't take him yet. *Please* don't take him yet."

29

S kyler's phone rang when he was only halfway to Amarillo. Rhett's name came up on the display, and the ring nearly deafened him as it came through the speakers and his device.

He hurried to tap on the button on the display and said, "Hey, Rhett."

"Where are you right now?" Rhett sounded winded, like he was running.

Skyler's first thought landed on Whitney. She was due any day now, and maybe she'd gone into labor again. He knew she did not want to have another baby at home, and he couldn't believe he'd forgotten about that and left town.

"Uh, I'm on my way to talk to Mal in Amarillo."

"Daddy's been in an accident," Rhett said. "Tripp was going to help him with some horse stuff, and he's just arrived at the scene. He's texting and calling, and oh, he's calling now. I have to go."

"Rhett—" Skyler tried, but his brother was gone.

Skyler eased up on the gas pedal, his mind racing. He pulled over to the side of the road, Rhett's words settling in his ears. When he came to a complete stop, he closed his eyes and bowed his head. "Dear Lord," he said. "I don't know what's going on, but bless Rhett and Tripp with a calm heart." He took a breath, his chest tightening. "Bless my dad, whatever's happened, that he'll be all right."

He didn't know what to add to the prayer, and his phone blared again.

"Rhett," he said once he'd answered. "What's happening?"

"Tripp is there with Daddy. He's riding in the ambulance with him back to Three Rivers. I'm calling everyone to ask them to pray, and to meet us at the hospital."

Skyler checked his mirrors and the oncoming traffic. None. "I'm on my way. What happened?"

"Near as Tripp can tell, someone crossed the middle line and hit Daddy's truck." Rhett's voice broke, and that nearly undid all of Skyler's carefully laced emotions. Neither of them said anything, and every muscle in Skyler's face felt so tight, so tight.

"He took some pictures," Rhett said. "It's not good. Daddy is not awake."

"Okay," Skyler said, because what else was there? "What can I do to help?"

"Tripp left his truck on the side of the road so he could ride with Daddy," Rhett said. "Someone will have to go get it later."

"Okay," Skyler said. "I'll call Mal, and maybe we can do that." But if the family was gathering at the hospital, that was where Skyler wanted to be.

"I know," Rhett said, but it wasn't to Skyler. "Evvy, get him. We have to go. Sky, I'll see you at the hospital."

"Okay, bye," Skyler said. "Rhett—" But his brother was gone. "I love you," Skyler said anyway. He gripped the wheel, wishing he wasn't at least thirty minutes away. He'd be last to the hospital. Last again.

"It's not a race," he told himself. And it wouldn't do any good if he got in an accident himself. "Please bless those working with my father." He continued to pray the whole way back to Three Rivers. When he passed Marcy's airplane hangar on the west side of town, he tapped to call Mal.

Her phone rang and rang, and Skyler hated with everything inside him that she didn't pick up. Her voice filled the cab when she said, "This is Mal Walker. Leave me a message, and I'll get back to you."

Mal Walker.

Skyler pulled to a stop sign while he waited for the beep. "Mal," he said, making the turn. "It's Skyler. My father's been in a bad accident. I was on my way to see you in Amarillo when I found out, and I turned back. Will you...?" He swallowed, trying to mask the emotions. But he didn't want to. He didn't want to cage his feelings, and he didn't want to hide them from his wife.

"I need you," he said, his voice full of agony. "Will you please come to the hospital in Three Rivers? We all need you."

With that, he hung up and continued along his way. Only minutes later, he pulled into the parking lot of the emergency room and got out of the truck. A strange sense of calmness came over him as he strode in, wondering where to go.

He shouldn't have wondered. The Walkers weren't a small—or quiet—group, and Wyatt said, "Sky," in a booming voice the moment he walked in. He detoured to his left, grabbing onto Wyatt like he was the only thing keeping him on the ground in that moment.

Because he was.

Everyone was crying. Positively everyone, and Skyler panicked. "I'm too late, aren't I?" He scanned the crowd, trying to find his mother. "Where's Momma?"

But Skyler couldn't get to his mother, who was flanked by Jeremiah and Rhett. They each held one of her hands, and Skyler let his own tears flow down his face.

"You're not too late," Wyatt said. "They brought him in about twenty minutes ago. Tripp is still back there with him. The nurse has come out once to say that he's alive, and they're working on him."

"Doing what?" Skyler asked.

"We don't know." Wyatt turned back to the crowd,

and Skyler went through it, hugging every person, one by one. Momma stood to receive his hug, and Skyler pressed his eyes closed as he clung to her.

"He'll be okay," Skyler said. "He will, Momma."

"Keep praying," she whispered, and she stepped back and wiped her eyes with a tissue.

"Tripp's coming," Liam said, and a whole new uproar started. Skyler edged to the side, well aware of how off-kilter he felt. He needed Mal there. He wanted to hold her hand and receive her steady assurance, the way Evelyn held Rhett's, and Marcy clung to Wyatt.

He knew all the in-laws loved his parents as much as the sons did, and Mal should be there. *She'll come*, he told himself, even pulling out his phone to check it real quick though Tripp had just arrived in their corner of the waiting room.

Really, they took up at least half of it, but no one seemed to care.

"He broke his back," Tripp said, wiping his face. "He never woke up on the drive back. They sedated him into a medically-induced coma, and they're taking him into emergency surgery." His whole face crumpled, and Momma stepped over to him to comfort him.

Fear like Skyler had never known entered his system. A man could drown in fear like this. It could take over his whole life, block out all that was good, and only leave room for worry and despair.

Skyler had been in such a place before, but this was

blacker. Bleaker. He could not imagine a world where his father didn't exist to tell him that he hadn't messed up too badly. That he loved him, no matter what.

And with that thought came a seedling of faith. A small ray of sunshine that chased away the darkness swirling through his entire soul. Fear was the opposite of faith, and Skyler didn't want to live in the darkness.

He wanted to live in the light. He wanted to believe that God would hear his prayers and answer them. He trusted that God was there, and he knew that whatever happened, God was in charge of it all.

That same calmness came over him again, and when Micah came to stand next to him, Skyler put his arm around his brother's shoulders. They didn't say anything, because they didn't need to.

"They said it'll be hours," Tripp said, reaching for his wife's hand. He pressed a kiss to her forehead. "Some of us should go home."

"I'm staying," Momma said, making her way back to her seat. No one else moved. Skyler didn't want to leave; he had nowhere to go.

So he sat down with a sigh, feeling weary all the way to the bone. His wife hadn't come home. She hadn't called. His father was in emergency surgery for a broken back. Life sure could kick him around sometimes.

"Sky," Micah said sometime later.

"Hmm?" He looked up from his phone, where he'd been playing a game.

Micah nodded toward the doors, and Skyler followed his gaze. Mal stood there, clutching her purse.

Skyler shot to his feet. Their eyes met across the space. Skyler didn't care who was watching, and he didn't care what they had to work out.

She'd come.

"Mal," he breathed, already moving toward her. He jogged several steps, sweeping her into his arms. "You're here." He breathed in the soft, floral scent of her neck, grateful beyond description.

"How is he?" she asked as he set her on her feet.

"He's in surgery," Skyler said. "He was in a bad accident with the horse trailer attached to his truck. The whole thing jack-knifed." After they'd all settled down, Tripp had shown them pictures, and there had only been six inches between the back of Daddy's seat in the truck and the steering wheel. The front half of it had completely collapsed, and their father was very lucky to even be alive. "He broke his back."

"Sky, I'm so sorry." Mal's tears made his start anew, and he hugged her again as they cried.

"You came," he said. "Thank you for coming. I'm so sorry for everything."

"You don't have anything to be sorry for," she whispered.

Skyler became aware of others getting near, and they probably wanted to welcome Mal to their family vigil.

"I do," he said quickly. "But we can talk later. I love

you. I love you, and I need you, and I don't want you to leave without me again."

That only made Mal cry harder, hold to him tighter. Skyler didn't mind, and everything between him and Mal washed away with their tears. When he released her, Marcy was there, and she hugged Mal. Then Wyatt.

When all was said and done, Mal sat next to Skyler in the row, with Warren in her arms. "I love this baby," she said softly.

"Yeah?" Skyler asked. "You think you want to have one of your own?"

Mal looked at him, and a dozen more apologies were said. "I'm sorry, Skyler," she said. "For telling my sister. I've really been praying that it will all work out for us."

"Me too." He smiled at her and looked at the week-old infant in her arms. "He sure is cute."

Mal looked at Warren again, who bore that strong Walker chin and a ton of fluffy, blond hair. "Yeah, he is. And yeah, I'd like babies of my own." She beamed up at Skyler, who could only lean his head back and smile.

30

Gideon Walker existed somewhere that was completely white. Every sound seemed to echo endlessly, all of them piling on top of one another.

Tripp had been with him for a while. *Stay with me, Daddy,* he'd said, and Gideon seemed to be able to recall everything the boy had said to him. Oh, how he loved that Tripp and Liam had followed his footsteps into the tech industry. They were both so talented with the coding and animation work they did, and Gideon longed to be able to tell them one more time how proud he was of them.

Push me higher, Daddy.

That was something Tripp had always said. The boy had never been afraid to take risks, and Gideon had drawn strength from his children when they were still very young. His own failures hadn't stopped him from trying again, but really, it was his sons that had inspired him. He couldn't let them down. He couldn't allow Penny to put all her trust in him only to have him fail.

So he'd picked himself up and tried again. He'd done his best to make a good life.

Everyone's here, Daddy. You'll want to see them all again. Hang on, okay?

Hang on.

Hang on.

Hang on.

Gideon couldn't see anything to hang on to, but he decided to do what Tripp had begged him to do.

He heard other voices, male and female, that he didn't recognize. They spoke about vertebrae, and blood pressure, and clinking metal seemed to accompany everything. He floated somewhere, unable to feel any pain.

"Gideon."

Joy filled him at the sound of his wife's voice. She was here, and everything would be okay now that she was. "I love you, you old cowboy."

I love you too, he thought, but he did not hear himself say it.

"The whole family's here, and you should see them, Gideon. They're everything we've hoped they'd be."

He remembered how shocked he'd been to learn that six of his sons had entered into their marriages under false pretenses. But they'd all obviously worked through their issues, their hang-ups, their problems.

Skyler? he asked, because he knew Skyler and Mal

had been going through a difficult time. He'd begged the Lord to build a bridge between them and guide their feet to the path they needed to be on to meet on that bridge.

But Penny didn't tell him about Skyler. She talked about Warren, and how the baby needed to be able to grow up in his grandfather's shadow, that Marcy had no grandfather for the baby on her side of the family, and that Gideon's work on this Earth wasn't done yet.

"Daddy, I love you." Rhett.

"Gideon, you are precious to me." Evelyn.

One by one, every person in his family told him how much they loved him.

"I love you, Dad." Jeremiah.

"You mean a great deal to me." Whitney. "I love you."

"You've been my hero my whole life." Liam.

"Please hang on, Daddy. We love you." Tripp.

"Thank you for everything, Daddy." Wyatt. "I love you."

Gideon smiled, because he could see his son waving that hat. Oh, how he'd loved watching Wyatt in the rodeo. He'd traveled with him when he could, and every time that hat came off his son's head, Gideon knew it was for him and Penny.

"My dear Gideon, I love you." Marcy.

"Daddy." Skyler, who sounded so broken but who was so strong. "I love you forever. You're the glue for us."

"Gideon, you've been so kind to me. I love you." Mal.

Micah did not speak, and Gideon really wished he

could see. He needed all of his sons with him. Restlessness filled his soul, and something akin to darkness flashed in his world.

"Daddy," Micah finally said. "You just can't go."

Gideon wasn't going anywhere. He was trapped in this place, but he wasn't going anywhere. His sons, their wives, their children, and his dear wife spoke around him, their voices combining into a quiet din that soothed him to the very core.

I love you all, he tried to say. *I love you all so much.*

————

"So that's it," Micah said. Gideon had no way of telling time in the white existence where he was. "She said she thought I was still hung up on Simone, which, if I'm being honest, I am." Micah sighed, and Gideon wished he could take his son in a hug and tell him everything would be okay.

He should go out with Simone, because anyone with even one good eye could see how much they liked each other. Gideon had liked Ophelia too, of course, but he wasn't all that surprised she'd broken up with Micah.

Still, breaking up was never easy, and Micah had seemed a bit more tormented than usual the past couple of months.

It'll be okay, he tried to tell his son.

"Anyway, Liam's here, and he wants to bring the kids in to see you. Love you, Daddy."

———

"We got the horses to the Shining Star, Daddy," Liam said. "I think even Momma was surprised by how many you had." His son chuckled, and Daddy wished he could hug him too.

Thank you, Liam.

"I mean, Dad, did you know you have fifty-two miniature horses? Plus the eleven new ones, none of which were harmed in the accident, by the way."

Accident.

The word rang through Gideon's head, and he tried to grasp onto wisps of movement. A horn. Light. A crash.

Pain.

Gideon tried to move, but he couldn't.

"You should see Callie and Denise out there with the ponies," Liam said, chuckling. "Denise goes everywhere with her mama, and they've been collecting the honey this week too. I'm still plugging away on the sixth film, and I think another week will do it."

Liam sounded tired, and Gideon wished he could take Liam to the side and tell him not to work so much that he missed the important things in life. Gideon had missed so much of the boys' lives growing up, and that was one of his biggest regrets.

Liam had two beautiful girls, and he should be out there getting the honey, and helping Denise learn to ride a horse, and plant the flowers.

"Here they are now," Liam said. "Denise, say hi to Gramps."

"Heya, Gramps," the little girl said, and Gideon's spirits soared. "Is he sleepin', Daddy?"

"Yes, right now," Liam said.

A baby babbled, and Callie said, "That was Ginger, Gideon. She wants you to take her out to the goats, so when you wake up, you're going to have to do that."

I will, he promised her, also promising himself. He'd never known as much joy as he had when he'd become a grandfather. *Will you ask Evelyn and Rhett to bring Conrad? And Tripp needs to bring his boys by too.*

Liam spoke with Callie, and Gideon pieced together that Callie was leaving with the children. Then his son's strong, steady voice started reading, "Old Billy Dunbar was down flat on his face in a dry wash swearing into his beard...."

Ah, Louis L'amour. Gideon had read all of the man's books, and extreme gratitude that Liam had brought one to share filled his soul. With his son reading, Gideon drifted again....

———

"Daddy," Jeremiah said, and Gideon immediately came back to his white place. "I brought your new grand-daughter to meet you."

Oh, how wonderful.

"She was born yesterday," Jeremiah continued. "And we named her Clara Jean. Jean was Whitney's great-grandmother. She has a ton of hair, Daddy, and you'd just love her." The love Jeremiah had for his daughter came through loud and clear, and Gideon so wanted to hold that new grandbaby. He wanted to hug Whitney for her part in carrying the baby for nine long months, as he'd seen his wife really suffer there near the end of all six of her preg-nancies.

Jeremiah told him about the ranch, the new baby, what JJ was up to now that he was fifteen months old. "And I'm tired, Daddy," Jeremiah said. "I don't know how you had seven kids. I'm drowning with just the two."

They're close together, Gideon told him. *You're doing great. You'll be fine. You're a good man, and a great father, Jeremiah.*

"I don't know what I'm doing most of the time," Jere-miah said, as if arguing with him.

No one does.

"I keep thinkin' about you, and what you'd do in any given situation. When the hay isn't getting mowed fast enough. When the blade on the swather goes out at exactly the wrong time. I'm stressed about the ranch almost all the time, and sometimes I bring that home to

Whit, who's been home with JJ—by herself—all day." He sighed, and Gideon wished he could take his son into his arms and tell him he was merely human.

But Jeremiah had always bordered on superhuman, and he had high expectations for himself.

You're doing great, he told him again.

"We're just gonna sit here with you for a while, Daddy. Is that okay?"

Totally fine.

Gideon listened to the baby make a grunting noise, and a few moments later, the even breathing of his son told him that Jeremiah had fallen asleep. Peace moved through him, because if he could give Jeremiah a few minutes of rest, he wanted to do just that.

———

"Conrad's giving you a hug, Daddy." Rhett's voice brought joy to Gideon's soul. Oh, how he'd loved becoming a father, and Rhett had been such a good first baby boy. He'd always helped his mother, led the other boys, and set the kind of example Gideon had hoped he would.

"Hey, Gideon." Evelyn was the perfect person for Rhett, and Gideon sure had enjoyed getting to know her. "You look good today. Doesn't he look good, Rhett?" The way she drawled Rhett's name reminded Gideon so much of how Momma said his name.

"You sure do," Rhett said. "More color in your face." Something scraped, and then Rhett added, "We came to tell you something big, Daddy. You're the first one to find out."

"And it's a secret still," Evelyn said. "So you can't be tellin' the nurses in the middle of the night or anything." She laughed, and Gideon hadn't heard someone laugh in so long. All of his sons had come. They'd brought their kids and wives, and Jeremiah had even brought Winston and Willow, his dogs.

But they didn't normally laugh. They talked to him. They read to him. They talked to each other. They didn't laugh.

He really craved the sound of laughter, and he wanted to reach for Evelyn and thank her for treating him like he wasn't one step away from death.

"Daddy," Rhett said. "Evelyn's going to have another baby."

"Not just one baby," Evelyn said. "Three babies, Gideon."

Triplets! Gideon felt like he couldn't breathe. *How wonderful. You two must be so thrilled!*

"His monitor is increasing," Rhett said.

"Of course it is," Evelyn said. "He's excited about the babies." Her voice got louder as she drew nearer. "Remember, it's a secret. And I'm scared out of my mind. How am I supposed to take care of three babies?"

Momma will help, Gideon told her. *God wouldn't give them to you if He didn't think you could take care of them.*

"And how are we doing, Mister Walker?" This time, one of the nurses was talking to him. They did that from time to time, and he knew one woman was having some trouble with her son. "Yep, his heart rate went up. What have you guys been telling him?"

"Nothing," Rhett said. "Just visiting."

Nope, they're having three babies. Three babies! Gideon felt downright jovial, and the nurse said, "Oh, there he goes again. Well, let's get the doctor in here to see him."

"This is good, right?" Rhett asked. "I mean, he hasn't done this before."

The voices faded, and once again Gideon was left alone. *Three babies. Wow,* he thought as he drifted.

"I'M BACK, GIDEON."

Gideon smiled at the sound of his wife's voice. Liam had finished the Louis L'amour book, and Gideon had told him to send Momma with a new book.

She had, and she'd been reading to him for a couple of chapters now. She didn't stay all the time, but Gideon understood. They had seven sons, and six daughters-in-law, and eight grandchildren. Penny was a busy woman.

"Can you squeeze my hand, dear?" she asked.

Gideon so wanted to see his wife again. So he put everything he had into trying to squeeze her hand.

"Oh," she said. "He did it, Doctor. He squeezed my hand!" Penny started to cry, and Gideon tried to reassure her that he was okay.

All at once, he could see, and everything wasn't nearly as bright as the white space where he'd been floating.

Penny's beautiful face slowly came into focus in front of him, and Gideon became aware of a sharp, clean scent, and a monitor beeping to his left. "Penny?" he asked. His voice actually hurt coming out.

"Welcome back, Mister Walker," a man said, and Gideon looked at him, noticing the white doctor's coat.

"Praise the Lord." Penny sobbed into his chest, and Gideon had no idea what to do, but he thought he had a very long road ahead of him.

31

Mal woke with a groan as she realized a phone was ringing. "It's Thursday," she complained. She didn't work at the bakery on Thursdays or Sundays, the only two days she got to sleep past two a.m.

"It's my mother," Skyler said, and that got Mal all the way awake. Guilt crept through her for complaining as he asked, "Momma?"

Mal looked at Skyler, finding tense anticipation in his face. Suddenly, everything sagged. "Oh, thank heaven." He pulled the phone away from his mouth. "Daddy woke up this morning."

Emotions surged in Mal. "That's great." She got out of bed. "Let's get over there." Gideon had been in a coma for over a month now, and while he wouldn't be coming home any time soon, him waking up was a miracle.

Thank you, she prayed as she hurried into the bathroom to get some clothes out of the closet.

"I'm getting in the shower real quick," Skyler said.

"Okay, I'll go make coffee." Mal dressed quickly as the shower started. In the kitchen, her hands shook as she measured the coffee grounds. Fifteen minutes later, both of them with a cup of coffee, Skyler and Mal headed to the hospital.

"Is it weird I'm nervous to see him?" Skyler asked. "I mean, I have a picture of him in my mind, and he's not that man anymore."

"He's the same man," Mal said.

Skyler didn't argue, and Mal chalked that up to nerves. They'd been getting along splendidly since she'd returned from Amarillo. He'd been teaching her to ride a horse on her days off, and they often clip-clopped along in the mid-afternoon heat, talking.

He spent mornings on the ranch after his solitary run, because it was cooler. He and Jeremiah got along great, and Mal could usually find the two of them in Skyler's office at the front of the house in the hotter afternoon hours. They went over the budget, planned for breeding season, market day, and more ranch talk Mal didn't completely understand.

What she knew was that Seven Sons had drawn their market day on the same day as her and Skyler's one-year anniversary. He'd said there wasn't much he could do about it, but that they could go anywhere in the world the day after.

Mal honestly didn't care all that much about the anniversary. She knew a life wasn't built around special occasions, but constant living, breathing, talking, and praying with someone day after day.

"We're going to offer to have him and Momma come live with us, right?" Skyler glanced at her as he got the truck going down the highway.

"Yes," Mal said. "But Sky, he's not going to come home immediately."

"I know that," Skyler said, his voice a bit wounded. "But I don't want them going back to that farmhouse. Momma can't handle what it will take to care for him."

"I agree," Mal said. "Our place is huge, and we have a bedroom right across the hall."

"Jeremiah will offer too," he said.

"He has two children under sixteen months," Mal said. "Your mother will come to our house, Sky." She wanted to tell him not to worry about it, but she knew that annoyed him. Skyler worried about things sometimes, and that was okay. He was allowed to worry.

He reached across the console and took her hand. After kissing her knuckles, he said, "I love you, Mal."

"I love you too."

"I don't think we're going to get to celebrate our anniversary the way I want to. Not if my parents move in with us."

"It's fine," Mal said, thinking of where she'd been a year ago. "Remember when you found me in my apartment?"

He cast a look at her. "Yeah."

"This new life *is* the celebration," she said, her voice quiet. "That apartment was infested with cockroaches and rats. I couldn't afford to fix my car. I had nothing. Less than nothing." She put a brave smile on her face, because they didn't talk about their lives before they'd gotten married very often.

"Now you get up at two a.m."

She knew he was trying to make light of the situation, because he didn't like it when she called him her savior. But he had literally saved her, and she was so grateful for him. "That's by choice, though," she said. "I do love the bakery."

"I know you do." He smiled at her. "We've almost made it a year, sweetheart."

"And we've heard nothing from the immigration agent."

"Well...." He glanced at her again.

"Well?"

"Wyatt said he did his interview over a month ago."

"He did?"

"Yeah," Skyler said. "He said it went well."

"What does that mean?"

"I have no idea," Skyler said. "I've been trying not to worry about it. Whatever happens will happen, but I believe they're going to decide our marriage is one-hundred-percent real." He looked at her fully then. "Because it is."

Mal smiled at him, so glad she wasn't his wanna-be wife. She loved being a Walker, and a rush of affection for Skyler's parents filled her. She knew a lot of the unity in the family came from them, and she'd happily taken her shift at the hospital with Gideon. Everyone had, as Mal hadn't heard a word of complaint.

"Here we go," Skyler said, pulling into the hospital. They walked inside hand-in-hand, and went to the intensive care unit. Of course, nearly the whole family was there, and Mal wondered if they ever got tired of having family reunions in hallways.

"They're only letting back two people at a time," Rhett said. "You're next if you want to go."

"You've all gone?" Skyler asked.

Rhett shook his head. "Just me and Evvy. Wyatt's back there right now. Jeremiah's not here yet."

"We're fine to wait," Liam said. "Ginger is almost asleep, and then we can pass her off."

Mal looked at Ivory and Tripp. "You guys don't want to go back?"

Ivory had her son pressed to her chest while he cried. "We need a few minutes," she said, smiling. "Ollie's a little emotional."

So Skyler and Mal went back when Wyatt and Marcy came out several minutes later. Wyatt wore a huge smile along with his signature cowboy hat. "He looks good, you guys."

Light filled Mal's soul as she walked with Skyler, but his hand just got tighter and tighter in hers. Penny stood at the door, and she hugged them both.

"Momma," Skyler said. "When Daddy gets out of the hospital, we want the two of you to come stay with us."

"Oh, I'm—"

"I'm really good at nursing someone back to health," Skyler said. "And he'll need a lot of help."

Penny looked at Mal, who just nodded. Her own emotions had formed a lump in the back of her throat she couldn't swallow back.

"I don't know...." Penny said.

Mal stepped up to her and took both of her hands. "You won't be putting us out. We *want* to help you. Please." She leaned into Skyler as he slipped his arm around her waist, and they both smiled at his mother.

Hope filled Mal, and she knew the moment Penny would say yes. She blinked, and her gaze softened. "You two are so good for each other."

"I know," Skyler said, planting a kiss on Mal's cheek. "So what do you say, Momma?"

"All right," she said. "I suppose it's the right thing to do. Daddy's horses are out there already."

"That's right." Skyler kissed his mother on the cheek too as he moved past her, already saying, "Hey, Daddy," as he went inside.

"Are you sure we won't be any trouble?" Penny asked. It was so very like her to be worried about such a thing when her husband had been in a coma for almost five weeks.

"Not at all," Mal said. "And we have main floor living, Penny. You belong there." She went into Gideon's hospital room with Penny, and she couldn't push against the wave of emotion for the man who had become her family. She marveled that these people had accepted her so readily, and her gratitude swelled as she bent down and kissed Gideon on the cheek.

She'd realized that Skyler might think he didn't fit with his family, but the truth was, he hadn't fallen far from the tree. He'd do anything for his family, and Mal admired his sense of loyalty and the way he loved them through thick and thin. It was a special kind of love that she enjoyed from him too, and she smiled warmly at him while he started asking his dad what he wanted to eat first when he got out of the hospital.

"Mal's chimichangas, of course," Gideon said, and that caused everyone to laugh.

Once the nurse had shooed them out of the room, Mal took Skyler's hand again, and they walked back to the waiting room. Only Rhett remained, and Skyler said they weren't going to stay either.

They walked back to his truck, and he drove them back to their house. They both paused in the doorway of the bedroom across the hall from theirs, and Mal said, "I'll order a bed. A king-sized will fit, I think."

"It will," Skyler murmured. "Micah showed me the plans."

"Are you okay? You want them to come stay, right?" He'd been adamant about it. What had changed in the past hour?

"Yes," he said. "I want them to come stay here." He turned toward her. "And I want you, Miss Mallery."

"Oh, okay." She giggled as he took her into his arms and kissed her. His touch had always been welcome, and he walked her backward into their bedroom. "Now, let's go start this morning off on the right foot." He closed the door behind them, and Mal smiled at this handsome cowboy husband of hers.

"I love you," she said.

"And I love you." Skyler didn't let a day go by without telling her he loved her, and as he made love to her, Mal had never felt more cherished, more needed, and more loved in her life.

32

Micah sat in his truck, his nerves running through him like a runaway train. The community theater didn't have the nicest building in the world to meet in. In fact, according to his online research, the theater only used part of the charter school, which met in a building that used to be used to store apples.

Plenty of cars sat in the parking lot, and the school had invested in some serious street lamps, so Micah felt safe being there. It was when he'd have to go face Simone that made his heart pulse too hard.

"She's not going to like this," he muttered. But he found himself getting out of the truck anyway. Walking toward the door. Once inside, he took a deep breath and glanced around. The hallway smelled like rubber and sweat, like the wrestling room had when Micah had tried a brief stint on the school wrestling team.

He'd found that he'd rather work on his grandfather's farm than try to pin someone to the ground, and that was when Micah had truly become a cowboy. The year after that, he'd taken a woodworking workshop for one of his Boy Scout badges, and that had been when sawdust had started flowing in his blood.

"Are you here to audition?" a man asked, and Micah blinked his way out of the past.

"Yes, sir," he said.

The man smiled at him. "We're down in room one-seventeen. There will be a brief orientation meeting, and then we'll head into the auditorium."

"Okay," Micah said, his stomach quaking with every slap of his cowboy boot against the tiled floor. Dozens of people waited in room one-seventeen, and the man who had brought Micah with him seemed to disappear the moment he entered.

Micah paused on the threshold of the room, trying to take in everything—and everyone—at once. His first instinct told him to turn right on around and go right on home. Growing up, his parents had taught him to listen to those instincts and obey them. Then he wouldn't find himself somewhere he shouldn't be, with people he didn't want to be with.

But now, he fought against that flight instinct, remembering something his father had said to him just last night.

Just go in there and do it, son. What's the worst that could happen?

Micah had thought a lot about his question in the past few hours. He'd never prayed as hard as he had the past few months as he begged God for his father's well-being and recovery. Daddy had woken up a month ago, but he still wasn't strong enough to leave the hospital. He'd had another surgery on his back, and he was walking around the hospital with one crutch now. The family continued to use a rotation to go visit him, and Micah had given him a hug last night and promised to call after tonight's audition.

So he couldn't leave.

And the worst that could happen was currently happening, as Simone Foster had seen him and was currently making a beeline straight for him. And she did not look happy.

"You cut your hair," he said. Why he'd chosen that to comment on, he wasn't sure.

She paused a few feet from him, one hand going up to pat said hair. "Yeah, a few days ago."

"Did you color it?" he asked. "It looks darker."

She folded her arms and cocked her head, her now-chin length hair bobbing with the motion. "What are you doing here?"

He lifted the sheets of paper he'd printed off the Internet. "I'm auditioning for *West Side Story*."

"No," she said. "You're not."

Annoyance sang through Micah's bloodstream. "Are you the director?"

She didn't answer, which meant no.

"It's an open audition," he said. "Says so right online. Says anyone can come audition, for any part." He started to move past her, though he had no end goal in sight.

"Who are you auditioning for?"

"Officer Krupke," he said over his shoulder. He found a seat in the back, frustrated that how he thought Simone would react had come to fruition. His fantasies were always so different from reality.

"All right," a man said a few minutes later. "I'm David Gonzalez, and I'm going to be directing the show. Welcome." He beamed out at the crowd, and the energy in the room could've fed Micah for days. David proceeded to give instructions for how auditions would go that night, when call-backs would be, and the rehearsal schedule.

"Lana will pass those out now," he said. "Everyone with any date conflicts must fill out a card tonight. If it's not on this card, and you're cast, you can't miss." He waved a stiff index card in his hand. "I understand emergencies happen, but folks, a birthday party isn't an emergency."

A few people twittered, but Micah decided the man was serious. Someone had tried to use a birthday party to get out of rehearsal. He took one of the schedules and looked at it. He didn't travel much, and he currently only had two clients for his general contracting business. He couldn't fathom a reason why he wouldn't be able to make it to evening and weekend rehearsals, especially since there was nothing scheduled over the holidays.

He looked up again when David started calling out parts and handing out music and lines. Micah had no idea how auditions went, as this was his first. But when David called for the detective and the officer, Micah took both of those parts. He wasn't a bad singer, but he wasn't great either. Tripp and Liam were definitely better than him, and the most musically inclined in the family.

He scanned the music and didn't find anything that would give him too much trouble. Besides, the parts he wanted weren't even singing parts. He wasn't sure why he'd need to sing at all.

"Who are you auditioning for, Simone?" Simone asked as she sat next to him in the previously empty seat. Their eyes met, and some of her earlier vitriol had fled.

A smile touched his heart, but he did not let it infect his mouth. "Who are you auditioning for, Simone?" he asked, repeating her question the way she wanted him to.

"Maria, of course," she said. "I don't quite have the range for her, but if I audition for the lead, I might be cast somewhere close to that."

"I see." Micah focused on his music again, because looking at Simone for too long got him a little too hot. "Who do you really want to be?"

"Maria," she said.

Micah looked at her again. "No, really."

She blinked, but she couldn't hide very much from Micah. "Anita," she said. "Or Consuelo or Rosalia. I'd like to be any of them."

He nodded and lifted the music. "My parts don't even sing. Do you think I'll really have to sing tonight?"

"You should go for Tony," she said.

"I'm not a tenor," Micah said.

"Oh, well, then, Bernardo."

"Nah, I'm going to stick to the detective or the officer. They don't have to sing or dance."

"It's a *musical*." Simone smiled. "You thought you'd come audition for literally a singing, dancing show when you don't want to sing or dance?"

Micah simply looked at her. Surely she knew why he was really here. Didn't she? She reached up to tuck her hair, but the shorter locks just sprang right back out from behind her ear.

"Simone, I came to audition because—"

"All right, people," David called. "We're moving to the auditorium, and I want all the females first. Ladies, to the stage!"

Excitement rose into the air as everyone stood up and started surging toward the door.

"Gentlemen," David called above the chaos. "To the seats. You'll be up next."

Neither Simone nor Micah moved with the rest of the crowd. She watched them mostly leave, and then she looked at him again. "Why did you come to audition?"

He started to shake his head, and then he remembered the way she'd shown up on his doorstep, months ago. He'd never gone to get those cookies. She couldn't shake the thought of stopping to see him, and he hadn't been able to shake this idea of auditioning to be in the same play as her.

It wasn't rocket science.

"I couldn't shake the idea," he said evenly. He took a deep breath. "And Ophelia broke up with me."

Shock covered her face as she pulled in a breath. "She did? When?"

"Ages ago," he said. "I'm surprised you didn't know."

"I don't get to town much."

"Is it that surprising?" he teased, reaching out to touch her chin. "You look like a codfish."

She snapped her mouth closed. "It's a little shocking, yeah."

"Why's that?"

"Why would she break up with you? You guys were so cute together, and you'd been seeing her for a long time." She looked like she genuinely wanted to know.

Micah once again thought about just shrugging. Instead, he said, "She knew...well, my family is big and loud, and I think they freaked her out."

"Oh, well, that's just ridiculous." Simone gazed at Micah, and she couldn't have given a more perfect response. Before he'd even realized it, Micah leaned toward her, and he might've been hallucinating, but she leaned toward him too....

"Simone," David called from the doorway. "Are you two coming? I thought you wanted Maria."

"Yes," she said, flying to her feet. "We're coming." She

walked away from Micah, though, leaving him to get up himself and follow her out of the room.

"Do you know Simone?" David asked as Micah passed him.

"Yeah, sure," Micah said. "She's my neighbor."

"Did she tell you to come audition?"

"Kind of," Micah said with a smile. He went into the auditorium while Simone continued down the hall and made a left turn.

"All right, ladies and gentlemen," David said, his voice echoing throughout the huge auditorium. "We're going to start at the top and work our way down. If you're auditioning for Maria or Anita, line up on stage right, please."

Micah took a seat near the other men, his eyes hooked onto Simone. She looked like she'd been born to be on the stage, without a single tremor of fear or anxiety. When it was her turn to step into the spotlight and sing, she did so with a smile affixed to that beautiful face.

And when she opened her mouth...no wonder Micah hadn't been able to move past her. She sang with the voice of an angel, and she projected confidence from the stage to the very last row in the theater.

He sat there breathless as she walked off and another woman took her place. And Micah was so glad he hadn't been able to shake the idea of coming to audition for her play. Even if he got cast as the water boy, he'd do it just to be near her.

And he wasn't leaving here without asking her out—again.

His heart balked at that idea, but he sternly told himself that this time was going to be different.

It will, he reassured himself. He and Simone were going to make the fourth time the charm. Oh, yes, they were.

33

Skyler stepped out of his front door and looked up at the top of it. "It'll fit, Mal." He reached for the wreath they'd bought that morning. It was shaped like a horse's head, the pine boughs folded and contained in a wire frame. The horse wore a Texas flag around its neck, and Skyler had loved it upon first sight.

Convincing Mal that it was Christmasy enough had taken some serious argument on his part, and he thought he should've become a lawyer with how well he'd presented his case.

"I can't believe we're hanging up a horse-head wreath." She moved out to stand on the porch and watch him while he stuck the wreath hook to the door. "Can you imagine what our former friends in Amarillo would say?"

Skyler snorted as he pictured that. "I would've never." With the hook in place, he took the wreath from where she'd set it on the ground and positioned it so it hung straight. "How does it look?"

"Ridiculous." Her voice carried a playful tone though, and Skyler simply grinned.

"I like it." He stepped back and put his arm around her waist. "It's awesome, Mal. Exactly what a cowboy would have on his front door." There was a reason the department store had horse-head wreaths, right?

She leaned into his side, and Skyler kneaded her closer. "I suppose," she said.

"All right." He looked at the oak tree several yards away. "Since Tripp is gone, Liam's family is going to decorate the tree. Our lights are up, and the wreath really completes things."

"The tree is up inside," she said. "Wyatt said something about having two at the homestead?"

"Yeah." Skyler didn't want to set up another tree. If he could avoid that job, he would. "Here at Casa Sky-Walker, we're just doing one tree."

"Skywalker." Mal giggled.

He'd had to name his house something, because everyone called the house where Jeremiah lived "the homestead." But Skyler had a homestead now too. So he'd started dubbing it Casa Skywalker, and the name had stuck. He didn't know much about Star Wars, but his house was a lot newer than the homestead, with a lot more upgrades, kind of like the spaceships in the science fiction movies.

No robots, though he had paid someone to come hang his Christmas lights.

"Let's see if we can get the front fence," Skyler said, turning to go down the steps. No one else had arrived at Seven Sons yet, so Skyler and Mal should be able to get the job they wanted. "Daddy will see that first, and we can make sure it's perfect."

"And we really do this in one day?"

"I think so?" he said, but it was more of a question. "I don't know, Mal. I haven't been here for the holidays before." He went down the steps, Mal following him. "Rhett says they get the ranch decorated the day after Thanksgiving, and Daddy's coming home tomorrow. So it has to get done today."

Skyler would stay up all night if he had to. He wanted everything to be absolutely perfect when his father arrived at this ranch, where he would spend the next several months recovering.

As he walked next door, Skyler ran through the list of things he and Mal needed to have ready. Bedroom. Check. Food. Check. Medical consultation with the doctor. Check. Medication chart. Check.

Skyler felt like he had everything ready, except the Christmas decorations. He desperately wanted this holiday to be the best one the family had ever experienced. They'd almost lost their patriarch, and every time Skyler let himself think too long about it, his emotions overwhelmed him. As it was, Daddy had been in the hospital since July—five months—and he still had a very long road ahead of him.

But his father was a tough old cowboy, and if anyone could make a full recovery, it would be him.

"Morning," he called as he entered the homestead. The scent of sausage and maple syrup met his nose, and Skyler's mouth watered. He rarely ate breakfast, because he spent mornings out on the ranch. He wasn't sure how Jeremiah had the energy, as all this ranch work had taken a toll on Skyler's ability to stay awake all day long. He was getting better and better about not taking a siesta in the mid-afternoon.

It was hard for him not to slip down the hall and climb into bed with his wife, who often took a nap in the afternoon. She got up at two a.m. so she at least had an excuse. Skyler's was that ranching was a lot harder work than going to college or forcing Wyatt to take a walk with him and then take his pills.

"Mornin'." Jeremiah stood at the sink, washing something. Whitney worked in the kitchen too, flipping fried eggs. Both of their kids sat in highchairs already, and Mal went over to the table to sit with them.

"Can we do the front fence?" Skyler asked, picking up a plate.

"Sure," Jeremiah said. "I pulled all the boxes to the front of the shed. They're marked."

"Great." Skyler smiled as Whitney put two eggs on his plate. "Thanks, Whitney."

"Sure thing." She cracked more eggs into the pan, and soon enough, they all had plates with food. Jeremiah stacked his eggs, sausage patty, and cheese onto an English muffin, and Skyler shook his head. He ate all the same foods, but not everything had to be made into a sandwich.

"Eat your eggs, JJ," Whitney said, nudging a few chunks of scrambled egg closer to the boy. He was looking more and more like a toddler than a baby these days, and Skyler smiled at him.

"Here you go," Mal said, forking one of the eggs and waving it around. "Open up." She zoomed the eggs toward JJ, who opened his mouth. Mal slipped them right in, and they both laughed. Skyler watched her with awe, thinking she'd be a great mom.

"Here comes Liam," Jeremiah said. "I'll get the eggs going again." He got up and moved back into the kitchen.

"Morning," Liam called as he came through the back door.

"Uncle Skyler!" Denise ran toward him, and Skyler barely had time to toss down his fork before the four-year old was upon him.

"Heya," he said, scooping her onto his lap. "Whatcha got there?"

"Clover honey," she said. "Mama and I made it."

"You made it?"

"The bees made it," Denise said, looking up at him. She reached for his cowboy hat, the way she always did. Skyler let her take it off, and then he took it from her so she wouldn't drop it on his messy breakfast plate. "But Mama and I collected it, and we spun it around real fast." She made a whizzing noise with her tongue and twisted in his arms.

He chuckled. "Well, that's awesome. I love honey." He held up the pretty bottle of pinkish honey so Mal could see it.

"You should see him," she said. "He almost drinks it."

Skyler laughed and shook his head. "I do not."

"Come eat, Denise," Callie said, and the little girl squirmed off his lap.

Skyler got up and took his plate to the kitchen sink. "I'll help her." He took the plate from Callie.

"You sure?" she asked.

"Yeah, sure. Tell Uncle Sky what you want," he said to the little girl.

"Scrambled eggs."

"Uncle Jeremiah is making those. Do you want sausage?" He picked up one of the links with a pair of tongs.

"Yes," Denise said.

"Scrambled eggs," Jeremiah said, and Skyler stuck Denise's plate out to get a scoop. The activity in the kitchen continued as Rhett arrived, and then Wyatt. Skyler didn't see Micah, which was surprising as he lived right down the hall from the kitchen. Tripp had gone to Tennessee to visit Ivory's family, and Skyler suddenly realized what he'd missed the past few years by not being here to contribute to the holiday decorating of Seven Sons.

"All right," Jeremiah said half an hour later. "Sky and Mal are doing the front fence. Liam and Callie are on the oak. I'm hanging the lights outside." He looked around. "Who wants to do the trees in here?"

"I'll help with the lights," Wyatt said. "Those fake trees make me break out in a rash."

"The mighty Wyatt Walker gets a rash from a Christmas tree?" Rhett teased. That caused some laughter, and more jabs were tossed back and forth. Finally, Rhett said, "Evvy and I will do a tree in here. She can't do much, and this way, she'll have access to a couch if she needs to rest."

Skyler looked at Evelyn, and he was surprised she could even walk. She was huge, being pregnant with three babies. She wasn't due until April, which was just over four months away. But she looked ready to pop already.

"I'll help with the trees," Marcy said. "I can lay Warren down for a nap that way."

"Where's Micah?" Skyler asked.

Silence filled the homestead, and he felt like he'd missed something important.

"What's going on?" he asked. When no one would say anything, he reached for his phone. "I guess I'll call him." He couldn't believe Micah himself hadn't told him what was going on, nor that literally everyone else in the family knew. That keen sense of being on the outside looking in hit him again, and he swallowed hard.

"He's probably at Simone's," Callie finally said. "Don't bother them."

"Simone?" Wyatt asked, and Skyler's gaze flew to his. He didn't seem to know what was going on either.

"They're...talking," Evelyn said. "We only know because she's our sister."

"Married to Callie," Liam said. "That's how I knew."

"Micah lives here," Jeremiah said. "I caught him sneaking home late one night, and he admitted he'd been at Simone's. That's how we knew." He indicated himself and Whitney.

"Well," Wyatt said. "I guess Sky and I are the only ones who really respect his privacy."

Another beat of silence passed, and then Skyler and Wyatt both burst out laughing. He was surprised that Micah hadn't said anything to him. He'd been fairly distant since Ophelia Montgomery had broken up with him, and Skyler had thought he just needed some space.

"Sounds like we need another breakfast," he murmured to Wyatt as they went out the back door to get the Christmas decorations they needed.

"I'll send the text," Wyatt said, already tapping on his phone.

Skyler smiled, and he and Mal loaded up the back of his truck with all the boxes labeled FRONT FENCE, and they got busy hanging garland, looping Christmas balls over rungs, and stringing lights so Daddy would be welcomed to Seven Sons Ranch when he got released from the hospital tomorrow.

When they finished, Skyler sighed and stood down the road a bit. "It's awesome," he said.

"Skyler?" Mal asked.

He turned toward her as she came to his side. The day was bright, though not terribly warm. Winter in Texas was his favorite time of the year, that was for sure. Even the humidity was bearable today. "Hmm?"

"I love you, and I love your family."

Happiness moved through him, and he took in the two-homestead ranch, the waving fields, dormant for now, and the many Christmas decorations going up right in front of him. "Me too," he said. He took her into his arms and kissed her. "And I love you the most."

34

Momma inched along beside her husband, her hand out to his side as if she could catch him should he stumble. She couldn't, and they both knew it. A sense of drowning overcame her, but she pushed against the feeling. She'd raised seven boys, sometimes by herself as Gideon was off working. She could do this too.

And she wasn't alone. Her sons had rallied around her in a way she couldn't even imagine. They'd brought her food without her asking them to. They'd show up at the house just when she thought she couldn't be alone for another moment. They'd sat with Gideon when she needed some fresh air or a break. They'd taken care of her lawn, her house, the farm, Gideon's horses, all of it.

Her daughters-in-law had all been simply wonderful, and Momma had thought she'd never have enough room in her heart for more than her husband and sons. But she'd been wrong. They'd found wonderful women, and they were all raising families of their own.

Not all of them, she reminded herself. Poor Micah was still searching for that just-right woman for him. She amended her thinking, because her youngest son would not be happy she'd thought of him as "poor Micah."

He came over several times a week, and his visits both at the farm house and at the hospital had increased since his break-up with Ophelia. He'd told Momma once, "I'm fine, Momma. You don't need to worry so much about me."

"I know," she said. "But it's what mothers do."

"Okay," he said, and he hadn't been happy. "But I'm doing great. I've got my new business, and I'm busy on the ranch, and I'm okay."

She hadn't pushed the issue, though she was sure Micah would love to have a girlfriend and then a wife to bring to all the family functions.

"There he is." Skyler's voice filled the air, and Momma smiled at him. "How ya doin', Daddy?"

"Good," Gideon said. "Good." He wore a smile, and he definitely had more pep in his step than any other day. He was still using the single crutch on his right side, and the doctor had said to use it for several more weeks too.

Skyler enveloped his father in a hug, and Momma tried not to let her emotions rear up. She had a long day ahead of her, and she couldn't be crying before they even left the hospital. She didn't succeed in keeping all the tears back, and she swiped quickly at her face before anyone but Mal could see.

Mal squeezed her hand, and said, "Let me take that bag, ma'am." She took Gideon's bag from her and put it in the back of the van. "You get to ride back here with me." She wore such a pretty smile, and Momma smiled back at her.

"Thank you, dear." She got in the van easily while Skyler helped Daddy get in the front seat. Once everyone was in, Momma couldn't help having a chuckle at the two, broad-shouldered cowboys riding in the front seats of a minivan. But Gideon couldn't get in and out of a truck right now, and she'd bought this van last week for them to use until he healed fully.

"Here we go," Skyler said. "Who wants a churro? Mal made them herself this morning."

"I'll take one," Daddy said, and Momma watched him take two. She took one as well, and the crispy, crunchy outside was sweet and delicious.

"Mal," she said. "These are amazing."

"Thank you."

"Jeremiah is feeding everyone lunch at the homestead," Skyler said as he got the minivan moving. "And we've got anything you could want at our place." Skyler filled the van with conversation on the way out to the ranch, telling everything about their dog, Rosie, and the decorations, and where he and Mal were going to go for a late celebration of their anniversary.

"All right," he finally said. "Here we go. Are you ready for this, Daddy?"

"Oh, I don't know," Gideon said with a slight laugh.

"Well, we're just so glad to have you home for Christmas," Skyler said, making the turn and going down the lane to the ranch.

"Look at that," Gideon said. "Lights and garland all over the fence." He sniffled, and Momma nearly lost her own composure. "I love seein' those seven stars."

Momma did too, and while she hadn't been sure what Rhett was doing when he'd bought this place, she now knew it was the perfect place for their family to be.

"What's going on across the lane here?" Momma asked. "Surely you're not getting a new neighbor out here."

"Yeah," Skyler said. "That's Micah's place. Didn't he tell you about it?"

"No," Momma said.

"He told me," Gideon said. "He bought the land, and he designed the house." He looked to his left. "It's comin' along."

Maybe Micah had mentioned it. Momma wasn't as good at holding facts and bits of conversation in her mind as she used to be. Several trucks sat in the driveway, and Skyler veered right to go around them and up to the gorgeous house where he and Mal lived.

"I love that wreath," Gideon said, and Skyler made a triumphant sound.

"Stay there, Daddy. I'll come around." Skyler jumped from the van and went to help Gideon, and Momma and Mal got out of the back by themselves.

"Momma."

She turned at the sound of Jeremiah's voice, and she hugged him fiercely though he held Clara in his arms. "I'll take her," she said with a little bit of weeping thrown in.

"You sure?"

"It'll give me something else to focus on," she said, taking the baby from her son. Clara was a beautiful girl, one of the calmest babies Momma had ever encountered. She probably knew that JJ had already caused quite a bit of stress for their parents, and she wanted to give Jeremiah and Whitney a break.

Greetings began, and Momma hugged everyone who even got near. It sure was nice to have this big family gathering somewhere besides a hospital, and after Liam and Callie had shown Gideon the tree, they all went into Jeremiah's house.

Gideon took the stairs very slowly, and Momma was glad Skyler had considerably less than Jeremiah. The homestead was warm, filled with cheer, Christmas music, and the scent of good food.

Momma didn't want to admit it, but she was so tired that she went straight to the couch instead of into the kitchen, where she usually helped Jeremiah. He didn't say anything, and Whitney, Callie, Marcy, and Evelyn joined her with their kids. With all the babies and kids on the floor, Whitney got toys out of the toy box next to the couch, and they started playing happily.

"How are you feeling, Evelyn?" Momma asked.

"Good." Evelyn sighed. Or maybe she was just breathing out. Breathing with that many babies up in her lungs would be hard, and Momma had a flash of empathy for her.

"How are *you*, Penny?" Mal asked, stepping over babies and toys to hand Penny a cup of tea.

She looked around at all the women watching her. She couldn't lie to them, and she didn't even want to. "I'm hanging in there," she said. "The best way I know how." She glanced into the kitchen, where Gideon had settled at the huge dining room table where they'd all eat.

"We're all here," Callie said. "Literally three of us on the same property. If you need something, all you have to do is send a text."

"I go to town every day," Mal said. "I can bring you anything."

"Wilde and Organic delivers now too," Whit said.

Momma felt so loved among these women, and though she was a generation older than them, she felt like she'd been thrown back into her community in the Hill Country, where she and Gideon had started their family. All seven boys had been born there, and they hadn't moved to Austin until Gideon had sold the ranch, lost his business, and they'd lived with his parents for a year.

No matter where Momma went, she managed to find a

group of women to form a community with, and she wouldn't have chosen any differently than the women surrounding her here in Three Rivers.

Whitney, the perfect compliment to Jeremiah's rough side.

Marcy, the softer, serious side of Wyatt.

Evelyn, the fun-loving, whimsical side to Rhett's more analytical mind.

Callie, the nurturer to Liam's tech-minded brain.

Mal, the outgoing friend-to-all when Skyler just wanted to hide.

Ivory wasn't here, and Momma missed her in that moment. She was serious when Tripp wasn't, and she kept his big head grounded.

The back door opened, and another woman entered. Momma nearly burst from her seat when Simone Foster entered. The woman looked around as if no one would see her, but Momma felt certain everyone had already glanced at her at least once.

Micah certainly knew she'd arrived, and he went to greet her. Simone looked into the living room, but her eyes skated past Momma's to those of her sisters'. She didn't come join them in the living room, though Momma very much wanted her to. So she got up and went into the kitchen for a refill on her tea.

"Come tell us about your play, dear," Momma said, sliding her arm through Simone's. "Micah said something about you being the lead?"

"Oh, no, ma'am," she said. "I mean, I'm Anita, and she's a star role, I guess. I mean, not a *star* role. That sounded arrogant. She's a—"

"She's a lead," Micah said, smiling at Simone. "Don't let her be modest, Momma. She's phenomenal."

Simone threw Micah a look, but Momma couldn't decide if it was playful and appreciative or communicating to him that he needed to stop talking. Now. Women's looks could be two-sided, and it might take Micah a while to learn all of Simone's.

Momma, in her advanced age, didn't see everything that she used to. But Simone let her lead her into the living room, and Momma finally felt like her circle was complete. Well, if Ivory were there, that was.

"Merry Christmas," one of her sons bellowed, and a cheer went up in the kitchen. Not long after that, Jeremiah called them all together for dinner, and they gathered round the big table as a family.

Momma looped her arm through Gideon's and leaned into him. "Look at them, Gideon," she whispered. "Aren't they wonderful?"

"They sure are," he said back. He pressed a kiss to her forehead, and she leaned right into the touch. "I love you, Penny."

"I love you to the moon and back, even if you have over sixty miniature horses now."

Gideon started to chuckle, and Penny couldn't help laughing with him.

"What's so funny?" Wyatt asked, but Penny could only shake her head.

Forty-nine years with Gideon Walker. That was what was wonderful, and funny, and full of love.

"Nothing," Gideon said, still chuckling. "Who's sayin' grace?"

35

Mal woke early on Christmas morning, a habit she'd developed over the past eleven months of getting up while the world still slept. She could take a nap later, and for Christmas Day breakfast, Skyler had proposed the bright idea to have the entire Walker family to Casa Skywalker.

She slipped away from Skyler, who breathed in slowly and then out. She liked listening to him in his sleep, and sometimes he had a nightmare that woke her. She'd lay very still for a moment, trying to work out what he'd said, but he was mostly unintelligible. Then he'd wake, and he'd reach for her. Mal would roll into his side and place her hand right over his heartbeat, imagining that her touch could soothe whatever plagued him.

He normally did settle right back to sleep after that,

and he'd never mentioned anything about what he night-mared about.

This morning, she quietly pulled the door closed behind her and glanced at the bedroom across the hall too. That door was closed, too, and she hoped Gideon and Penny slept as long as they wanted.

Breakfast wasn't until ten, so she didn't head into the kitchen to cook. She tiptoed into the kitchen and flipped on the light right above the sink, which cast quite a bit of light throughout the space. She opened the drawer next to the sink and pulled out an envelope she'd been keeping there for a few weeks now.

Skyler had taken twelve hundred head of cattle to market on their anniversary. They hadn't taken a trip afterward, because the work on a ranch never ended, and Skyler had wanted to coordinate everything for his father's release from the hospital and his return to their family.

But Mal wanted to show him how much she loved him. How grateful she was that even if their marriage had started out as a favor, it was definitely more than that now. She stood in the wee morning hours, staring at the enve-lope, wondering if she and Skyler would've ever gone out if she hadn't filed the wrong paperwork.

She'd like to think so. They did get along extraordi-narily well, and her love for his hardworking manner and good spirit grew in the semi-darkness.

She opened the envelope and took out the brochures she'd requested. She'd always wanted to see the northern lights, and she and Skyler could go to Fairbanks in Alaska to do just that. She'd been saving her money at the bakery, and she'd talked to Jeremiah in the barn for quite a while as he checked his calendar.

Seven Sons was right in the middle of calving season, and Skyler worked every day. Even today, the cowboys would be out in the barns and fields to make sure the pregnant heifers didn't have trouble giving birth. Every cow was money for the ranch, and though the Walkers were all billionaires, Skyler and Jeremiah had it in their heads that the ranch should support itself.

She brought up the origami how-to videos Heidi had shown her, and she got to work folding the brochures into swans and dogs and even a squirrel. With the few things folded and ready, she looked up, trying to decide where to put them so Skyler would see them. She could leave them on the counter for him, next to the coffee maker. He'd see them there.

But he'd obviously been up later than her, playing Santa Claus, as their Christmas tree had several more gifts under it than it had when she'd gone to bed last night. There would definitely be a brief gift-opening ceremony, and she wanted him to get this gift when they celebrated by the tree.

She opened the drawer again and rummaged around for a moment. She kept a needle and thread in almost every room in the house, because she never knew when she might need it. She hadn't been sewing as much as she would like, because of her work at the bakery, but that was okay. She'd bought the sewing machine for something to do, and her life in Three Rivers barely gave her a spare moment for a hobby.

She was busy at the bakery, or around the house, or napping, or learning to ride a horse with her husband. A smile came to Mal's face, intensifying when she finally found the needle and thread.

Getting them working together quickly, she pierced the top of her little animals and made ornaments out of them. She moved over to the tree and hung the three paper ornaments on the boughs of the Christmas tree, which they kept lit all night.

She admired the lights and looked down at the neatly wrapped presents, a sense of pure gratitude flowing over her. She loved Christmas and always had, but this year, it held something special.

"Thank you," she whispered, hoping the Lord would know exactly what she was thankful for. Was it too vague and not special enough to not be able to identify specific things?

She hoped not. "Thank you for everything," she whispered.

"Hey," Skyler said, and Mal jumped about a mile.

"You scared me."

A soft smile came to his mouth. "Sorry. What are you doing out here?" He reached her and wrapped her in his arms. "Couldn't sleep?"

"Yeah." They rocked back and forth together, and Mal closed her eyes and moved with him.

"Did you get the money off to your family for the holiday?" he asked.

"Yeah," she said again, tipping her head back. "Thanks, Sky."

"No thanks needed," he said, smiling softly at her. "They're family, and *we* can send them whatever they need, whenever they need it."

Mal marveled at the goodness in him, something she'd suspected lived in him, dormant somewhere. But now she saw it every time she looked at him, and she tucked herself against his chest again, absolutely content and full of pure joy.

———

HOURS LATER, Skyler and Mal had walked over to Jeremiah's to watch JJ open his presents. Clara was still too little to really get what was going on, but Whitney put the baby's gifts in her lap and let her rip at the paper until the toy or stuffed animal was revealed. Penny laughed and took a million pictures, and Gideon couldn't stop smiling through it all.

Then they went back to Casa Skywalker while Whitney and Jeremiah cleaned up and got their kids ready.

"Okay, we have some presents too," Mal said. "I know

it's kind of boring with just adults, but well, it's Christmas." She moved over to the tree and knelt down to start handing out the presents. "In my family, my father would hand out all the gifts, and we had to wait until everyone had their pile. Then we'd go around and open them one by one." She handed out the gifts and realized they'd done exactly what she said.

"We don't have to do that." She looked at Skyler for direction.

"I like it," Skyler said with a smile. "Let's let Momma go first." He looked at his mother, who picked up one of her gifts. She ripped the paper off with a smile tainted with anticipation to reveal a binder.

"Mal," she said, drawing the name out.

Giddiness pranced through Mal, but she just smiled.

"Is this what I think it is?"

"Open it," Mal said, and Penny flipped open the front cover of the binder. A gasp followed, and she looked up, her eyes glassy.

"It is," she said. "Your family recipes. Look, Gideon, all the things Mal comes from." She got up and hugged Mal, and once again, Mal held her tight, imagining her own mother to feel and smell the same as Skyler's momma.

"I love you, Mal," she said, and Mal's throat closed.

"I love you, too, Penny," she said. She cleared her throat and glanced at Skyler, who watched with that sexy, joyful smile on his face.

"Your turn, Gideon," she said. He opened a kit Skyler had found at the antiques expo in town.

"It's a knife-making kit," he explained, getting up and going over to bend over his father and show him the instructions. "You pick the wood you want for the handle, see? And the blade. And you put it all together. This one is supposed to be the best one for someone who has horses, and you have a million of those, so."

"It's great," his dad said. "Thank you, son."

Around and around they went, until they'd opened all the presents.

"Thank you, everyone," Penny said. "What an amazing day already."

She started to get up, but Mal said, "We have one more." Mal jumped out of her seat and went over to the tree. "Sky, this one's for you." She plucked one of the ornaments from the tree. "And this one. And this one."

"Would you look at that?" He took the folded origami figures from her. "I see what you were doing in the middle of the night now."

Mal just smiled at him and sat next to him on the couch. "Open them."

He did, carefully unfolding the dog first. "The northern lights." He looked at her.

She nodded to the next one. He opened the next one and smoothed it on his leg. "Fairbanks."

"I can't really travel to Iceland," she said. "And they

might not be great this year. Apparently, 2017 was the best year for the northern lights for a decade."

"I'm sure it'll be great." He picked up the squirrel. "What is this? A monkey?"

"It's a squirrel," she said, swatting his arm as she smiled. "And that one's the most important."

"Why's that?" He started unfolding the squirrel's tail.

"You'll see."

He finished opening it and scanned it. "We're going in two weeks?"

"Yep."

"Calving—"

"I talked to Jeremiah already," she said, pointing to the bottom of the sheet. "Look, Jeremiah-approved." He'd signed the paper for her, and Mal grinned.

"Jeremiah-approved," Skyler repeated, taking in the signature. "You had him sign it?"

"I want to go on an anniversary trip with you," she said. "So yes, I made him promise that you would go, no matter how many cows go into labor the night before. Rhett can come help. Or Liam. Or Tripp. Or Wyatt. Or—"

"Okay," Skyler said, laughing. "Point taken. Someone else can help."

"That's right." Mal leaned forward and kissed him. "Merry Christmas, Sky."

He kissed her back, his way of saying Merry Christmas.

Mal didn't let the kiss go on too long, because his

parents were sitting right there. She turned toward them and said, "And don't worry. Micah is going to come stay here with you."

"Oh, we don't need—" Penny started, but Skyler cut her off with, "Momma, yes you do."

She didn't argue again, and Mal got up. "Okay, we better get started on breakfast, Penny. Everyone will be here soon."

They stepped into the kitchen together, and Skyler got his father up and out of the house for another walk. When they returned, he gave his father his medicines, set him up with a piece of toast and a cup of coffee before he came into the kitchen and started getting out the plates and silverware.

When ten o'clock arrived, so had every other Walker. The kitchen was hopping, as Mal had had to figure out how to get enough tamales in the steamer baskets to feed everyone. Not only that, but they were serving fried eggs, and everyone wanted one straight from the pan. At least Mal did.

"Welcome to Casa Skywalker," Skyler said, and everyone started to gather in the kitchen. Men and women bounced babies. Mothers and fathers tried to get their older kids to come closer. Skyler waited for Daddy to get to the corner of the counter and rest his hand on it.

"We have so much to be thankful for this year," Skyler said. "I know for me, this year has been twelve months of spiritual growth, and I just want to say how grateful for I am for the Lord." He paused for a moment. "And all of you." He nodded. "Mal and Momma will explain the food, but I know we have a tradition of announcements at Christmas dinner." He glanced around. "So, who has an announcement?"

Everyone looked around at everyone else.

"Everyone knows our news," Evelyn said. "I mean, I'm the size of a bus."

Rhett put his arm around Evelyn as the family chuckled. No one raised their hand. No one said anything else. Mal distinctly remembered Skyler's announcement last year, and surely there wouldn't be anything as drastic as a secret wife.

For some reason, she looked at Micah, but he said nothing. He stood next to Simone, but he wasn't touching her, and Mal glanced away.

"Nothing?" Skyler said. "All right, Mal. Take it away."

"Okay," she said. "We have breakfast tamales. There are some with a little spicier sausage called chorizo. Those are the ones with the orange masa." She held her hand over one of the baskets. "There are more mild ones that have scrambled eggs and bacon and cheese. If you get one of the chorizo ones, we have fried eggs for the top."

"Mal also made Mexican hot chocolate," Momma said. "And we have French toast sticks for the kids." She smiled at everyone, and Mal was grateful she'd let Mal incorporate some of her traditional dishes into Christmas morning.

"I have an announcement," someone said, and Mal's pulse jumped.

Micah stepped forward, and she wondered what he could possibly say. "I think most of you know, but Simone and I are seeing each other again."

"That's not an announcement," Wyatt said with a laugh.

"It is for me," Simone said, stepping next to Micah and claiming his hand. She nodded at him, and Mal thought they were just perfect for each other. There was definitely an air of tension there too, and she hoped they'd be able to find their own happily-ever-after.

"I have an announcement too," Daddy said.

"Gideon?" Penny asked.

"I've decided to sell the miniature horses," he said.

"Daddy, they're fine at the Shining Star," Liam said.

"Gideon, you don't have to get rid of the horses."

More voices joined the fray, and Mal stayed out of the way. The tamales would keep, and it felt like a conversation they needed to have.

"I just can't be a burden," Gideon finally said. "Anymore. I'm already living with my son, and he has to get a babysitter for me so he can go on a trip with his wife."

"Daddy," Skyler said. "You're not a burden. The horses are fine." He looked at her, and Mal felt their trip to Fairbanks slipping away from her.

She didn't want to, but she said, "We don't have to take our trip," she said, stepping to his side and linking her arm through his. "You are not a burden. We love having you here."

He looked at her, and Mal tried to convey without words how much she wanted him around.

"Okay," he finally said. "Okay. Let's eat."

"Daddy—"

"I'm fine. Let's eat. The eggs are getting cold."

None of the sons protested again, and Skyler said, "Okay, Wyatt will you say grace?"

———

LATER THAT NIGHT, Mal sat on the front steps with Rosie watching the sun set. Penny and Gideon sat in the swing on the porch, and the constant squeak of it behind her reminded her of how important family was to her.

Rosie sat up and looked next door as Skyler came out the front door.

"Go get 'im," she said to the dog, and Rosie streaked across the lawn and driveways to greet Skyler. He laughed and bent down to scrub the dog, and then they both continued toward them.

He groaned and sighed as he sat next to her on the front steps.

"All good?" Mal asked.

"Yeah," Skyler said. "I should go to medical school for how much I'm taking care of people."

Mal linked her arm through his. "I don't think going to

the store and getting pain medication is quite the same thing that doctors do."

"No?" Skyler grinned at her.

"No." Mal laughed as the sun dipped lower. Jeremiah had called and said all four of them next door hadn't felt well that day and they were out of children's fever reducer. So Doctor Skyler had gone to the grocery store for them.

"It's so beautiful here," Skyler said.

"It sure is." Mal leaned her head against his shoulder.

Skyler kissed her, and the moment was so sweet. "Love you, sweetheart."

"I love you too."

———

Keep reading to find out if another Walker brother can get his happily-ever-after in Three Rivers! Now that Micah and Simone are openly dating, can they make this fourth attempt at a relationship work? Chapter one and two of **MICAH** are next! Keep reading.

Sneak Peek! Micah - Chapter One

Simone Foster left her cabin, glad she'd put a jacket on this morning. She took a long, deep breath of the February air as she walked past the row of country cabins that housed the ranch's cowboys and cowgirls. She usually made the quick trek from her cabin to her she-shed, where she had fifteen hundred air conditioned square feet of antiques, varnishes, shelving, pottery, upholstery, power tools, and ideas.

She loved her job with everything inside her, even if it had grown a bit stale in the past year or so. Another couch to be reupholstered. Another dresser to sand, paint, and repurpose. Another sideboard she could turn into a cabinet that would go right over a toilet and house all necessary bathroom supplies.

To keep things interesting, Simone had started buying

brand new notions and adding them to the old items to make a blend of past and present. Her prices had gone up because of this, but she hadn't had any problem selling her inventory. People seemed to love her creations, and she couldn't keep her online store stocked for very long. She got daily messages about when more pictures would be available, and if she had another of those burnt orange settees....

Honestly, the weight of her business accompanied her around almost all the time. She fought the urge to work fourteen hours a day, because she didn't want to be a robot that churned out "modern antiques for every Texas home," even if that was her shop's motto.

She wanted to be human too. She wanted to spend time with her sisters, their husbands, her father and grandmother...and Micah Walker.

Her step lightened as she reached the yard of the homestead where her sister, Callie, lived with her husband Liam, and their two children, Denise and Ginger. Her heart didn't feel like a lump in her chest either. She'd made a bold move over the summer by stopping by Micah's house and telling him she didn't like the silence and distance between them.

But he'd been dating someone else, and it wasn't until several months later when he'd shown up at her community theater auditions that something new had started between them.

Simone couldn't help wondering if they had what it took to make a relationship work. *Not them*, she amended in her head. *You. Just you, Simone.*

"There she is," Callie said, opening the back door. "Go on and be sure to say thank you."

A little girl said, "I will, Mama," and burst out of the door, already running toward Simone. She grinned at Denise as she got closer and closer, finally lifting her up and into her arms as the girl threw herself at "Auntie Simone!"

"Heya, Deni," she said, giggling with the girl. "You got your jacket?"

The girl had just turned five, and she'd be starting kindergarten in the fall. Callie and Liam had enrolled her in some reading classes already, as well as a playgroup, as she'd come from a language-poor background and had been quite stunted in her verbal and written language when they'd gotten her, over a year ago.

Denise puffed out her chest. "It's pink."

"I can see that," Simone said, setting her niece down on the ground and taking her hand. "Now, you have to stay right by me today."

"I will," she said solemnly.

"You can't touch anything without asking me first."

"I won't."

"You can't ask her to buy you stuff," Callie called from the doorway, where she stood with her two-year-old clinging to one of her legs. Ginger had been born addicted to drugs, but the toddler didn't seem to have any problems now. Liam and Callie had been the best parents, and Simone could admit that she loved being the favorite aunt, and she babysat whenever either of her sisters asked her to.

She also wanted a family of her own, and while she would turn forty at the end of the year, she held out hope that she could be a mother. Maybe if she and Micah could make this fourth attempt at a relationship work for them.

"And you can pick where we go for lunch," Simone said with a smile. She waved to her oldest sister, who waved back and closed the back door. Simone continued around to the side of the house, where she parked her delivery truck. "Get in, Tiny." She helped Denise climb into the truck, and she went around to the other side. "Seatbelts."

She put hers on and took a moment to orient herself to the bigger vehicle. She took it on all of her scouting expeditions, because she could load two queen-sized mattresses in the back and still have room for a bookcase if it wasn't too wide. The pull-down door in the back locked, and she could drive through wind, rain, and sleet and nothing would get damaged.

Yes, this delivery truck was the best thing Simone had ever purchased for her business. Her favorite thing was the pottery wheel and kiln she'd added to her collection a year or so ago. And her first love would always be taking a piece of furniture that had been carved for a particular purpose, used lovingly for many years, and then transforming it into something completely different. She loved breathing new life into something old, something someone wanted to throw away, something that didn't get used anymore.

It was like giving a table a second chance to become a bench in someone's flower garden, and Simone thought everyone—and everything—deserved a second chance.

"Do you like dogs?" Denise asked, and Simone glanced over at her.

"Yes," she said.

"Daddy says I'm too little to take care of one, but I think I could do it."

"Oh, I see." Simone smiled at Denise. "What does your mama say about the dog?"

"She says nothin'," Denise said. "Maybe I could keep the dog at your house."

Simone laughed, because she'd often thought about getting a dog. A little one, not one of the big ones Jeremiah had next door, or the cattle dog Skyler Walker and his wife Mal had.

No, Simone wanted a lap dog. One that would curl up right next to her—or on her—and keep her company at night. At the same time, she couldn't put together more than a couple of her waking hours where she was home. She worked in the shed, or helped Callie at the homestead, fed the donkeys at the ranch, or went to her theater classes and practices.

She liked being busy, that was for sure. An idle Simone wasn't a happy Simone, which was why she and Denise were driving an hour south of Three Rivers today, to a small town that had a huge swap meet every weekend in January, February, and March.

Simone went every year, sometimes more than once. After all, she needed old things to make into new treasures, and while the residents of Three Rivers held plenty of yard sales, she didn't want to simply recycle their things back into the community.

Of course, her online commerce had far surpassed her in-person sales at festivals and fairs for a couple of years now, and she'd had to learn about shipping costs, timelines, and ways to ensure her hard work didn't get ruined on a truck from Three Rivers to Lexington.

Her brain felt stuffed with useless information, and she let Denise talk about dogs and cats and rabbits while she hummed along or asked simple questions like, "What do rabbits even eat?"

The little girl sure seemed to know *all* about it, and Simone sure did love having her along, at least for the drive.

They arrived at the swap meet, and Simone wasn't surprised to find many, many cars in the huge field they were using as a parking lot. "Tell me the rules again," Simone said. She'd never brought anyone with her on her finding endeavors. She knew the hours could slip away like smoke—for her—and she hoped the little girl wouldn't be too bored.

"Stay by you. Don't touch....um."

"Those are good," Simone said. "Your mom didn't want you to beg me to buy you something. But if you see something really good...." Simone shrugged with a smile. "Let's go."

Denise struggled to open the door, and Simone had to do it for her. She helped her down and took her hand. "Okay, so I'm looking for anything that can be transformed into something amazing."

She realized that wasn't a good description of what to look for, even for an adult. But Simone would just know what she should get when she saw it. "There's a lot of walking," she said. "Should we get a drink first?"

She'd been to this swap meet at least a dozen times, and she knew the best entrance to access the meet. It had bathrooms and concessions right inside, and she paused. "Do you need to use the restroom?"

"Nope," Denise said, and Simone remembered how Callie had told her that Denise would always say no to that question.

"Let's go anyway," Simone said, leading the girl into the bathroom. Afterward, she bought Denise a lemonade while Simone opted for water, and they set off down the outer circle of the swap meet.

Simone almost always stuck to the outer circle, because

the further in she went, the less desirable the items were until she was literally looking at someone selling power tools from their garage or groceries at a deep discount.

She liked potato chips that were practically free as well as the next person, but they were not the reason she'd made the drive today.

"Let's see what treasures we can find," she said, eyeing a booth several down that she'd bought from before. "Maybe Bill will have something new." And he'd load it up for her for free, always a plus in Simone's book.

She walked slowly, scanning the booths on both sides. But she didn't want jewelry or handmade vases. No, she was looking for something old she could make new.

"Look at that," Denise said, and Simone looked to see where she was pointing. Inside the booth, which sold barn wood that had always interested Simone, Denise seemed to be pointing to a mirror.

"Do you see yourself?" Simone asked, detouring under the tent of the booth.

"No, that barrel," Denise said, looking from it to Simone. "Do you need something like that, Auntie Simone?"

"Hmm," Simone said, taking a step around the old barrel. She'd never done anything with a barrel before, because she saw them every day. Most people did too.

In Texas, she told herself. And not all of her customers lived in Texas these days.

"We have 'em all over the ranch," Denise said. "Maybe you could just use one of those."

"What would you use it for?" Simone asked, trying to see what the child could. She put her fingers on the wood, and it was old, sure. For some reason, the barrel did speak to her creative soul.

"Daddy puts me on the barrel to eat lunch."

"Like a table," Simone mused. She looked up to find the booth master. "Do you have more of these?" She indicated the barrel, and he looked from it to her. The idea forming in her mind to make a counter-height table with the barrels at the ends, split in half height-wise and all this barn wood for the top. She could sand it, fit all the little pieces together, stain it…. "And how long is the longest piece of barn wood that you have?"

"How many barrels do you need?"

"Just two," she said. "They come from a real ranch?"

"The oldest one in the county," the man said. "The owners—my family—are doing a major renovation, with all new everything. I can probably get you twenty barrels."

Simone had never made a table the size of what she was currently envisioning. "Let's start with four," she said. "And how far is the ranch? Could I come pick out the wood?" She reached into her hip pack and pulled out a card. "I'm Simone Foster, and I create household furniture from old items. I'd love to feature your ranch on my listings."

The man took the card and smiled. Simone had been

using a different design until very recently, when Micah and Whitney had helped her photograph her best pieces and make new cards that were more like a postcard than a business card.

"I'm Easton," he said. "And the ranch is only about twenty minutes from here." He looked at her and added, "We'd love to have someone like you out."

Simone stood in the booth and bought the two barrels, as well as enough barn lumber to make the two tables. She chatted easily with Easton, and they made arrangements for her to come visit his ranch later the next week.

She had no idea how much time had gone by before she'd finished, and this was only the first booth, only feet from the entrance.

Denise had been patient, but she'd soon spied a dog behind the table in the back of the booth, and Easton hadn't minded if the little girl played with his dog.

"All right, Deni," Simone said, her stomach growling. Was it lunch already? "Let's go." She took the girls' hand, and they merged back into the flow of traffic outside the booth.

"Ma'am," someone said, and she turned. "I think you've stolen my niece."

"Uncle Micah!" Denise shouted only a moment before the sexy cowboy scooped her into his arms, nearly wrenching Simone's arm as he did.

Warmth and surprise filled her as she watched him hug Denise. The fact that the little girl had rightfully called him "Uncle Micah" wasn't lost on Simone. He was her uncle. She was her aunt.

It was weird.

Simone wished it wasn't, but for her, it still was.

"What are you doing here?" she asked.

"Yeah," Denise said, pulling back and looking into Micah's handsome face. "What are you doin' here?"

Sneak Peek! Micah - Chapter Two

Micah Walker carried his niece on his hip, unsure if the look on Simone's face was happy or neutral or negative. But they talked every day, sometimes all day long via text, and she'd told him she'd be at this swap meet today.

He'd told her this already, but he said, "I had a meeting down this way this morning, remember?"

"Oh, that's right. The Rhinehart place," Simone said, finally smiling.

Micah reached for her hand, feeling claustrophobic with all these people pressing between the two rows of booths. She slipped her fingers between his, and Micah squeezed. "Yeah, the Rhinehart's. I think they might hire me too."

"That's great, Micah."

"Yeah." He could use the business, that was for sure.

He'd known going into his general contracting endeavors that he was catering to a ranch or family with a lot of money. Three Rivers had some wealthy families for sure, but not everyone needed a new, high-end home, which was what Micah had decided to specialize in.

He'd built Skyler's house last year, and he was halfway through his own place across the lane from Seven Sons. He'd managed to get the land there, and he had ten acres all along the highway. He had no plans to do anything with it, though. He liked how wild it was, and he could keep his horses at the ranch he owned ten percent of.

He'd designed and built two more houses in the towns and land surrounding Three Rivers, and if he could land the Rhinehart's ranch, he'd be well on his way to filling his days with good, hard work.

"Have you found anything good?" Micah asked.

"A bunch of wood," Simone said.

"Wow," he teased. "You drove an hour for wood?"

She grinned at him, and Micah's whole world grew a little brighter. He'd enjoyed this fourth relationship with Simone, which was entering their fourth month. Things were moving considerably slower than before, and he hadn't quite kissed her yet.

His mind wandered down previously forbidden paths, when he'd snuck over to her she-shed and kissed her despite her objections and complaints that he distracted her from her work. So he'd back up and turn to leave, only to have her grab his shirt and pull him back for another kiss.

A smile stayed on his face as they walked down the aisle, Simone looking for something only she could see. She indicated a booth on the left she wanted to go in, and Micah followed her as she said, "Bill usually has something good."

And Bill obviously knew her, because his face lit up when he saw Simone and he abandoned the shelf where he'd been adjusting some pots. "Simone." He took Simone into a hug, causing her to drop Micah's hand. "It's good to see you. What are you looking for?" Bill couldn't be much older than Micah who had a birthday in a few weeks and then he'd be thirty-four.

Simone was older than him too, and they'd celebrated her thirty-ninth birthday at the theater in Amarillo. He'd debated with himself for the entire drive home if he'd kiss her then, but in the end, he hadn't.

Why he was thinking so much about kissing was beyond him, and he really needed to stop. It would happen when it was meant to happen, Micah knew that. He'd learned to rely more on the Lord's timing than his own the past couple of years, but that hadn't eliminated any of his frustration.

He'd simply learned how to be slightly more patient than he'd used to be. And he still wasn't perfect at it.

"Oh, you know," Simone said, glancing around. "I'll know it when I see it."

"Well, look around, and if you think you might want something, let me know. I can't bring everything I have."

Simone nodded, and Bill turned back to the bookcase. Micah watched her look at the items in the tent, which included ratty end tables, a brass headboard, and a pair of lamps that looked like they'd once belonged to his great-grandmother.

"These are nice," she said, almost to herself, indicating the lamps.

Micah's eyebrows went up, and he looked at Denise. "I do not think those are nice," he whispered.

Denise giggled and she took his face in both of her hands. "Auntie Simone makes old things into new things, Uncle Micah."

"Oh, is that what she does?" he asked. "I didn't know." He grinned at the little girl, who wiggled out of his arms. He set her on the ground and said, "Don't touch anything, Denise."

"I know," she said. She wandered around while Simone did too, each of them inside their own worlds. Micah had no idea what Simone was looking for, as she seemed to really examine some things while others her gaze skated right past.

She picked up a candlestick and said, "Bill, where did this trunk come from?"

The shopkeeper approached, saying, "I don't have a trunk."

Simone pointed to something Micah couldn't see,

because a couple of pieces of furniture separated him and where Simone stood. "What's this, then?"

"That's an Army locker," he said. "And I bought it in an estate sale."

"How much?" Simone bent down, really looking at the Army locker now. Micah stepped around the ragged armchair still blocking his view to find Simone crouching in front of what looked like a very old box. A very old box with a very rusty latch. All of it should be thrown away.

Still, a general sense of excitement filled him, because he knew exactly what Simone did in that she-shed of hers. She made gold with her bare hands. He couldn't imagine what was going through her mind in that moment, but he had the very real feeling she knew exactly what to do with that beat-up box.

"Twenty," Bill said.

"I'll take it," Simone said, and she peeled a bill out of her pocket. She wore a pair of black slacks and a dark, long-sleeved blouse covered in bright flowers. She was classy and sophisticated, and exactly everything Micah wanted in a woman.

He'd seen her in dirty jeans and cowgirl boots too, her shirtsleeves pushed up on her shoulders as she worked in a pig pen, or shoveled out a stall, or rode a lawn mower around the Shining Star Ranch.

He liked her soft side, her rustic side, her blunt side, all her sides. And he decided right then and there that he was going to kiss her today.

Today, he vowed.

Almost as quickly as he decided, his insecurities kicked in. *Maybe not today*, he amended. *We'll see how things go.*

Simone led him and Denise through several more booths, and she bought a few more things. On the way back through, she got the shop owners or their assistants to bring all her purchases to her delivery truck, where she stood back, not getting an ounce of dirt on her hands while she directed them.

"Thank you," she said with a smile to each one. Some got handshakes, others hugs, and she kissed Bill's cheek as he left. Then she drew a deep breath and looked at Micah. "So I guess you'll be unloading all of this for me later."

"If you need me to," he said, lifting his cowboy hat and reseating it.

"Do you want to come to lunch with us?" Simone asked, taking Denise's hand. "I promised her a day with me and then lunch. She gets to pick the place."

Micah looked from Simone to Denise, and he had the very real impression that he should let them have their girls' day. He knew Simone had girls' nights with her sisters too. No husbands. No kids. The Foster sisters were very close, and the one time he'd tried to ask what they did at girls' night, she'd just looked at him.

"You don't know?" he'd asked, teasing her.

"I know," she said. "It's just...stuff. Sister stuff. What do you do with your brothers?"

"We ride horses and talk about the rodeo and...stuff."

"Yeah," Simone had said. "We do stuff too."

And he hadn't asked again.

"I have to get back," he said. "I said I'd send some paperwork over to Wade, and I've been here for a couple of hours." He stepped into Simone and put one arm around her waist. "Good to see you, sweetheart. I will come unload this for you later, if you'd like."

"Okay," she said, pressing into his kiss against her cheek. "I'll text you."

He nodded, bent down to hug Denise, and then he tipped his hat and walked away. He heard Simone ask, "So, Deni, where do you want to go to lunch?" as he left. He wasn't sure why he felt like he shouldn't crash their lunch; Denise obviously didn't care.

Does Simone?

He couldn't answer himself, so he simply walked back to his truck and got on the road back to Three Rivers.

MICAH PARKED in his own driveway and looked at the shell of the house. He was building it himself, though he had contracted with Stephania to do the plumbing, and Dylan to do the electrical and HVAC. He'd hire people to come install the carpet and flooring too, install the appliances, and make sure the gas fireplaces in the house and in the backyard wouldn't explode and blow up the whole ranch.

He wanted to see how long it took to build a house by himself, with custom finishes, when he relied on other experts to do what they were best at doing. He didn't work on his place day and night, though, because he did have ranch chores to do each day. Feeding and watering the llama herd wasn't hard, but he'd been helping Liam with their father's miniature horses too. And Daddy had a lot of those.

Micah also pitched in around the ranch when big events happened, like calving, breeding, branding, and haying. Jeremiah was just one man, and while they employed four cowboys, they really needed a dozen hands to keep up during the busy times on a ranch. With Skyler back now, things on the ranch were improving, and Micah was glad to have his best friend in Three Rivers with him.

He got out of the truck and cast a glance toward Skyler's house, which he'd also designed and built. He'd purposely chosen a radically different design for his place, and the first thing that included was the size.

Skyler's house was easily a second homestead on the ranch. It was sprawling and big and bold and open. Micah liked that concept, but he wanted more of a farmhouse, like his parents, and like the place where he'd been born and had grown up for a few years.

So his house utilized more outdoor space, with a massive porch that spanned the front of the house and wrapped around the side, continuing to a large patio in the backyard. The front door opened to a small foyer—much smaller than Wyatt's or Skyler's homes—where a hall led back into the kitchen. The homestead where Jeremiah lived currently did this too, but there were two offices off the front there.

At Micah's house, the stairs went up, and through a doorway was another bedroom and bathroom, as well as the office or formal living room.

The kitchen and dining room weren't enormous, though he could probably host the family with enough folding tables and chairs if he needed to. But he didn't need to, and not everyone had six brothers and their wives, children, and dogs to host for Christmas.

The laundry room veered to the left, as did the master suite. That was it for the main level, and while it wasn't huge, it was almost two thousand square feet. Upstairs, he had a large living room, three more bedrooms, and another bathroom, as well as a common area for his weight machine and a treadmill.

It felt cozy, and he wanted to show people that luxury didn't always mean huge. It just meant custom, with the unique touches a family could want.

He'd put up the walls, put on the roof, and today, he needed to get some sheetrock up. The electric and plumbing had gone in last week, and he was ready to cover it all up. He affixed a mask to his face and put on a pair of work gloves.

He judged time by his stomach, working until he had to stop and get something to eat. He took off his mask and his gloves, set them on his workbench and started down the steps to the main level. He'd taken a couple of steps down to what would eventually be the yard before a bloodcurdling scream filled the ranch.

Micah took off running, going past his truck as he scanned the yards, driveways, and homes in front of him. He saw nothing.

Guide me, he thought, desperate to reach whoever needed help before it was too late.

Read **Micah** today, which is available in paperback! Get it here by scanning this QR code with the camera on your phone.

Seven Sons Ranch in Three Rivers Romance™ Series

Rhett (Book 1): To save her business, she'll have to risk her heart. She needs a husband to be credible as a matchmaker. He wants to help a neighbor. **Will their fake marriage take them out of the friend zone?**

Tripp (Book 2): She needs a husband to keep her son. He's wanted to take their relationship to the next level, but she's always pushing him away. Will their trivial tie take them all the way to happily-ever-after?

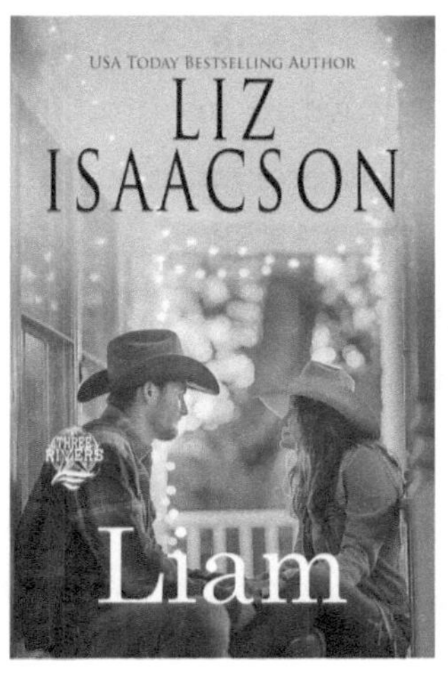

Liam (Book 3): She's desperate to save her ranch. He wants to help her any way he can. Will their invented I-Do open doors that have previously been closed and lead to a happily-ever-after for both of them?

Jeremiah (Book 4): He wants to prove to his brothers that he's not broken. She just wants him. Will a fake marriage heal him or push her further away?

Wyatt (Book 5): To get her inheritance, she needs a husband. He's wanted to fly with her for ages. Can their pretend pledge turn into something real?

Skyler (Book 6): She needs a new last name to stay in school. He's willing to help a fellow student. Can this wanna-be wife show the playboy that some things should be taken seriously?

Micah (Book 7): They were just actors auditioning for a play. The marriage was just for the audition – until a clerical error results in a legal marriage. Can these two ex-lovers negotiate this new ground between them and achieve new roles in each other's lives?

Gideon (Book 8): It's 1971, and Gideon Walker is on the cutting edge of all the technology coming out of Texas. He has big dreams and wants to make something of himself. Then he meets Penny Aarons, and everything changes. He only has eyes for her, but she's got plans and dreams of her own...

Read this origin romance for Momma and Daddy from the Seven Sons series today!

Second Generation in Three Rivers Romance™

Step back into the heartwarming small Texas town of Three Rivers! Get ready to experience a small-town saga like no other, where the legacy of the past meets the promise of the future. As you journey through these heartwarming stories, you'll not only fall in love with the next generation of cowboys and ranchers but also have the joy of revisiting beloved characters from Three Rivers Ranch, Seven Sons Ranch, and Shiloh Ridge Ranch!

The Cowboy Who Came Home (Book 1): He's been serving in the military for a decade. She's been quietly grieving a devastating loss. When Finn and Edith reunite in small-town Three Rivers where they grew up together, can their second chance romance provide hope, healing, and the happily-ever-after they both crave?

Three Rivers Ranch Romance™ Series

Escape to Three Rivers, Texas for small-town charm, sweet and sexy cowboys, and faith and family centered romance. You'll get second chance romance, friends to lovers. older brother's best friend, military romance, secret babies, and more! The Three Rivers cowboys and the women who rope their hearts are waiting for you, so start reading today!

Second Chance Ranch (Book 1): After his deployment, injured and discharged Major Squire Ackerman returns to Three Rivers Ranch, wanting to forgive Kelly for ignoring him a decade ago. He'd like to provide the stable life she needs, but with old wounds opening and a ranch on the brink of financial collapse, it will take patience and faith to make their second chance possible.

Shiloh Ridge Ranch in Three Rivers Romance™

Meet the cowboy billionaires in the southern hills outside of Three Rivers! They love God, horses, the land, and family, and all 12 of them are looking for love in the small Texas town where they grew up. Start this Christian family saga romance series and spend time with people you'd be happy to call YOUR family too!

The Mechanics of Mistletoe (Book 1): He can be a teddy or a grizzly. She's a genius with a wrench. Can the pretty mechanic tame this cowboy's wild side, or will they both be left broken-hearted this Christmas?

About Liz

Liz Isaacson writes inspirational romance, usually set in Texas, or Wyoming, or anywhere else horses and cowboys exist. She lives in Utah, where she writes full-time, takes her two dogs to the park everyday, and eats a lot of veggies while writing. Find her on her website, along with all of her pen names, at authorelanajohnson.com